D0498176

BLAZE AWAY

The Harpur and Iles Series by Bill James

YOU'D BETTER BELIEVE IT
THE LOLITA MAN
HALO PARADE
PROTECTION
COME CLEAN
TAKE
CLUB
ASTRIDE A GRAVE
GOSPEL
ROSES, ROSES
IN GOOD HANDS
THE DETECTIVE IS DEAD
TOP BANANA
PANICKING RALPH
LOVELY MOVER
ETON CROP
KILL ME
PAY DAYS
NAKED AT THE WINDOW
THE GIRL WITH THE LONG BACK
EASY STREETS
WOLVES OF MEMORY
GIRLS
PIX
IN THE ABSENCE OF ILES
HOTBED
I AM GOLD
VACUUM *
UNDERCOVER *
PLAY DEAD *
DISCLOSURES *
BLAZE AWAY *

* *available from Severn House*

BLAZE AWAY

Bill James

This first world edition published 2015
in Great Britain and the USA by
Crème de la Crime, an imprint of
SEVERN HOUSE PUBLISHERS LTD of
19 Cedar Road, Sutton, Surrey, England, SM2 5DA.
Trade paperback edition first published
in Great Britain and the USA 2015 by
SEVERN HOUSE PUBLISHERS LTD.

Copyright © 2015 by Bill James.

All rights reserved.
The moral right of the author has been asserted.

British Library Cataloguing in Publication Data

James, Bill, 1929-author.
Blaze away. – (The Harpur and Iles series)
1. Harpur, Colin (Fictitious character)–Fiction. 2. Iles, Desmond (Fictitious character)–Fiction. 3. Art thefts–Investigation–Fiction. 4. Police–Great Britain–Fiction. 5. Detective and mystery stories.
I. Title II. Series
823.9'14-dc23

ISBN-13: 978-1-78029-072-0 (cased)
ISBN-13: 978-1-78029-555-8 (trade paper)
ISBN-13: 978-1-78010-637-3 (e-book)

Except where actual historical events and characters are being described for the storyline of this novel, all situations in this publication are fictitious and any resemblance to living persons is purely coincidental.

All Severn House titles are printed on acid-free paper.

Severn House Publishers support the Forest Stewardship Council™ [FSC™], the leading international forest certification organisation. All our titles that are printed on FSC certified paper carry the FSC logo.

Typeset by Palimpsest Book Production Ltd.,
Falkirk, Stirlingshire, Scotland.
Printed and bound in Great Britain by
TJ International, Padstow, Cornwall.

ONE

'Here's the house,' George Dinnick said. They were looking at laptop photographs, George, Liz Rossol and Justin Benoit. 'Probably the squire's a few centuries ago. What might be called a *gentilhommière* – an English gentleman's pad. Much refurbished and altered, but the dignified and graceful shell, as it always was. Additional stables. Obligatory paddocks. Six or seven bedrooms, bathrooms galore, butler's pantry, larder, wine cellar, three big reception rooms downstairs, one where he usually hangs the stuff and does his deals. We think a concrete strongroom alongside the wine cellar for the pictures when they're not on display. He's a careful lad. Several probably fakes, but, as ever, Justin will do a pre-visit as Mr Ardent Private Art Collector and make sure the job is worth the trouble.'

'Always available,' Justin said. 'Always ready to apply instinct, acting ability, experience and knowledge. And the greatest of these is instinct. In my case.'

Some people in this game resented having to rely on advice from a scholar and expert, particularly an expert as young as Justin Benoit, not long out of college, his face boyish, chubby, readily insolent. Liz regarded this kind of hostility as narrow and foolish. She knew George did, too. Almost all business enterprises had to call on professional guidance now and then to deal with a difficult problem or difficult problems. It should not be regarded as a creeping challenge to the leadership. If anything, George appeared to recognize that Justin brought real quality to the firm, though he certainly was very self-assured, even vain. Never mind: Liz considered these seemingly negative qualities could, in fact, be seen as the opposite – as supremely positive. Again, she thought George would agree. Justin's flashiness came from interminable, brazen confidence, and such confidence could be a necessary asset when trying to convince a collector that a particular work was brilliantly genuine and absolutely worth its gorgeous price tag of six, seven, even eight figures. Of course, Liz was mightily biased in Justin's favour. She rather liked his cockiness. Yes.

Dinnick said: 'We take and then transfer our trove to that jolly friend in Ghent by customary methods, and it disappears into the great, shadowy, magnificently efficient arty elsewhere. Obviously, it would be best if we could get there while the stuff is actually on display, easy to unhook and multi-filch. The strong-room could cause difficulties – delays, and the need to force the door-combinations from him. We all hate that kind of blood and bone-break thing, I believe, but Jack Lamb's not some innocent, pure at heart, pictures' fan, is he? We've dealt several times with similar obstructiveness. Lamb has chosen risk as a colleague. That's us. Risk can move in on him and become not risk at all but authentic, professionally delivered pain. He's hardly going to call the police, is he, running the kind of business he does?'

Liz thought that George, sleek, sixty next birthday, no convictions, probably realized that as an argument to justify possible thuggery and worse this might appear very rough-and-ready and touched by self-interest. But they were in a very rough-and-ready trade, where self-interest dominated. They had met today in George's Kensington, London flat. These apartments did not come at give-away cost, nor did the suitably fine furniture, carpets and general fittings. Nor did his wife's clothes and hairdressing, nor their son Oliver's education. People like Lamb could not be allowed to thwart decent profits for the firm. That would be blatant unkindness – as George would see it. Lamb might have set himself up as a feudal lord, but this didn't mean he'd be getting any fealty from the George Dinnick organization.

The laptop picture changed and showed two women, one young, one not so young, cantering in woodland on Welsh cobs. Dinnick said: 'Liz has been there doing a bit of unobserved surveillance and photography.'

'We *hope* unobserved,' Liz said.

'I'm sure,' Dinnick said. 'You're brilliant at seeing and not being seen. We consider you as much an expert in fieldwork as Justin is at judging the status and value of a picture.'

Liz was about Justin's age, mellow-voiced, alert-looking, mousy to blonde hair cut short and tufted, squarish face, neat nose, brown eyes wide apart, tall, unbony, reassuring breasts. Naturally, George knew she and Justin had something good going. George didn't seem to mind. She and Justin took care the relationship never interfered with their work. The reverse, perhaps: it could produce a binding-together element in the firm. George Dinnick seemed to have trained himself to see the plus side of situations. What was that old song about a silver lining to every dark cloud? George would second that, she thought. In a commercial career, optimism and initiative gave strength to each other. But George could turn very unpleasant.

Liz said: 'There seemed to be three of them in the house, beside staff: Lamb himself; what I gather is his live-in girlfriend – I have her as Helen Surtees, about twenty years old; and then this other, elderly woman riding with her here. Possibly, Jack Lamb's mother. There was some information, I think, that his mother lived in the States, had a divorce there from a second husband, and reverted to her previous surname, possibly wanting to forget that US marriage had ever happened. Maybe she comes over for a holiday occasionally.'

'They could be an extra way of persuasion if he's backward about giving the strongroom combination codes,' Dinnick said. 'Once more, not a nice thought, but these women are part of that risk game. Jack buys them a lifestyle. The lovely house with views all the way to the sea, the nags and bathrooms and so on. They can't expect immunity or tenderness.'

'Here's a car on its way to the house,' Liz said. 'Can we stop the pic a minute?' The screen showed an oldish looking VW Golf. There appeared to be a man at the wheel, burly, fair-haired. 'You can make out the reg,' Liz said. 'But it's a reg that doesn't exist. I paid X, who has that mate, Y, who has a chum, Z, who can get access to the computer, and we collect a blank when it's offered this number plate.'

'Standard police trickery,' Dinnick said. 'It'll be from their special stock. I said Lamb couldn't call the police for help in a crisis, but there might be a special arrangement with one officer.'

'Yes, I thought maybe police,' Liz said.

'But why the anonymity?' Justin said.

'An understanding between our *gentilhomme* and the cop?

Perhaps an informing set-up. The cop keeps in touch, but doesn't want it known he keeps in touch,' Dinnick said. 'A kind of bargain? The cop gets tip-offs – good for the career – and in exchange doesn't intrude on Lamb's business. In fact, is asked up to the house to look at the works and so becomes sort of a party to what's going on. He's corralled, he's compromised. This is a routine tactic by big-time snitches. It's in the informants' handbook under the chapter heading "How To Enmesh Your Dick".'

'Could be,' Liz said.

'Artfully compromised,' Justin said.

'There's a Latin quote on the gate of the grounds meaning, if I'm recalling right from school, "we are all driven along the same road",' Liz said.

'"Driven"?' Dinnick replied. 'But it doesn't go on to say "with a heap of snatched daubs in the back of the estate car en route to Belgium", does it?'

TWO

Twice lately Jack Lamb had invited Harpur out to Darien, his sixteenth-century manor house, near Chase Woods, to look at some art. This was new art – 'new' meaning it had only lately reached Jack, not that the artist had only just finished it. In some ways, asking Harpur to Darien was a crazy, dangerous break from their usual drill. Normally, they'd meet in discreet, sometimes remote spots: an old, reinforced concrete, coastal defence blockhouse left over from the war; likewise ex-wartime, a former anti-aircraft gun site on a hill at the edge of the city; or they'd each take a bag of washing to a suburban launderette somewhere and talk quietly among the other customers while watching the clothes jostle in the suds.

But Harpur recognized that Jack had a special purpose when he suggested the visits to his home. Harpur played along. In case Lamb was being watched, though, Harpur always drove a doctored car from the police pool to Darien, lately an old VW

Golf, sometimes a comparably old Focus, like today, their registration plates a fiction. Some people knew other people who knew someone else who, for a fee – cash only – could persuade someone at the Vehicle Licensing Centre to link a registration to an owner, for a fee – cash only. The pool-car reg if fed into the computer would produce an answer along the lines of: 'Not recognized in UK, try Mozambique.'

When Lamb wanted to show a collection he hung it in one of his big, high-ceilinged drawing rooms, where special lighting presented the works at their best for potential buyers. At other times he kept the items in an air conditioned bombproof, fireproof, multi-lock, concrete bunker he'd had built in the cellars. Harpur had looked at the Planning Authority application. Jack described it there as a Safety Room, in case of intruders, and/or an anti-nuclear attack shelter. And it *could* have functioned as either. Obviously, Jack would not have alarms fitted in Darien because, if activated, they might get him and his business awkward attention, police ferreting about legitimately all over the house, cellars included. '*Could you open-up the shelter for us, please, Mr Lamb, so we can check all's tickety-boo?*'

No picture ever stayed long enough on display to cause discoloration of the drawing room's green and gold flock wallpaper. If Harpur had only just met Lamb, and never been to his home or discussed decor, he thought he would have guessed Jack was a flock wallpaper person; though Harpur didn't go presumptuously further and imagine he could have sixth-sensed the green and gold. Both drawing rooms had minstrels' galleries, from a time when that kind of entertainment was all the thing and home-grown. Occasionally, Lamb would go up into one of the galleries and play a harmonica tune for Harpur, usually something from the First World War – say, *Pack Up Your Troubles in Your Old Kit-Bag* or *It's a Long Way to Tipperary*. The drawing room had an echo, and these jolly, easy-beat tunes would hang in the air, like moments between bouts of whiz-bang, no-man's-land shelling.

Lamb used to say, 'Colin, would you like to come and take a peek in Darien?'

Harpur had discovered long ago that this was some sort of joke. Jack loved the occasional quip and would keep returning doggedly to his favourites. For instance, it amused him endlessly that a room he'd turned into a kind of gallery, showing paintings and drawings for sale, was actually *called* a drawing room! He believed a good joke should do plenty of regular, steady work – 'like waitresses or trawlermen, Col,' he said, often.

Jack had explained to Harpur that the name of his property – Darien – came from a poem learned at school. He would recite parts of it in a special, fluting, shrill tone, to imitate, to recapture for a minute or two, those classroom days. Over time, some of the words had become imprinted on Harpur's mind. The verse said that far back in history explorers reached Darien in Panama. They stood silent 'on a peak' there, staring with 'a wild surmise' at each other, dumbstruck at finding the Pacific, which, up till then, they'd never even heard of, although there was so much of it: quite an eye-opener, and bound to cause wild surmising. Jack delighted in that peak-peek word-play, the notion of this group on a peak taking a peek at an ocean – yes, an eye-opener.

Harpur always had a loud, congratulatory chuckle when Jack asked him to 'come and take a peek in Darien.' Lamb had continually put his balls and the rest of him at very major risk of pain and obliteration, entirely on Harpur's behalf. So Harpur would never – *could* never – harshly, brutally, ask Jack for fuck's sake to replace peak-peek with a fresh witticism, capable of taking on the next three or four years' tour of duty. Although Jack had a great, slabby, quadrangle of a face, stood six feet five and weighed about 260 pounds, he possessed true sensitivities, and his spirits could be severely hurt. Harpur had come across the term 'mojo' lately, meaning, as he understood it, someone's selfhood and personal aura. He always went very gingerly with Jack's mojo. An individual's mojo gave him or her uniqueness, and Harpur certainly acknowledged Jack's uniqueness and felt determined to safeguard it. Yes, his piping recitation voice might seem all wrong for someone grown so bulky and solid, but Harpur realized Jack had surprising complexities.

Harpur thought that quite a few of the paintings on show at Darien today might be genuine, not fakes, though he couldn't tell whether Jack knew which. That kind of niggling question from Harpur, a cop, a detective cop, a top detective cop, would be considered by Lamb disgracefully uncivilized, especially if asked on his own historic property. Uncivilized or 'inappropriate' and 'unacceptable', as Jack might say. These were vague, weaselling, bromide terms he'd picked up from somewhere and came back to frequently, just as he did to his most cherished, gnarled jokes. 'Tell me what you think of *Heures Propices – Halcyon Hours* – Col,' he said, pointing at a small, surreal item in a wide, silver frame, an anti-comprehensible, frantic work featuring fractured layers of red, ochre, purple, blue-black and dun.

'Understated yet richly purposeful,' Harpur replied.

With his vast right fist Jack struck his vast left palm to signal excited harmony. 'So true, but this is the secret of its mesmerism, isn't it?'

'That's what I was getting at.'

Lamb said: 'We have here an artist familiar with the rough ways of the world, who can bring us a coded glimpse of them through the manipulation of tints and particularly ochre. The ochre has its own rally-round, drumbeat eloquence.'

'It's the ochre that speaks to my centre, too,' Harpur said. 'I thrill to that drumbeat.' He knew Jack prized this kind of ramshackle, barmy conversation. Lamb obviously thought it made Harpur a more or less happily enmeshed associate of Jack's brilliantly prosperous, profoundly dodgy vocation as fine arts huckster, sales online or by appointment. Website business boomed, apparently. Jack had mentioned something by an American called Hopper that went for nearly ten million dollars online. '*Heures Propices* will sell for a six-digit sterling sum, and the first of those digits won't be one and could be seven or eight,' Lamb said.

These visits to Darien, apparently to look at, and lunatically chat about, Jack's most recent acquisitions, had another, unspoken side. Jack Lamb was the greatest informant Harpur had ever dealt with – might be the greatest informant any police officer anywhere had ever dealt with. Jack had, in fact, ended this arrangement not long ago; or, at least, put it into abeyance. He'd apparently come to feel there was something rotten and base about informing. Harpur could understand that attitude.

There were a lot of deeply contemptuous terms for those who whispered into the ear of a detective – 'stool pigeon', 'grass', 'tout', 'nark'. Although Jack had always confined his informing to crimes and criminals he considered especially disgusting, it was still informing, and his conscience had moved in lately and stopped him bringing prompts to Harpur. But Harpur kept contact, still followed his side of the bargain, because he felt indebted to Jack for what had happened previously. And because he couldn't be sure whether Jack would have another change of mind in the future and resume his brilliant tip-offs. A further consideration gripped Harpur: although Jack might have stopped whispering in a good cause, there were still people locked up because of his arrangement with Harpur in the past. One or two or more of these would be getting out soon, and some of them might suspect they had been fingered by Jack and feel vengeful. Harpur believed he had a duty to look after Jack, as far as that could be done – not very far, most probably.

The working connection between Detective Chief Superintendent Colin Harpur and Jack Lamb had been unusual in that no actual one-to-one *dealings* occurred, if 'dealings' signified Harpur bunging money to Lamb for information. Jack would have regarded that as a despicable, furtive, ignoble relationship, even then. What he did favour, though, in return for his exclusive, marvellously reliable tip-offs, was the benign, cultivated, bull-shitting involvement of Harpur in his high-priced, shady, ochre-graced trade. He seemed to believe this would come via thorough, cheerfully puffed-up wordy, vaporous commentary sessions such as this afternoon's.

But it had to be only a marginal, token involvement. Jack had wanted, and got from Harpur, a guaranteed, holy understanding that not too much aggressive poking and delving into the financial and more general aspects of Lamb's bonny career would take place. Jack whispered prime information – meaning gloriously relevant information – though only to Harpur and to no other detective. Such whispers could be perilous – perilous for Jack. Villains didn't like whisperers, hated and despised whisperers, in fact, and would try to torch their home, and/or maim or kill them and/or their families. In the Press not long ago, Harpur had spotted an example of how totally contemptible grassing was considered by career crooks. The multi-murderous Boston racketeer, James 'Whitey' Bulger, didn't bother to dispute at his trial that he'd killed many enemies, but angrily denied he had ever been an informant for the FBI. He claimed this would be grossly dishonourable and shameful under the gangster code he lived by, like the slaughter of women. He yelled 'fucking liar' when an ex-FBI officer told the court from the witness box that Bulger had been an informant. Of course, that might have been partly because he feared violence from other convicts when he was sent to jail if they thought him a snitch.

Revenge against stool pigeons was regarded as an obligation, as well as a right. Harpur recognized that Lamb would naturally feel due some return, some quid pro quoism, from him. Jack was vulnerable in several areas: his plentiful skin, the grand house, a mother and a long-term live-in girlfriend. His mother spent most of the year in her condo not far from Jack's sister and brother-in-law in San Francisco, but was over on one of her mouthy annual visits currently and was probably somewhere in Darien today. She had changed her name back to Lamb, though there had been a second marriage in the States. It lasted only months and, as Harpur had heard her put it, she 'didn't want to be tagged with any reminder of that sicko'.

'And what about *Amelia With Flask*?' Lamb had moved a couple of paces along. 'Very famous, of course.'

'The fame eminently deserved!' Harpur said, joining him. So, was *Amelia* kosher, and, if she was, how exactly had she come to Lamb? Prospective buyers liked to know the 'provenance' of a painting, to establish authenticity. That is, its history, its *proven* history, right back to when the artist put his or her signature on it, and then a no-gaps record of all the subsequent owners. Harpur would have liked to know it, too. Naturally, Jack abominated, and bridled at, the word 'provenance'. He refused to take part in that type of disclosure, regarding such curiosity as pettifogging and an insult – an insult not just to him and his company, which was hurtful enough, but to art in all its forms worldwide.

Harpur assumed that some of the paintings had been stolen and given a name-change, like 'Mrs Lamb'. He'd heard that for crooked international profitability art theft now held third place, just behind drugs and arms. And, as with drugs and arms, the money involved could lead to violence, killings included. Paintings might be relatively small, easy to hide and to transport. Harpur remembered a film on one of the TV movie channels, where without much trouble the hero nicks a hugely valuable water-scene classic from a New York museum. Stolen art could be used as more or less a currency-equivalent to buy a brilliant lifestyle. Or it might fund terrorism groups. Alternatively, it could have a sweet role in money laundering. That is, paintings might be bought with stolen loot, held for a while in the hope of a price rise, then offered to Jack, or someone not too legalistic, like him, to buy and sell on, in some cases to legitimate collectors; or possibly to other gangsters with their own laundering needs. Some paintings went on a kind of non-stop circuit. Occasionally, convicted crooks could bargain for a shorter sentence by offering to reveal the whereabouts of a missing picture or sculpture. There was more to art than hanging on a hook.

For the sake of victims, auction houses and insurers, Interpol and national police forces, as well as private companies, ran databases and registers that aimed to keep track of stolen works. Successes were minimal. Rumour, and more than rumour, said that Belgium in particular maintained the fastest record for making thieved daubs conclusively vamoose. Some theft victims refused to report a loss, fearing this might mean it got buried even deeper in the underworld system; or because they didn't want publicity that showed how poor security was on the rest of their collection.

An experienced art expert might have been able to trace some recent ownerships in Jack's present lot. But, of course, that would be possible only if the expert knew what Jack had at Darien. Harpur sensed this was the kind of information Lamb expected him to keep eternally quiet about, and he did. Inevitably, it compromised Harpur, turned him into a kind of see-no-evil accessory, if not a virtual partner; gave Jack a hold on him. That was a ticklish but essential feature of their relationship. Possibly, Lamb got more out of the arrangement than Harpur.

Jack was very choosy about what information he gave. He would never identify his business customers or suppliers. Jack only whispered when a crime or possible crime appalled him; or when some crooked behaviour threatened seriously to disturb the basis of day-to-day existence in the city. Jack liked life to be nice and steady, no disruptions. Harpur respected his quirks – had to. Jack's art, true or counterfeit, stayed private between them.

Jack pointed at *Amelia*. 'We're talking real quality and proper money here. The "Dutch School", as it's known, seems always to impact directly, head-on with me. I couldn't tell you why, Col.'

'The unmatched flatness of Holland is a big plus for those artists,' Harpur replied wholeheartedly. 'Plenty of good, level ground to perch their easels on, no steep slanting that would cause paint to run and splotch. A "Darien School" is impossible. Too many peaks. God knows what tint the Pacific would come out as.'

As for the counterfeits, there would naturally be no provenance for them, or no respectable provenance. They might have been turned out in someone's garden shed a couple of weeks ago, possibly by the dozen. Of course, their creators would refer to them as 'copies', rather than 'fakes'. Harpur gathered that in the art game there was an almost decent tradition of copying, even of Old Masters. He'd heard, though, that copying/faking Old Masters had become increasingly difficult to get away with because science could date a work pretty accurately by analysing the paint and canvas. Moderns were preferable.

'I shall need to know the buyer reveres *Amelia With Flask*, and reveres it for all the right reasons. That's the chief consideration, Colin, not the mere act of making a sale.'

'Like insisting they're going to "a good home" when getting rid of kittens,' Harpur replied.

'I want a purchaser who can see in a portrait such as this what is taking place, between, so to speak, the lines, as well as the obvious: there must be communion with its hinterland. This is the product of a particular society at a particular period. Due recognition should be given. Notice the graded shadowing on her eponymous flask, Col. This is perception. This is brush control. This is empathy with the very essence, with the very soul, of flasks. On the face of it, the flask is an inanimate article. The artist, though, shows its one-off identity, gives this object a distinctive personality to complement the distinctive personality of *Amelia* – a flaskish personality, yes, yet of a one-off, gloriously individual flaskishness.'

'Its mojo,' Harpur replied.

'Parting from *Amelia* will depress me. But that's to sentimentalize. Unprofessional. Putting it baldly, Col, I am a merchant venturer, and merchant venturers exist to buy and to sell, not to disable themselves through intemperate affection for a particular work, however worthy of that intemperate affection a particular work might be. Rigour is essential, detachment. Always this dilemma in the art game – a spiritual side, certainly, a commerce side, also certainly. The critic and scholar Bernard Berenson's life gives forceful examples of this, doesn't it?'

'Does it? Who?'

'He loved pictures but also took nice and sometimes dubious cuts from art deals he middle-manned.'

'Venturing always has its tricky side, Jack, especially when a flask is involved.' Harpur didn't object to taking part in this long-winded idiocy if it made Lamb feel more comfortable, more autonomous. Like everyone else, Lamb was entitled to a quota of self-deception. Life would be a bummer without it. He had to be indulged. So far. But, eventually, Harpur's mind would refuse to put up with any further evasion and absurdity and, suddenly, now for example, when Jack was continuing to spout a fond, bonkers lecturette about the floral background of *Amelia* – 'observe, Col, the implied argumentativeness of these hyacinths' – Harpur would see for a moment on the canvas not Amelia, the flask and the cluster of chopsy flowers, but an image of Jack himself: Jack dead and with his throat deeply, ostentatiously cut, in the way grasses sometimes got their throats deeply and ostentatiously cut as a warning to others, grey eyes open, staring out at Harpur from that gargantuan face, full of agony and blame for failing to protect him; almost as if he believed Harpur had supplied the serrated knife and a diagram showing the between-chin-and-chest and ear-and-ear target region. The little pink hillocks, plateaux and dunes of the wound gave an easy-to-understand illustration of how flesh was constructed.

Occasionally, Jack liked to dress up in military garments he hired from a costume shop or bought at some army-surplus car boot sale. In Harpur's present vision of him he had on a John Wayne, US, green commando beret and a light-grey tunic with medal ribbons, possibly German SS officer gear from the Second World War. Death didn't take sides. No blood from the havoc seemed to have stained the tunic, and the beret remained securely in place although there would probably have been a bit of a tussle when he was killed.

'It's a bold reversal of how I would normally think of hyacinths, but this is surely the function of great art, Col – to reappraise, to see eccentrically, to see, indeed, afresh.'

'A daunting obligation, Jack.' That vile hallucination Harpur experienced made him think not so much of John Wayne as a scene in *The Sopranos*, a TV gangster series, when Tony Soprano has a breakdown and believes fish displayed on a market stall are hectoring him in the voices of people he knows. Tony Soprano could go off and get wise treatment from his leggy woman psychiatrist though. Harpur had to cope on his own and fight his way back to full sanity and contentious hyacinths.

Jack said in a big, jolly tone: 'This one – *Amelia* – intrigues you, doesn't it, Colin? I can tell – your fixed, sort of hypnotized gaze, like, probing it for detail.'

'Well, yes.'

'If you had a spare million or two about your person you'd be making me an offer for it, wouldn't you?'

'Absolutely.' Harpur had sworn to himself never to use this word. It had been taken over by BBC news reporters on television replying to soft, feed questions from a colleague. Harpur realized he must have been pushed gravely sideways by sight of that cavernous injury.

'You could hang it in your bedroom, and it would be a delight to wake up to in the morning, wouldn't it?' Jack said.

'Well, yes.'

'You and your sweet, undergrad girlfriend, Denise.'

'Well, yes.'

'What is it that strikes you most tellingly about *Amelia with Flask*, Col?'

The extreme artisan competence of the neck butchery, Jack. There'd be no need for you to shout, 'Touché!' like in fencing, to acknowledge a hit. In fact, you wouldn't be able to shout anything, your voice-box severed. But Harpur actually said: 'The Dutchness.'

'Yes! Oh, yes!'

'I can imagine those hyacinths growing alongside a canal, of which there are many in Holland, and possibly disputing with other flowers the right to adequate soil.'

'This is why I say the purchaser must be capable of looking beyond the superficial. Hyacinths are all very well, obviously – are entirely valid Nature – but these are hyacinths that have been chosen to send out a theme, an intimation.'

Harpur hurriedly turned his back on *Jack with Incision* and made for a large painting of cargo ships grouped in port as if waiting to join a convoy during the war. They looked utterly themselves, as ships ought to look – real, rust-prone, angular, ugly, U-boat sinkable, entirely non-Jack-like. But, even so, as Harpur approached, he thought he might see Lamb hanged at a yardarm for treachery, and still intermittently radiating that awful reproachfulness when his face came around every so often as his body caught the wind and spun.

But, no, the masts stood proud, thin and empty, thank God. Harpur felt so relieved that he would have bought the painting to hang in his bedroom instead of *Amelia*, if he'd had the money, and so restore normality for him, and for Denise, who did sometimes sleep there. He would like her to sleep there more, instead of at her student hall of residence, but she probably wouldn't if she awoke to find a fairly unfavourable picture of Jack Lamb in attendance.

Harpur's two daughters loved it, also, when Denise slept over and cooked breakfast. It seemed to make them feel they belonged to a proper family again, after the loss of their mother.[1] This was another of those thoughts that Harpur kept to himself: Denise, a student at the city's university, hadn't quite turned

[1] See *Roses, Roses.*

twenty yet. She wouldn't want to be regarded as a sort of parent by two teenagers, thanks very much.

Jack Lamb had moved again, away from the ships. 'And now this gouache, Col,' he cried, 'cryptic, defiant, optimistic, feral. I don't think "feral" is to overdramatize. Do you?'

'From a gouache we might not be expecting a feral element, yet when one sees it now and ponders the overall effect, then "feral", it can be stated, is a major characteristic, an inevitable characteristic, yet only inevitable on, as it were, reflection – on a kind of hindsight. It—'

Jack turned towards the door. 'Why, here are Mother and Helen! How opportune!'

THREE

Jack Lamb knew several people who regarded his mother as entirely charming, and he would be quite willing to name them, if they didn't mind. Their attitude really pleased him, and they were definitely entitled to it. Tastes varied sharply, and life would be a lot duller if they didn't. He, personally, could see quite a number of nice qualities in her, and he was always willing to put her up for a month when she came back to Britain from the United States on holiday each year.

Jack believed it would hardly be natural for a son to refuse temporary lodgings to his mother, whatever she might be like. 'Temporary' was not an arbitrary, harsh term here, simply factual: she arrived for a break, a change, and a month would be just about right, all things considered. To her credit, Jack felt she sensed this and never tried to sneak an extra week, or weeks, on to her stay by feigning illness or terrible sorrow at having to leave Jack. Perhaps, despite what he would describe as her 'all-weathers ego', she had some occasional lapses into silent self-criticism and even suffered galloping spells of humility. His mother seemed to realize she had a flair for causing deep discomfort to those living close to her in the same house and, for a while, often very unexpectedly, she would become more or less completely tolerable – none of the worst-words swearing or loud belittling and sarkiness. She was tall, aquiline, regal, but, in Jack's view, fairly clueless about fashion and quack-quack voiced when war-pathing. Her physical height meant she could get extra, downwards force into this mouth-blare if dealing with people smaller than herself. That didn't include Jack, of course, nor Helen Surtees, Lamb's live-in partner, who stood eye-to-eye with Alice, used softer tones and dressed better, sometimes repro-punkish, sometimes formal-severe. Helen would be twenty soon. She and Harpur's student girlfriend, Denise, around Helen's age, had met at ballet lessons in the town and stayed pals.

Jack's mother loved riding, and he had extended the Darien stables to accommodate a couple of extra horses so she'd have a good choice when she went out, sometimes with Jack and Helen, sometimes with Helen only, sometimes alone. She could develop a roaring enmity towards a particular animal, perhaps because it had behaved poorly in some way while she was aboard; or perhaps because at a random moment she had a stack of spare hatred looking for a taker, and this horse might as well get a fair whack of it. Duty compelled Jack to have a replacement always available. It greatly pleased him that he could fulfil that duty. He realized, of course, that many sons would be unable to offer their mother a choice of horses, supposing she rode, which not every son's mother did. Jack could not expect her to pick a mount which, at the time, she loathed for good reasons, or, alternatively, and maybe more importantly, for no reasons at all, just pure, free-range, inexplicable loathing. It made him anxious when she went solo, not because she might have a fall and lie undiscovered in the woodland near Darien: improbable – she rode too well. But there were dangerous, watchful people about.

He knew this didn't make much sense. If someone wanted to do damage, *he* would most likely be the target. Perhaps she'd actually be safer alone, rather than with him present. That was logic. It didn't convince Jack, though. Something less than logic, or a lot *more* than logic, told him he and/or Helen should be there or thereabouts when his mother was in the saddle, exploring. A mother brought responsibilities, regardless.

The two women were in riding gear now, Helen with jeans tucked into calf-length brown boots, tight tweed jacket, black helmet; Mrs Lamb, in proper jodhpurs and boots, similar jacket and helmet. In contrast to her usual clothes, she looked totally right for that gear: jaunty, commanding, trim. Jack thought she would possibly regard the art as in competition with her, displaying itself so damn blatantly on the walls, claiming classical distinction, clamouring for attention, trying to sideline her. As she'd said lately, she didn't know much about art, but she did know what she detested: most of it. On none of her previous visits had he ever heard her swear at one of the pictures, but she would walk past them in the drawing room, facing unwaveringly frontwards as if to avoid seeing something, to right or left, that was distasteful or even obscene, but not obscene *enough*. She did swear quite a bit, including 'motherfucker', abbreviated to 'mother'. He felt she wanted to show how at ease she was now with US day-to-day, domestic conversation. She'd told him that the way many artists chose and applied colour made her think of someone 'blind bloody drunk and part concussed conducting an orchestra in a notoriously difficult concerto by Schoenberg'. She had a mind that could move adroitly between different art-forms, rubbishing both or more en route.

'Well, hello there, Mr Harpur,' she cried with a terrific, welcoming smile, her head slightly to one side, apparently trying to see round him. 'Is that a Castellani I glimpse behind you?'

Of course it wasn't a fucking Castellani. It infuriated Jack when she pulled this kind of palsied tactic. He'd seen it frequently before. She'd go about claiming art meant nothing to her, or less, and then come out with a name she'd read somewhere, liked its foreign tinkle, and memorized it, so that when she saw a chance she could chuck it into the chat to astonish and confuse people. It wrong-footed them. She loved seeing that effect. They wouldn't know whether they were dealing with the kind of ignoramus she claimed to be, or someone who knew plenty and was therefore licensed to have widespread contempt for most art, but didn't want to go on about the extent of her knowledge, out of English-fashion modesty.

She seemed to have a strange effect on Harpur, though. He turned and glanced at the non-Castellani and said, 'Possibly.'

'Ah, you cops – guarded, cagey, non-committal,' she cried with a genial woman-o'-the-world chuckle.

'Possibly,' Harpur said. Then Jack saw him seem to grow very unsettled. 'But I'd like you to come with me to look at *Amelia with Flask.* Would you, please?'

Jack thought he heard a kind of plaintiveness in the 'please'. Maybe it should have been, 'Please, oh, *please*!'

'Why?' she said. She'd stopped smiling now and gave Harpur a sort of interrogation bark.

'Do you mind?' he said. 'There are matters of interest.'

'Which?' she said.

'Some matters of interest,' Harpur replied. He went and stood in front of *Amelia* but seemed, yes, seemed to Jack scared to view it head-on. Harpur gave the picture little, nervy side glances, as if to check bit by bearable bit what was on show, and as if he couldn't risk eyeing it all at once, in toto, because . . . because . . . But Jack couldn't think of a reason. People who were old enough to remember said Harpur looked like a fair-haired Rocky Marciano, undefeated world heavyweight boxing champion, who must have been fearless and physically daunting. That seemed all wrong for Harpur now, though. He appeared terrified. But of what? A picture of a woman? Why? Harpur beckoned Mrs Lamb. She shrugged and in a while came with Helen and stood alongside him. 'It's *Amelia With Flask*, isn't it?' he said. 'I need a sort of independent opinion.'

'Well, sure it bloody is,' she said.

'There's a name plate,' Helen said, gently.

'What else could it be?' Mrs Lamb asked.

'Yes,' Harpur said. 'And you're OK, Jack?'

'Right,' Lamb said.

'Definitely OK?' Harpur said.

'Completely,' Jack said. What the hell was this about?

'Yes, you are, you are!' Harpur muttered, but a gloriously happy, relieved mutter.

The four of them stood in an arc facing *Amelia*. Alice Lamb pointed laboriously, wearily, as if explaining something to a particularly thick child: 'Here's Amelia. OK? It's a woman in a crimson robe. Still OK, Harpur? You following?' Slowly, she shifted the direction of her finger. 'And there's the Flask. So we arrive, you see, at *Amelia With Flask*. "QED", as they say in mathematics – meaning "which was to be proved".'

'Yes, yes,' Harpur said. To Jack he sounded full of gratitude, as though he'd been saved from some bewildering, immensely distressing experience, 'It *is* Amelia, and it *is* the Flask,' Harpur murmured contentedly.

'What did you think it was, a pig's arse?' she replied. Jack noticed that although his mother had picked up some Americanisms in her talk, she'd remained faithful to the British pronunciation of arse, rhyming with farce, rather than the shorter, sharper, US, 'ass', rhyming with lass. She gave Jack no consistent impression. Her slang was nomadic, cosmopolitan. But he would agree that 'a pig's arse' seemed somehow – he thought he saw why – yes, seemed somehow to give a better idea of a pig's arse than a 'pig's ass' would have. 'Pig's ass' sounded only matter-of-fact, like 'pig's ear' or 'pig's trotter'. 'Pig's arse' caught the amplitude and topography of it, and the absence of house-training. It was good to think she still clung to some Britishness. Obviously, though, he wouldn't want foolishly to over-encourage that in case she decided to come back permanently, intending to live with or near him and Helen. A well-known term for his mother's Anglo-Americanism existed – 'mid-Atlantic'. Jack felt fond of this map reference. There was a Victorian popular song, *Alice, Where Art Thou?*, used as an introduction to a BBC TV series a while ago. Jack thought that 'mid-Atlantic' would be an excellent answer.

'So, you're very keen on *Amelia With Flask*, are you, Harpur?' she said.

'The juxtaposing,' Harpur said.

'Of what?' she said.

'Yes, the Dutch can always get juxtaposing right,' Harpur said.

'The Germans do it, too.'

'I don't argue,' Harpur replied.

'Think of *A Lady With A Squirrel And A Starling* by Hans Holbein the Younger.'

'I do.'

'It's a red squirrel, not one of those vicious grey hellers you've got so many of in GB.'

'They exterminated the reds.'

'The squirrel, the starling – Nature. Of course. The lady is in the kind of formal attire demanded by the thinking of her time – bosom just about covered, matching white scarf and headpiece. So, we have creatures of the wide outdoors alongside someone who shows the cultivated, imposed refinement of her social class.'

'True.'

'Sometimes I wonder about you,' she replied. 'Both.'

'In which respect?' Harpur said.

'The juxtaposing,' she said.

'Of what?' Harpur said.

'The relationship. You and Jack,' she said.

'This is an association going way back,' Jack said.

'Yes, way back,' Helen said. 'Art and other interests.'

'I don't mean gay,' Alice said.

'No,' Jack replied.

'Friendship,' Helen said.

'You look after each other?' she asked.

'In which sense, Mother?'

'*You* tell *me*,' she said.

'Tell you what? Harpur said.

'Do I get a whiff of snitch?' Alice said.

'If you do it's a dud whiff of snitch,' Jack said.

'This is a big-job cop up in your property looking at a haul of pics from who knows where?'

'Me,' Jack said. 'I know where.'

'Jack is meticulous on that kind of thing,' Helen said. 'Sources.'

'Meticulous?' Alice asked.

'Tirelessly scrupulous,' Helen said.

'Famed for it,' Harpur said. 'Mention the name Jack Lamb in artistic circles and someone will automatically comment, "Meticulous."'

'You help Jack with his business; he helps you with yours? The rattletrap car you come in, parked outside, has "Untraceable" written all over it,' she said.

'Spelt all right?' Harpur said. 'Is there an e after the c?'

'How do you think he looks?' Alice Lamb said.

'Who, Jack?' Harpur said.

'I come back after a gap of nearly a year and what do I see?' Alice replied. 'Possibly, I'm more likely to notice changes.'

'With regard to Jack, you mean?' Helen asked.

'With regard to Jack,' Alice said.

'Well, he's fine, as ever, surely,' Helen said.

'Yes, surely,' Harpur said.

'But you sounded anxious about him just now,' she said.

'Did I?' Harpur said.

'You know you fucking did,' she said.

'Did I?' Harpur replied.

'Shall I tell you what I see?' Alice replied.

'Why not?' Harpur said.

'I see fear, I see cringing, I see shame, I see suffering, I see doom,' Alice said. She swung her head about giving each of the other three a bit of special, dogmatic gaze. Jack had experienced that kind of thing from her often as a child and later. It didn't upset him now. The other two could probably cope with it.

'I just see Jack as Jack,' Harpur said.

'You're not his mother,' Alice said.

'Well, no,' Harpur said.

'I see an onset,' Alice said.

'Of what?' Helen asked.

'Dread of retribution,' Alice said.

'For what?' Helen said.

'Dread of punishment,' Alice said.

'For what?' Helen said.

'Dread of hatred, dread of contempt, dread of that final, savage injury,' Alice said.

'Which?' Helen said.

'Do you know the name "Whitey" Bulger?' Alice replied.

'"Whitey"?' Harpur said.

Jack thought he sounded utterly puzzled, and so most likely wasn't.

'Once a gang lord in Boston, responsible for a dozen or so murders. He was on the lam without a final b for years, but they caught him at last, put him in court. What do you think seemed to trouble him most?'

Helen said: 'Well, I suppose—'

'Not the blame for those murders. No. But an ex-FBI guy said Bulger had been an informant. Whitey screamed a denial. For him, informing was a much more disgusting crime than murder. A snitch was filth. Perhaps some of his murder victims were informants. He wouldn't regret their deaths. That's what informants deserved. And, now, perhaps some informants realize this and the funk is in their faces. Have you noticed, Helen, when we're out riding how he's staring about the whole time, nervy, tense, terrified, like expecting pay-off for his betrayals?'

'No,' Helen said. 'What betrayals?'

'Yes,' Harpur said. 'What betrayals?'

'Yes,' Jack said.

'Oh, Helen, he's your man. You have to stand by him,' Alice said.

'He's your son,' Helen said. 'You should stand by him, too.'

'I want him safe, intact. I didn't bring him up to have his throat cut,' Alice said.

'Not wise to let imagination run away with us,' Harpur replied. 'Enjoy the tranquillity and beauty of great art instead, such as *Amelia With Flask*.'

'He's got two kinds of worry, hasn't he?' Alice said. 'First, there's the betrayals. People see the lovely house, the grounds, the horses, all of it, and they deduce he's got it and is allowed to keep it because he's built a nice connection with a cop. This nice connection has put some of their relatives or mates in jail. That's very irritating for them. And then, second, he has all this stuff on the walls, some of it valuable. Maybe all of it valuable. There will be hard, knowledgeable folk out there who'd like to get hold of it.'

'It's here for them to get hold of, Mother, if they have the price.'

'I'm not talking about paying for it. You know I'm not talking about paying for it,' Alice said. 'If you get in their way, Jack, what do you think will happen to you? There might be no time for you to call out Mr Harpur in one of his old cars. I hear art theft is up there for profitability with drugs and guns.'

'All trades have their risks,' Jack said. 'I keep alert.'
'Jack keeps very alert,' Harpur said.
'Oh, God,' Alice said. 'So play naive.'

FOUR

George Dinnick's art firm had three main people. First, obviously, himself. Then, equally valuable for their different skills, Liz Rossol and Justin Benoit. Managing them into useful cooperation with each other was how George saw his chief role as head of the company. Useful cooperation with each other didn't mean making love to each other, which they might or might not be at. They wouldn't need an impresario for that. But this Jack Lamb project illustrated pretty well how the two of them, Liz and Justin, should function together. They had their specialities, like consultants and football players.

What George called Liz's fieldwork had provided the original tip that now and then Lamb might have some good stuff at his country house. George didn't ask who the tipster was and knew he'd have got no answer if he *had*. He caught a half hint the guiding voice might have been Danish. That was as much as would be forthcoming. Liz did a lot of travel, particularly in Scandinavia, Belgium, the Low Countries and Luxembourg. Art was like that – cosmopolitan. Liz had at least the basics in a handful of languages, fluency in three, and knew how to listen and, more important, how to find people it was worth listening *to*. In only a few years she'd built up an excellent network of what she called 'friends' in the art game, but who were actually clients or customers. By now she had quite a hold on some of these, enabling her to apply a kind of genial, irresistible pressure – Liz's kind of genial, irresistible pressure, which could reasonably be translated as outright blackmail, even menaces. She had a round, cheerful, almost jolly face and features, which helped a lot.

The thing about the art business was that in matters of legality and/or morality there existed considerable areas of vagueness.

Nobody known to George Dinnick was better at exploiting this vagueness than Liz. She thought of it as her habitat. Her relationships with her *friends* could be very complicated. For instance, there were collectors who considered themselves utterly law-abiding and honest in buying and/or selling their paintings and sculptures. They wanted all their dealings to be entirely transparent – a modish term that George found deeply unreal. And then one of Liz's friends would get offered something he or she particularly greatly desired and which he or she was willing pay the asking price for; and was willing, also, to assume that the work came validly on to the market. That is, it had been properly sold by a previous owner, who had previously properly bought it, 'properly' here signifying the work at no stage had been stolen. The friend of Liz would probably long to believe everything was immaculate but might not have the time or ability or inclination to do a real look into its history. Liz could make use of this reluctance.

Naturally, if there had been publicity about a spectacular robbery of works named in the media, perhaps with photographs, it would be mad for any collector to act as if ignorant of where the items came from. But Dinnick knew matters weren't always so clear, thank God. Consider booty: the Nazis confiscated art works from galleries, museums, private collections in every occupied country, and there were a lot. Marshal of the Reich, Hermann Goering, cornered a heap of looted works. After the German surrender in 1945, some paintings, sketches and sculptures were traced and returned to their owners. But some were not. They came on to the market with their histories obscure, often deliberately *made* obscure. 'Ownership' turned into a tangled, very shifting and shifty term.

More modern theft might also present special problems. Some collectors didn't like reporting they'd been robbed. They feared that, if a police search were started, the work would get pushed further into hiding, to avoid detection, might even get destroyed, to be rid of evidence. Also, disclosing a loss could indicate poor security and bring more trouble.

Liz knew how to get an abiding plus for the firm from all these various, gloriously helpful sources of doubt. She might have handled the sale of a painting to one of her friends, giving the impression, of course, that the transaction was totally pure and legitimate. But later, when Liz, perhaps, required some less pure and legitimate help from the friend, she would hint that, in fact, the life story of the piece or pieces in question was now known to be exceptionally dodgy, the sale possibly criminal/Hun tainted. Liz would also hint that, naturally, she wouldn't be disclosing anywhere that the friend's right to ownership could be dubious. *And, oh, by the way, would this so-far reputable and apparently blameless friend mind doing Liz – the up-till-now ever so discreet, careful Liz – a minor favour by getting on the phone to another reputable and blameless collector, Jack Lamb, for instance, in his handsome, resoundingly named property, Darien, and vouch for the genuine, cash-backed interest of another friend who'd like to visit Darien with a view to adding to an already distinguished collection?* In this fashion, Liz would apply her admirable flair.

Justin had charm and persuasiveness but couldn't just roll up at Lamb's place and say he'd heard there might be some fine items on offer at Darien occasionally, and could he please have a dekko, if a selection were in house at present? Lamb would almost certainly know about all the shadowy and very hazardous factors in this kind of trading and would need some sort of assurance that Justin, or whatever he called himself for this operation, was of true, authentic standing, or, at least, not a cop or private investigator engaged by a victim to search for lost treasures. Liz created this status for him: perfect collaboration. As a matter of fact, Justin would possibly stick with his proper name, because nobody in this sort of potential double-cross on double-cross was going to complain to the police. Here was the essential element in Liz's brilliantly productive fieldwork. She had a good degree in the history of art, but it was her instinctive tactical nous that made her such . . . well, such an artist herself, and one not easily copied, as some were. Dinnick had named the firm 'Cog', because of the way it helped the machinery of art commerce to function efficiently.

FIVE

Ralph Ember had been thinking quite a bit about art lately. Not any particular piece of art, but art in general. Everybody would agree this was some topic. He'd been thinking about art in what he would regard as a good and mature way, good and mature meaning here that he felt totally in favour of art. He wouldn't describe himself as a fan of art, because the word 'fan' suggested half-daft, hysterical enthusiasm like screaming groupies for a pop star, not his kind of thoughtful, well-founded appreciation. What Ralph had, in his view, was a steady, quiet, unshowy *reverence* for art. Some of the amounts paid for paintings were bound to attract massive respect. The international rich had become hooked and pushed prices up and then further up. He'd read that a famed work called *The Scream* went for $120 million. Apparently, inside the art trade a battle was going on because certain auction houses would handle only stuff from established painters and sculptors, since that's where the big, reliable loot was. Ralph could understand that attitude, but he did see the other side of it too – the unfairness to new, modern people. Regardless of whether a high quality painting had been around a while and given a tasteful frame, or still stood on the easel, Ralph was sure to delight in it. If he'd been asked, he would have replied that his appreciation was wide-ranging, very wide-ranging. Frames could do a good job, but they were not the essence, only a presentation gimmick, like pastel-shade silk knickers.

One of his constant, major ambitions was to raise the quality of a social club he owned, The Monty, at present unquestionably a lovely building but, because of the membership, also unquestionably a scrap-heap, crap-heap. And, naturally enough, he considered one of the fine arts could help him bring change. He did what he could by other methods, also, to spruce up the club's grubby character, but they didn't really work. For instance, Ralph issued every member on joining with a booklet of Monty rules, as a positive and thoughtful guide towards reasonable behaviour, this to be renewed annually with any amendments. The first, most important, most prominent, most non-variable of these club laws stated that no weaponry 'of any kind whatsoever. REPEAT – any kind whatsoever' should be brought into The Monty. Page One carefully listed the banned items. Ralph wanted thoroughness and total clarity. Named in alphabetical order were: baseball bats, bayonets, bludgeons, finger-irons, grenades, handguns, knives, nail bombs, Samurai or any other type of sword, shot guns, sawn-off or not, skewers, tasers. He didn't specify the make of handgun because some devious moronic sods in the membership would find a type of revolver or automatic not mentioned and pretend they assumed this particular piece must be OK. They'd turn a ban into a permit, a no-no into acceptable.

Of course, some people ignored the booklet. They could read all right, the majority of them, but rejected even the most well-intentioned, sensible orders. Behaviour? They wouldn't know what decent behaviour even looked like, and if by some momentary fluke they did, their immediate response would be to fuck it up somehow. Ember had witnessed several very unpleasant episodes in the bar featuring disallowed weapons. He recalled, especially, that disgusting use of a .38 automatic pistol by Basil Gordon Loam, the 'Gordon Loam' occasionally spoken as one surname, though not hyphenated.[2] He was known also as Enzyme. His family – either the Gordon part or the Loam – used to add up to something an age ago, apparently, with a fortune in tea. Now, though, he scuttled about doing sleazy jobs for odd sleazy people and being casual and perilous with guns.

As Ralph saw things, art – paintings, sculptures – obviously involved the creation of images. A wheat field in a painting was, plainly, not the wheat field, only a likeness of it, an image of it. That's what art was all about – turning the real into what could be put on to canvas. But art also created a different, secondary kind of image, Ralph believed, and this could have a real impact on his attempt to get the club up towards at least respectability, and possibly eminence. He meant the image, the

[2] See *Disclosures.*

personal reputation, of whoever bought the picture or pictures or sculpture. As long as the work or works represented definite top rating, the individual they belonged to received a true boost to his or her personal image, reputation, by possessing them; the way owning a Rolls Royce or big diamonds, like that bonny ring Richard Burton gave Liz Taylor, brought someone notability. A collector of high-calibre art acquired not just the art but high public regard for (i) recognizing in a great item what in fact made it great; (ii) admiring, even thrilling to, this excellence; (iii) coming up with the oodles of boodle required to buy it.

Ralph reasoned that if he could only get some of this distinguished, personal reputation, this notability, The Monty would inevitably share some of the hiked esteem and glory. Ralph had read somewhere about a famous hotel in New York which was originally of high reputation as a centre for an extremely worthwhile experiment in communal social living. But it was gradually taken over by druggies and petty crooks and lost all its prestige. Ralph aimed triumphantly to reverse this process in The Monty. He would brilliantly raise the quality of his club, not permit its sad moral collapse.

However, possessing top-grade paintings didn't guarantee absolutely that everyone thought the sun shone out of the owner's art appreciation. Ralph naturally realized this. In the art game there was something called 'provenance', a very important something. It meant: where did the owner of this or that piece of art get it, and how? Was crime involved – that is, theft? Was violence involved – that is, brutality during the theft, gunplay, hijacking? Violence had often been associated with art in the past, such as when the painter Vincent van Gogh cut off his own ear, as a bit of a saucy jape.

Despite these questions, doubts and the ear outrage, though, Ember continued to believe very firmly in the beneficial side of art.

What he wanted, and badly wanted, was some aid in bringing that licensed club he ran in Shield Terrace up to the kind of outstanding cultural level enjoyed by, say, The Athenaeum, in London, or Boodle's. He'd admit his club certainly didn't fall into this sort of category at present, too many members being dregs and/or arseholes. Ralph speculated, though, that if people heard he, individually, had become familiar with true and distinguished art and possessed renowned examples of it in respectable, tasteful, ungaudy frames, his own and the club's status would certainly benefit. He and The Monty were powerfully, almost mystically, linked, like the Queen and her corgis.

Once the club had begun to emerge in its new elite form, he might hang the pictures there now and then, as long as security seemed OK. Just to be credited with buying the art, though, would most likely be enough to hint at an alteration in The Monty's standing. His next step then must be to block membership renewal for all lowlifes, all slags, all slappers, for Enzyme and those like him. That might seem cruel, perhaps snobbish, but Ralph felt it vital to his noble development plan, his quest, his unique mission. For too long The Monty had been a rubbish tip. He would transform it, this transformation to go much deeper and further than what might be called a fresh coat of paint. But, yes, he planned that paint should be involved, the fine pallet paint of old masters or mistresses, and their modern successors.

In fact, Ember had already introduced an art element into the club, though of a minor form and not with complete success; to be honest, it was the cause of a disgraceful disaster. Owing to the grim, non-stop possibility that he would get shot dead, or, at least, permanently wheelchaired, or put into an eternal coma by business colleagues when sitting at his little accounting shelf-cum-desk behind the Monty bar, he'd had a rectangular steel barricade tailored and suspended tactically between pillars at the club so that nobody could draw a line on him just by stepping in through the main doors – set slightly higher than the bar – and letting go with a multi-round burst, then exiting fast. One main area of risk had been closed by this very original, made-to-measure fitment.

But Ralph realized it gave a rather coarse, frightening, killing-fields impression of The Monty, and although that might, regrettably, be deserved in some aspects, it was blatantly not the kind of flavour – the kind of *image*, to recycle the term – not the kind of image Ralph sought for The Monty, whether in its future shape or now. It couldn't be usual or desirable for a proprietor to fear having his chest and/or head smashed open by a pop-in visitor's barrage. *Hello, Ralph. Goodbye, Ralph.*

To disguise the life-preserver's true, disturbing purpose, Ralph had turned to . . . had turned to a type of art, though not the out-and-out sort he'd been thinking about these last couple of months. He'd arranged for some enlarged illustrations from a famed work, *The Marriage of Heaven and Hell*, by the poet William Blake, to be pasted on to the steel, giving, Ralph thought, an attractive and scholarly touch to the hovering bulwark, while not in any way impairing its actual anti-hitman readiness.

But, naturally, there'd been members of The Monty who considered this literary reference a bit of aerial Ralphy swank. These retards wouldn't even have heard of William Blake. Ralph had come across him during the Foundation Year of a mature student degree programme he'd begun at the university up the road, though he'd had to suspend the course because of increased business pressures, especially a brilliant, sustained boom in Charlie sales. Gordon Loam was banned instantly and for ever from the club in any of its forms following flagrantly imbecilic behaviour towards the Blake. He had opened fire with a Smith and Wesson handgun on the illustrations when pissed out of his skull one night, not on tea, causing what Ralph regarded as very unseemly damage to the beard of a figure in *The Marriage of Heaven and Hell.*[3] There'd been further acute hazards and breakages in the crowded club below, because the bullets ricocheted from that impenetrable, two to three centimetres thick metal comforter.

Skilled, urgent repairs to the Blake were put in hand, without reference to the insurance company in case of delays and/or ribaldry, but Ralph had come to feel that, in a way, the contemptible, ill-disciplined volley carried a message for him. It was: to acquire art that scored in its own right, not merely as cover for something crudely, ominously practical, such as the elevated rampart, but wholly, genuinely, glorious itself. Great paintings had a fundamental, independent worth and one-off identity. For instance, Ralph thought it would be philistine to stand before,

[3] See *Disclosures*

say, a Rembrandt or a Gauguin and exclaim, 'This could do a great camouflage job in my club!'

At the time of the Blake attack by Gordon Loam, Ralph had bellowed The Monty ban on him and added, to crush and punish him further, 'I'm going to install real, wonderful art in the club, and I will not allow you ever to get near it.' Ralph knew great pictures did get attacked at times by nutters. They were usually trying to publicize some selfish political point, about postage rates or wind farms. Gordon Loam, aka Enzyme, didn't need that kind of motive. Downright malevolence was enough. He had plenty of it, probably brought on by permanent rattiness at the way his family had slid in wealth and position. He probably loud-mouthed to cronies that he'd turned *The Marriage of Heaven and Hell* into a shotgun wedding. The Smith and Wesson wasn't a shotgun, of course, but someone as crude, insulting and bombastic as Gordon Loam wouldn't let a need for basic accuracy stop what he'd regard as a hilariously witty jibe.

Ralph was OK with that third requirement he'd listed for someone moving in on serious art – an ability to cough enough to pay for it. As a matter of fact, Ralph quite regularly had barrel loads of cash from his other business, much larger than the club. This was the supply of recreational substances on an expanding, big-city scale, chiefly Charlie and weed, but also all the rest. Ralph peacefully, beneficially, shared that trade with another local firm belonging to someone Ralph naturally knew very well, Mansel Shale. Their organizations were separate from each other, but mutually tolerant. This concord suited each of them and the police. Almost certainly, it would not be Manse or any of his people, or a gunman hired by Manse or by any of his people, who might slip into The Monty one day or night and try to see off Ember; but some jumped-up sod or sods who wanted to jump up higher and had decided that Ralph dead would make a great springboard. Or a pro hired by some jumped-up sod or sods. Or someone like Enzyme, enraged by the public humiliation of his ban and set on payback.

Ralph had an idea that Manse disposed of some of his profits into art. Although he lacked refinement by the metric tonne and, speechwise, sounded as if education hadn't been invented yet when he was a kid, Shale did have what seemed an authentic taste for Pre-Raphaelite works, usually young, skinny women with unchubby elbows, long ginger hair cascading down on to their neat breasts, bright, glossy, purplish dresses, and a look on their faces indicating plenty of the most gut-churning intensity about emotional problems. Ralph believed he could – even should – follow Manse Shale in the pictures aspect, though not specifically with Pre-Raphaelites, which Ralph found rather brash and samey. He felt pretty certain the models for those Pre-Raphaelite men artists got fucked.

Probably quite a lot of UK business folk with earnings they could hardly tell the Revenue about did some serious laundering in the paintings and sculpture areas. Ralph knew Manse bought sometimes from a local dealer, Jack Lamb, who lived not far from Ralph. They both had ancient, modernized country manor houses. Ralph could feel a kind of neighbourly fellowship with Lamb because of their properties and, in addition, Ralph had discovered a further strange resemblance. Each had inherited from a previous owner – probably someone upper-crust and learned way back – a Latin quotation on a blue tablet fixed to the gates of each estate. Lamb's said '*Omnes eodem cogimur*', which Ralph had heard meant 'we are all driven to the same end'. The maxim at Ralph's home, Low Pastures, read '*Mens cuiusque is est quisque*', translated on the internet as 'a man's mind is what he is'. Ralph preferred his. He didn't want to think of himself as 'driven'. *He* was the driver, and by means of his drive he'd eventually manage a lift in rating for The Monty. His made-up mind on this was what he was, in Latin or any other lingo.

These similarities would make an approach to Lamb much easier than it might have been. They'd talk in English, of course, not Latin. Ralph felt that because of their lovely, historic dwellings, grounds, paddocks and the classical mottoes, he and Lamb had become sort of squires hereabouts, though not via family succession. Jack had arrived at that position through the purchase and sale of items of true beauty, the bulk quite possibly genuine; Ralph through gifted, energetic marketing of the various well-known relaxing commodities, which he recognized had enemies, but which he knew would prevail: all sorts of top people, including Iles, the Assistant Chief Constable here, backed legalization.

Ralph could fantasize about things a few centuries ago and

imagine the local peasantry who had discovered the meaning of that Latin on the gate idolizing him and saying respectfully among themselves while harvesting the curly kale, 'Squire Ember of the Big House, Low Pastures, has certainly got a mind, and that mind is what Squire Ember is, so if he didn't have a mind he wouldn't exist, and who would be in the Big House then?' Unfortunately, people like those would have swilled back too much home-produced scrumpy cider over the years for their brains to cope efficiently with philosophical points.

This morning, seated at his accounting desk behind the bar, as the first staff members turned up to start the day, Ralph glanced fondly around at the mahogany panelling and well-polished brass fittings and thought – as he'd often thought – that The Monty looked like a place of real, solid, traditional quality. It was the ropy membership who let it down. He knew now he should have been more careful when he first bought the club about the type of people he'd let join. But it was a mistake that could be corrected, thank God. He yearned for the time when the effects of that error had been reversed and the protective Blake was no longer needed – would, in fact, seem quaint and laughable. So far, that time had not arrived.

Enzyme did arrive, though.

Barmen and chefs had come in via the staff entrance at the rear of the club, and Ralph left his seat and went to unlock the main doors on to the Terrace ready for the day's first customers. He was returning to his desk when he heard the door pushed gently open behind him. Ralph turned to offer a landlordly greeting to the early birds. Basil Gordon Loam, late thirties, green cord trousers, brown leather jacket, dark hair worn longish covering the top of his ears, gave Ralph a smile full of heartiness, friendship and purpose. Ember had the odd notion that Gordon Loam's features looked only temporary, as if he could fit a different combination tomorrow. Ralph wondered if that's where the nickname came from: in science an enzyme was a substance concerned with causing a reaction – with causing change.

Enzyme said mildly: 'No need to rush to your chair and special cover, Ralph. I haven't any bad intent. I come to apologize, to heal wounds, not cause more. It's true I carry a Smith and Wesson, *the* shamed Smith and Wesson, admittedly against wise Monty precepts. But it is a gun I bring only to hand over, a symbol of my wish for reconciliation. It is crucial to our present proceedings. I hope you will accept it, Ralph, in the kind of large spiritedness I know you capable of.' He moved as though to bring out the automatic from its shoulder holster.

'No! Leave it where it is,' Ralph yelled. 'I don't want any fucking symbolism here.'

Enzyme gave a great, comradely chuckle.

SIX

On the train, Liz Rossol did some careful rereading with her breakfast. An emergency: she needed to take another look around the Darien area. At home yesterday she'd had a bit of a shock. Always, after conducting fieldwork for the Cog firm, Liz paid for issues of the local newspapers, dailies and weeklies, to be forwarded to her London address so that she could update her researches, particularly with anything to do with art; or exceptional police activity in the area; or with road works that might demand diversions for a getaway vehicle; or, of course, with news reports or features about a target property or person, in the present instance the country house Darien and its owner, Lamb, and other occupants. A gossip column, 'I Spy', in one of the tabloids, which turned up by post the day before, had troubled Liz. She'd decided she must do some more on-the-spot nosing. She had the piece in front of her now in the dining car as she ate a plump pair of kippers with a pot of middling quality coffee.

SAUCY ART FRACAS AT THE MONTY

> I hear of an unusual, even explosive, happening the other night at The Monty, Mr Ralph Ember's ever-interesting and stimulating social club in Shield Terrace. The starting point for the incident was, apparently, art, not usually a presiding topic at The Monty. Sources tell me that a suspended collage based on the poet William (*Tyger, Tyger*) Blake's work *The*

Marriage of Heaven and Hell was severely damaged during a deeply unfortunate and, indeed, perilous few moments at the club, for damage was not confined to the collage.

Enraged by this grossly uncivil, philistine breakdown of decent behaviour, El Cid lookalike Mr Ember summarily banned one member for ever from The Monty, not simply as punishment for tarnishing the club's precious character, but also to safeguard in advance distinguished pictures he intends displaying at The Monty soon. These, he confidently hopes, will raise the club's reputation for culture to a level even higher than it occupies at present, which is saying something. Yes, something.

A bottle of Worcestershire sauce – obligatory in the preparation of 'bloody Mary' drinks, containing vodka, ice, tomato juice and the sauce – was shattered, badly splashing the surface of a pool table and the T-shirt of a club member. I am told that one long-time regular at the club, Mr Basil Gordon Loam (pictured below at a previous Monty convocation), offered at once to pay for any damage caused, whether to the collage, the pool table or the 'FASHION IS MY LONG SUIT' T-shirt. Repairs were immediately put in hand by Mr Ember, and he promised to have the T-shirt laundered. I understand the club will foot the bill for all these services. He declined the offer from Mr Gordon Loam on what were described by other members as 'grounds of principle'.

The collage is displayed on a hefty metal girder installed between pillars of the bar, either to increase the effectiveness of the air conditioning system (official explanation), or to protect Mr Ember, when he is seated at his accounting desk, from a fusillade by competitors in the general commercial scene (another explanation). It is known that Mr Ember does not care for this alternative version because it makes The Monty sound like an underworld battle ground and hardly the spot to hang great works of art in. Most people will see why Mr Ember resents this harmful reflection on his popular and normally refined, well-ordered, tranquil club. The white beard of a naked male figure on all fours, one of *The Marriage of Heaven and Hell*'s

> endearing personnel, suffered the worst rips, and I'm sure Mr Ember was greatly relieved when assured by decor experts that it could be undetectably restored. No proprietor would want his club famous for a shattered ancient beard with literary connections.

Yes, this account had made Liz uneasy and still did. She could put up with the customary flippant, skittish style for such personalized journalism, but she disliked the evasions, the deliberate concealment. That phrase 'even explosive', at the start of the piece – what did it mean? Just boisterousness? Noisiness? Or was this a kind of code? If the collage hung on a girder between pillars, how could it have been damaged? The 'I Spy' column didn't say the girder had fallen, which might have brought harm to the collage – and to anyone underneath. Was the smashed Worcestershire sauce bottle and the unhelpful scatter of splashes linked in some fashion with the assault on *Tyger, Tyger* Blake's work?

In Liz's view, the only sequence possible was that some member in the bar, maybe drunk, takes pot shots with a handgun at the collage and the bullets ricochet off the girder, one of them splintering the Worcestershire sauce bottle into shrapnel and causing havoc stains. The 'I Spy' columnist might not want to spell this out because gunfire in a club must become a police matter and the journalist could get pulled into their inquiries. Most people would probably work out that the incident involved shooting, but it could be blind-eyed since nobody seemed to have been hurt, despite 'perilous' moments.

Liz assumed that the man banned for ever was Basil Gordon Loam ('pictured below') though the column didn't say so, perhaps scared of libelling him. It named Gordon Loam only because he offered to 'foot the bill' for putting things right and was turned down by Ember. She thought this gesture by Gordon Loam seemed like someone regretful and appalled at what he'd done in a stupid, *jeux d'esprit*, mischievous outburst and, immediately afterwards, eager to make amends. The proprietor wouldn't have it, 'on grounds of principle', the principle being that the gun play, flying glass shards and cavorting sauce undermined club dignity, and repentant money could not buy an excuse for this. She did a long gaze at the picture of Basil Gordon Loam.

Was he familiar, half familiar? Had she seen someone very like him around galleries and auction houses, mostly in London but elsewhere in Britain, too – Glasgow? Birmingham? Cardiff? – and possibly on the Continent – Ghent? Antwerp? Dark hair, long over the ears, wide nostrils like drift mines, late thirties. 'Basil Gordon Loam' – was that name stored in her subconscious from trade gossip, or even from the fringes of a deal?

The Monty sounded a dump, all the seeming praise obviously sarcastic – 'refined', 'well-ordered', 'tranquil', its already brilliant cultural level maybe due for a lift, 'which is saying something. Yes, something'. The 'Yes, something' to be interpreted as the opposite of what it seemed, just as the 'convocations' referred to probably didn't properly describe the sort of louche shindigs customary in the club. Because of its unclassy nature, the owner, Ralph Ember, might be all the more committed to a campaign of improvement. Gordon Loam – if it *was* Gordon Loam – had in an unforgivable spasm disrupted that campaign. Ember wouldn't want his obnoxious cash.

Liz thought she might have heard of The Monty while working in the area previously. As far as she could recall, it wasn't a flattering mention. But the club hadn't seemed relevant to her researches on Lamb and Darien and so had not been worth investigating. 'I Spy' changed that, though. She felt that this almost farcical incident with art as its theme might affect local atmosphere. In its sneering way, the 'I Spy' column had spoken about this – 'art not usually a presiding topic at The Monty'. The 'I Spy' readership, including, most probably, the people at Darien, would be alerted to fancy work of some sort affecting pictures, although there was no connection she could yet see between the club and Lamb and Darien other than geographical nearness.

In these new circumstances, the thought of sending Justin to find what works Lamb had and their value made her anxious. It might – *might* – be possible for Justin to do these inquiries safely, posing as a genuine collector eager to see paintings held at Darien. He would very probably roll up at Jack's place with a sparkling recommendation from one of Liz's impeccable, obliging, knowledgeable, arm-twisted friends. But Lamb had been in this game a long time and wasn't likely to be stupid and/or naive. He might sense what was Justin's actual role and purpose – reconnaissance for an imminent raid on Lamb's collection – and dispose of him; or get some hired heavies to dispose of him. Art could be very big money. Of course it could. Would there be firms like Cog if not? Come to that, would there be operatives like Justin and herself if not? Very big money brought very big, life-threatening risks. There was the human frame to think about as well as the other kind, hanging on the wall.

Yet the situation hadn't really changed, had it, from when the Darien project was first considered? That is: Jack Lamb from time to time had some authentic, high-cost items among the fakes and maybe fakes at his country house, and the house might be broachable. Were her fears special to Justin because of the beautiful way things had developed between them recently? Had her judgement been pushed off kilter by that lovely relationship? This wouldn't be very professional. What she was going to try to discover now was whether any extra hazards to the Darien project had been produced by that blast-off insult to *The Marriage of Heaven and Hell*, if her guess at what had gone on was correct.

She'd arranged for a hire car to be waiting for her at the station, and she ought to be able to start her new survey right away. On her first visit she'd bought a street map, and she found Shield Terrace on it now. First thing, she meant to drive out for a look at The Monty. She finished her breakfast, thoroughly clearing the fish skeleton of all flesh, drank the remains of the coffee regardless, and gave her mouth a long, anti-kipper, deodorizing squirt from her breath freshener. Spying had its special hygiene.

SEVEN

Yes, Ralph regarded the Enzyme chuckle in the Monty bar this morning as 'comradely' – false comradely, tactical comradely, devious comradely.

'I love that,' Enzyme said.

'What?' Ralph said.

'I love the way you slice through things to the core, Ralph,' Basil Gordon Loam said, voice big, precise, warm, reeking with homage, false homage, tactical homage, devious homage, Smith and Wesson-backed homage.

'Which things? Which core?'

'It reminds me of what I've read about Winston Churchill during the Second World War. He'd tell his generals and admirals and air marshals to give him: "ON NOT MORE THAN HALF A SHEET OF PAPER (Repeat: ON NOT MORE THAN HALF A SHEET OF PAPER)" their plans for, say, the D-Day invasion of Europe, or the fire bombing of Dresden. The nub. He was interested only in nubs. You strike me as a nubs person yourself, Ralph. I've always thought so. There's me sounding off just now with noisy notions, woolly, inflated words like "symbol", but you . . . as I say, you just slice through it to the essential, expose it as the blab it is by a sweetly placed profanity. This is your powerfully demotic, indeed, *democratic* answer – the way strong, man-o'-the-people words might dismiss flowery, highfalutin' jabber from someone like me. Classic.'

'I had to fucking stop you getting your fucking mad fucking fingers on a fucking gun,' Ralph said. 'Are those profanities sweetly placed and democratic, too?'

Enzyme drew his hand back from the shoulder holster. He gave a sort of generous, even noble, you-win wince. Ralph felt satisfied. Enzyme had been flattened, like Dresden.

'I'd like you to go now, Basil,' Ralph said. He used his proper first name, not Enzyme, to keep distance between them, avoid familiarity. Ember knew that some people called him in secret 'Panicking Ralph' or even 'Panicking Ralphy', because of foul, false rumours about his behaviour at crisis moments in the past. But nobody, however malicious and slanderous, could possibly have found any trace of panic when the crisis centred on The Monty. Cool, effective, unflinching – that was Ralph then. He could surprise even himself by his powerful staunchness. Ralph thought it had some of that bulldog quality associated with Churchill during World War Two, so, perhaps the taste for nubs was not the only common characteristic they shared. True, Ralph had reacted a bit sharply when Enzyme was going for the Smith and Wesson just now, allegedly to bring it out as a sign of defeat, but that wasn't panic on Ember's part, just wisdom, taking into account Enzyme's previous sick spasm with a gun.

'I especially recall one of your statements on that collage evening,' Gordon Loam said. He spoke with awe, as though he'd been granted a unique revelation, possibly even up to full epiphany standard, too massive and incandescent to be defined straight off. It had to be gradually eked out in manageable portions or it might damage the listener, like feeding a starving child too much too soon.

'Which evening?'

'Oh, Ralph, but that's kind of you. *So* kind.'

'What's kind of me?'

'*Typically* kind,' Enzyme said. He touched the quantity of hair over his right ear, shifted some sheaves of it slightly, as though to clear a passage, so he'd hear properly any further fine kindnesses coming his way.

'Kind how?' Ralph said.

'To talk as though that evening wasn't still prominent and deeply resented in your memory: my absurd, over-exuberant, disrespectful ploy towards the flying collage.' Gordon Loam did a kind of hitch-hiking gesture, pointing with his left thumb up towards the *The Marriage of Heaven and Hell.*

'That was a ploy, was it?' Ralph said.

'So glad to see the beardy's been put back to rights.'

'Do you call that respectful, then?'

'What?'

'"Beardy". This is someone who brings dignity, stature and

intellectual depth to the club. Is "beardy" a proper term for him? Bugger off, Basil. You've no right to be here.'

'What you said then about art,' Enzyme replied. 'This gripped me. It was something I could not pursue with you at the time, the circumstances being unconducive – your very reasonable rage. But I filed that reference away, and here I am this morning to discuss it. I could be of help to you in that, Ralph. It would be a privilege.'

'Help in what?'

'Art.'

'You?'

'Ralph, you said you'd be getting some real art for the club. All right, in that understandably angry spell, you also said you would never let me near it, the suggestion being that I might put a .38 bullet through the work or works, I suppose, following that dire precedent.' He had what Ralph measured as a twenty-second further chuckle at the sheer preposterousness of this idea. It was as if Enzyme considered himself someone absolutely different now from the shoot-bang-fire jerk who peppered beards. Ralph had often seen this kind of schizo attitude in drunks. They'd ask you to tell them how they'd behaved when sloshed and laugh or groan when they heard, just as they might have if the antics had been someone else's. But Ember didn't go for it. Enzyme was Enzyme, and a fucking menace. The double barrelled surname didn't mean he could be two people: sober Gordon Loam, stinko Gordon Loam.

'I long to compensate for my foolishness, Ralph. I long to be taken back into the club.' He grew meditative. 'I think of that gospel chorus about the ninety-and-nine sheep "that safely lay in the shelter of the fold. But one was out on the hills away, far off from the gates of gold". I see myself as that lost, needy sheep, Ralph.'

'Which sheep-pen has gates of gold?'

'My selfhood seems diminished without The Monty,' Enzyme replied. 'Your glittering achievement, Ralph, has been to make it central to the contentment and completeness of so many, like the Vatican, or the Long Room at Lords cricket ground. I want to offer my gratitude in practical shape. I lead a life which could fairly be described as *très mouvementé*. Yes. *Très*.'

'Out on the hills away?'

'I get about, I meet people,' Enzyme said.

'Which?'

'Oh, yes.'

'Which?'

'Various.'

'We all do.'

'People of relevance.'

'To what?'

'Art. Or, to put it another way, Ralph, of relevance to you and your plans for The Monty, those plans focused splendidly and positively on art. Art with a capital A. Art as unfettered, worldwide, visionary.'

'I'll look after my own plans.'

'I'm talking about the kind of people I associate with on well-established, comfortable terms. But you'll ask in your justifiably sceptical, pragmatic fashion, "What are they like, what is their, as it were, ruling passion, their *raison d'être* – their reason for being alive?"'

'No, I won't. I won't ask anything about them. They're nothing to me.'

'And I'll answer at once, Ralph, that above all they prize and practise discretion,' Enzyme replied. 'Absolute, wholesome discretion, so crucial in this kind of dealing.'

'Which kind?'

'This.'

Ralph thought he might be seeing some of the ancient aristo arrogance Enzyme must have inherited a trickle of, despite the overall rubbish ranking he had now. Here was the Gordon Loam lineage on show – that casual, lofty way of ignoring anything inconvenient said to him, and pushing on with his own stuff, like an ice-breaker's bow, smashing through frozen seas. The two main cops around here, Assistant Chief Constable Iles, and Detective Chief Superintendent Harpur, behaved something like Enzyme. One of them would ask the other a question and either get no answer, or an answer that was another question, or even an answer to a different question that hadn't been asked and had no relationship to the one that had. This was not caused by subconscious obedience to the uppish family past and genes, though, as with Enzyme, but by a playful, vicious determination in both Iles and Harpur to piss on the other's peace of mind, confidence and sanity. That's what policing at the highest levels must be like: conversations which were not; which were sessions of attrition and lively insult.

Club members began to arrive and made their way to the bar. Ralph kept to the front of his mind the thought that when somebody brought a gun, apparently to hand it over as a goodwill sign, there was one central fact: the somebody had the gun. This was the 'core', to take Enzyme's own term. Strip away the folderols and flimflam: goodwill and symbolism might be there, but the gun was the sole certainty, and *he* had it and *you* didn't. Ralph considered this analysis showed the kind of methodical, unflustered, absolutely unpanicky appraisal he would exercise when the subject and/or the setting of a situation was The Monty. Above all, unpanicky: by contrast, someone *deservedly* called Panicking Ralph or Panicking Ralphy would be incapable of this cool thinking.

An obvious question now followed: was the gun fucking-well loaded? If Enzyme had genuinely brought the Smith and Wesson to hand over as a peace and would-be reconciliation gesture, the automatic might have no bullets in the chamber. Its emptiness and, therefore, harmlessness could be regarded as part of the armistice gesture. Enzyme wished to surrender the Smith and Wesson but, not only that, the automatic lacked an obvious essential of effective Smith and Wessons – ammo.

On the other hand, Ralph thought the gesture would be even more telling if the gun *was* loaded and *not* harmless. Enzyme would be depriving himself of something that could kill and, as a matter of fact, was ready to kill *now*. It needed only a finger on the trigger. And, Ralph had already mentioned Gordon Loam's fingers. To be giving up this readiness and actuality was surely more meaningful than giving up a weapon that amounted only to a husk, unable to do the slightest damage; a castrated gun. This piece had blazed off at *The Marriage of Heaven and Hell*. But if, now, it were not loaded, the Smith and Wesson would have little resemblance to the gun that had put two rounds into the portrayed beard, and therefore could not be an adequate emblem of regret and request for forgiveness. Enzyme might have thought like that, and consequently the automatic would have bullets.

This meant that if Ralph tried physically to silence the slippery sod and his snippets of cliché French, and chuck him out of the club, Gordon Loam might discard the supposed, original wish to say sorry to Ralph and to assure him there'd be no repeat if he, Enzyme, were reinstated. Instead, he'd possibly get the gun out of the holster and splash Ralph over the bar and wall behind, point blank, unmissable. Ember reckoned that here was another instance of how his mind could work rationally, methodically, precisely during a crisis.

However – and, oh, God, what a 'however' – this time his sharp brainwork produced the conclusion that he could get shot now if Enzyme suddenly went for firepower. The faultlessly conducted analysis seemed to do the extreme opposite of what it was supposed to do, and for a couple of filthy seconds Ralph did get the rotten symptoms of a panic, although the surroundings and topic were The Monty. He had a scar high on his face and occasionally when stressed, as now, he would get the impression that the old wound had opened up and was gratuitously shedding something medical and yellow-brown down his cheek and on to the collar of his shirt. Also, sweat formed across his shoulders in a sizeable, rectangular, cold pool.

A TV history programme lately showed a battery of old field guns, one with an inscribed metal label fixed to its barrel, the words in Latin and English: '*Ultima ratio regum*. The final argument of kings.' Meaning, stuff argument and logic: time for the simplification of shot and shell. And this was what seemed to happen here now. The prospect of Enzyme blasting him had destroyed Ralph's usual solidity and steadiness – and his logic. Maybe the Smith and Wesson should have '*Ultima ratio Enzyme*' inscribed on it. Ralph felt his personality fracture. His cherished, previously unwavering Monty-based resolve left him. Part stammer, part despairing gasp, he said: 'If you've got something serious to discuss, Enz, you'd better come up to the office.'

'How I yearned for that kind of reaction, Ralph.'

'Best not to let antagonisms drag on and fester.'

'Here speaks someone of generous spirit and wise understanding.'

EIGHT

And so it became clear to Ralph that he would have to kill Enzyme – a matter of survival: Ralph's.

But no, no, no, he realized the decision hadn't happened as instantly as this, nor as mechanically. That would have been glib, and glibness he loathed above all. It offered false simplicities. Ralph liked to think that, when people discussed him, somebody would point out, and the others would gladly agree, that if there was one thing Ember wasn't it was glib. For starters, he couldn't think of Enzyme as Enzyme, or, even worse, Enz, when considering his death. The man he intended getting rid of was Basil Gordon Loam, and that's how the name must appear on the funeral Order of Service sheet, and on his gravestone, if he had one: it would need to be nice and broad to accommodate that lot. Ralph didn't want any doubt about identity of the corpse, like in *The Third Man*, on video. The name required would be Enz's official passport and jail name. He was entitled to a satisfactory degree of correctness when dead. Decorum. Ralph regarded himself as hot on that. He saw decorum as one of the foundations of any properly ordered society.

Obviously, Enz and his carnage pistol didn't have much to do with decorum while alive. But once dead he'd qualify for a slice. Ralph might permit a post-crem send-off party for him in The Monty; his necessary absence from the celebrations would mark a quality versus impulse victory for *The Tyger* author, William Blake: Basil, Basil burning bright.

The nickname should not be used anywhere, full or foreshortened, on paper or sculpted, not even in brackets. A death deserved some dignity, some of that decorum, despite the fact that, in this case, it would be the death of a fucking arrant prat like Enzyme who could open fire on a harmless figure from the great mystical work by Blake and subsequently refer in a totally offhand, brazen style to that scrupulously and lovingly repaired figure as 'beardy'. True, the figure did have a beard, but this could categorically not excuse Enzyme for calling him 'beardy'. On the other hand, Enzyme had a mouth and could certainly be called mouthy. Many males in those primitive, pre-razor days had beards, so to call a man beardy would be purposeless, mad. Now, it was a childish insult.

The way Enz had pointed at the Blake with a jerk of his thumb, rather than more normally using an index finger, Ralph found outrageously casual. Apparently, Enzyme was here now to apologize, but then added to the original offence by suggesting in this type of coarse gesture that nobody could worry much about some old beardy getting shot, anyway. The beardy was taking part in something called *The Marriage of Heaven and Hell*, so he'd better get used to some hellish bits, i.e., .38 bullets. That seemed to be Enz's heartless thinking, if it could be called thinking.

As Ralph and Enz talked now in the club office, Ember suspected that Gordon Loam would never understand why it was vital for Ralph to wipe him out as soon as it could be managed, though not on Monty premises, naturally. Loam lacked that sort of subtle insight. He plainly believed life could be a matter of loud, showy outbursts of monstrous behaviour, such as the Blake atrocity, followed by a flagrant attempt to bargain for forgiveness with grandiose, but so far, undefined, promises to Ralph. Enzyme was hardly somebody who'd recognize that Ralph had been forced into choosing between two options, and only two, owing to exceptional sensitivities:

(i) He could cave in to Enzyme and the Smith and Wesson now and retract his permanent ban from the club on Enz. This would obviously bring about the virtual destruction of Ralph as he had been – the upstanding, courageous Monty-type Ralph, the worthwhile, aspiring, impressive Ralph. It would be the annihilation of somebody who, until today, had found much of his stature and glow in The Monty. And yet he'd possessed enough of that very stature and glow to want the club to develop into something different and better. His stature and glow would help with this mission and, crucially, be entirely suitable for the eventual splendidly enhanced and, yes, transformed Monty. Victory for Enze would mean all that Ember brilliance was extinguished. Embered.

Or (ii) – the second option – by seeing off Enzyme he would also see off the kind of degradation and shame that Gordon Loam had created by turning up at the Monty with a gun and scaring Ralph shitless, despite goofy chatter about sincere regret and bygones being bygones. He'd forced Ember to wonder whether he really *was* Panicking Ralph or Panicking Ralphy, even when in the Monty and on Monty business, such as – in reverse sequence – the ban, the insulting levity of 'beardy', the unpardonable – absolutely unpardonable – bullets in the William Blake.

To sum up: it had become a choice between two lives: Ralph's or Basil Gordon Loam's. Only one could continue. Ralph had settled which one that should be, and he'd continue to be vigilant in case Enz had also decided which one it should be – Ralph. By planning to kill Enzyme and doing it, Ember would demonstrate that he remained capable of strong, uncompromising, cleansing action. All right, he'd admittedly had a bad, contemptible, flashback moment or two with the imagined weeping face scar and a cross-shoulder sweat gush, but that was all. Mere physical blips, mere dismal moments from history. He retained still the force and guts to maintain his true, precious selfhood. He would never accept, *could* never accept, the abjectness of the Panicking Ralph, Panicking Ralphy unwarranted slurs.

Ralph kept an index card for every member of The Monty. He had looked at Basil Gordon Loam's recently when putting a large X cancellation mark on it, plus a short note explaining the expulsion and ban: 'Extreme vandalism re club decor, (MOHAH).' A partner was named on the card as 'Irene, aged thirty-three', and they had three daughters, Dawn, Emily, Jessica. They attended the same private school as Ralph's children, so he already knew vaguely about them. As far as he could remember, Enz had never brought Irene to the club. Ralph decided he would certainly help her and the children along financially for a decent while following Enz's removal. Private schooling cost and was so important in these days of sliding educational standards. Enzyme would be the kind who when blasting off the way he did wouldn't at all have in mind possible retaliation for this foolishness and its effects on his family. The

Smith and Wesson was a .38. That thirty-eight figure just about matched his IQ.

'Well, am I really entering the holy of holies?' Enzyme had said, ladling on the supposed excitement as Ralph showed him into the Monty office. This patronizing smarm-merchant was building a case against himself, though he didn't know it – was making it even easier for Ralph to think of him as dead meat. Ember felt grateful for the assistance. It was a long while since he last needed to turn violent. (Death of Alf Ivis?)[4] To get back to that kind of thorough, purifying activity would take some determination, some renewed dedication. Enzyme's reference to 'holy of holies' came from the same sneer source as 'beardy'. Satirical. Slimy. Mocking.

When Enz said 'holy of holies' he was suggesting, of course, that Ralph considered he had a superior existence to the general membership of the club and could set himself apart and aloof in this special room, this sort of sanctified lair. That might be true, but Enz had no right to turn it into snide piss-taking. He most probably thought that with his kind of surname and heritage even the most distinguished bits of property owned by someone like Ralph, such as this Monty office, added up to bugger-all, could be grounds for a cheap, ridiculing giggle at a tin god.

Ralph had gone in for a happy mixture of styles in the furnishing of the office. The computer was up at the far end of the room. They'd wanted him to buy a so-called 'workstation' to accommodate the monitor, keyboard and printer, but he'd chosen to use an old, though well polished, Victorian Pembroke table, with a hinged flap to enlarge it if required, and a drawer: real mahogany. Workstations were made of what was proudly called 'authentic veneer oak'. Authentic veneer! During his Foundation Year at the university he'd been required to read a novel where one of the families was named the Veneerings. That is, they were all surface, nothing much else. Ralph could do without authentic veneer, thank you! His non-stop search in life was for solid quality.

'Stages, Ralph,' Enz said.

'Stages in which sense?'

[4] See *Pay Days*

'The art business. Things must be allowed to develop in stages.'

'Do you mean the actual work on the painting – not rushing to finish it and getting slapdash with the colours? Some painters do get overexcited, I believe, and wear dungarees and sou'wester hats.'

'Not so much that. The business side. The buying and selling of the finished, framed canvas.'

'So when you say stages, what kind of stages are you thinking of?'

'Opportunities.'

'Well, yes,' Ralph replied.

'Patience.'

'Well, yes.'

Ralph thought that many would find it hard to imagine Enz dead because at the moment he seemed so confident and positive. But in the past Ralph had witnessed several instances where someone as assured and full-scale gabby as Enz seemed today had suddenly caught a couple of bullets in the chest or head and lost all bounce. In fact, bounce was the last quality you'd think of when looking at them. A ball full of air could have plenty of jolly bounce, but there was nothing flatter and deader than a ball when all its air had gone. Ralph's career, on his way to a good and comfortable position now, contained some very rough and bloody episodes.

Ralph glanced around the office again to bring himself back to the achieved present. He loved the combination of contemporary electronic equipment, such as the computer etcetera, and something antique, traditional and authentically authentic, namely the Pembroke. It intrigued him to think that when the table flap was made all those years ago, the carpenter had no idea what would eventually be resting there – not a candelabrum or fly swat, but a keyboard able to put its owner in touch instantly with the whole world. Simply by typing in 'Pembroke tables', Ralph could get a screen description and pictures of exactly the Pembroke table he was typing in 'Pembroke tables' at, a piece of furniture that had been passed down through the decades and now provided the flap to Google from in this way. His head swam. Ralph had often noticed how time could bring about very strange results. Changes definitely took place as the years followed the years. Ralph wanted change for The Monty. Change equalled progress. This was another of his main beliefs. It drove him forward. Think of high-speed dental drills or drive-on ferries. Also, he would bring significant change for Gordon Loam, by getting him to swap life for death.

'This is what I mean when I say I know people,' Enz said.

'Which people?' Ember wished Gordon Loam had a beard so that when the appropriate moment arrived he could put a pair of shots through it up into his neck and fucking cryptic voice-box, as a neat answer to what had started all this when Enz violated William Blake.

'*They* understand about the stages, also,' Enz said.

'Who do?'

'The people I know. London. A kind of recognized practice has developed over the years,' Enz replied.

'Recognized who by?'

Enzyme paused, as if delighted. 'You've done what you always do in your clear-sighted way, Ralph,' he said, his grin vast in admiration. 'You've hit the crux.'

'I was brought up to believe that's what cruxes are for.'

Ralph had three leather easy chairs in the office. He'd heard that executives of real power didn't conduct negotiations from behind a desk or at a workstation, but in a more relaxed, comfy style. Not long ago, Ralph had seen a magazine article about the 1960s, illustrated by a photograph of John F. Kennedy nestling sideways in a chair like one of these, legs hanging over the arm, his black lace-ups pricey looking, while he talked on the telephone, perhaps to Khrushchev about Cuba, or to a girl the President intended shagging later. Poise, but without strain. Ralph prized that. There was a scatter of Turkish-type rugs in pastel shades on the strip-board floor of the office. A small chiffonier stood against one wall, and Ralph went to it now and took a bottle of Kressmann Armagnac and two glasses from a cupboard. He poured for both of them. They sat down facing each other. At this point Ralph didn't take the Kennedy position, sideways on, legs dangling over the arm. Enz still had the gun, and Ralph wanted a proper, direct view of all his movements. Ralph wondered whether Enz had ever experienced Kressmann's before. Almost certainly he'd never experience it again. The colour of the bottle's label had a message for him: black.

'Forgive me, Ralph, won't you, if I describe the fundamentals of art as a commercial commodity? Perhaps I'm telling you what you already know. But I'll push on. People learn from the media that some painting or sculpture has fetched a record price at one of the famous auction houses – Sotheby's, Beijing Poly, LA Modern Auctions, Christie's – and they assume that this, yes, was a spectacular occasion, but also a fairly simple one. They suppose that the previous owner for some reason needs a sizeable bag of cash and has to sell; or the owner has grown tired of the piece and wants to trade it in and get something new; or the owner has died and his or her collection goes to the market so the proceeds can be shared among legatees.'

Enzyme made his voice soft and gentle but dismissive when describing these three possible explanations, as though to say all of them were more or less sensible, but only more or less, and – sorry! – he would have to show that, overall, they were rubbish.

Ralph stayed quiet, took a sip of the Armagnac. Once more he had that weird feeling about Enzyme's features – that they lacked permanence and might have been rearranged by the next time he was around. Ralph knew he would detest them, however they assembled themselves. Enz's nose was so wide-nostrilled that Ember felt he could look up it and see what was in his head.

'Again I ask for your tolerance, Ralph. I'm going to be rather blunt.'

'We *are* adult.'

'Naive, Ralph.'

'What is?'

'Those standard attitudes towards big art transactions. Oh, yes, occasionally the passage of a work to and from one of the auction houses is a straightforward matter, but this is rare, very. I mentioned Beijing Poly. Think China, Ralph.'

For God's sake – this gabby twerp could go global. 'China?'

'OK, it's not Britain, and things are much darker and more chaotic in art trading there. I refer to it only as a vivid example of market intricacies. China is awash with fake paintings.

Thousands of auction sales never get completed because the "buyers" come to doubt the authenticity of what they've "bought". The emerging and emerged super-rich class there want something worthwhile to spend their money on. So they chuck bids about but then have second thoughts. To feed this new appetite, forgeries thrive. Because the Chinese revere the past there's always been a tradition of skilled copying in China – some jokingly call this repetition *l'art d'echo* – and now what used to be a fine, respectful tradition has been turned into a multi-mill racket. It's said that in twenty cities about two hundred and fifty thousand people are producing fakes. Art is used like money for backhanders to government officials – a practice known as *ya-hui*, elegant bribery.

'That's China, and a long way off, but I wonder if you realize, Ralph, that the art market here has its own problem areas. The people I associate with from time to time are in touch with the more roundabout, even mysterious, ways great works can disappear, reappear, disappear again, re-emerge, lie low, and finally, perhaps, show themselves openly at a point of sale.'

'Which people?'

'These are people known in the trade as "facilitators". Indeed, possibly, because of my relationship with some of them, I might be described as a facilitator myself. Or an apprentice facilitator, anyway. Art is something I feel very congenial with, Ralph. A natural response and affinity. It could be a genes matter.'

'From which side?'

'Which side of what?'

'Gordon or Loam?'

'The thing about art is it exists to be looked at,' Enzyme replied.

'True.'

'This is its sole function.'

'Right.'

'It's not like, say, a valuable, beautiful watch. The watch will also exist to be looked at, but its role goes beyond that. The watch might get looked at, but when it is looked at it supplies something – the time.'

'Point taken.'

'Art is different. Looking at it is the full experience, the whole experience, no extras, such as the time with a watch. True, I heard that the poet W.H. Auden was cold in bed and took down a framed picture and put it on top of the blankets for warmth. So you could say that in his case art did have a functional role. This is very unusual, though. If you see that Constable picture, *The Haywain*, you can enjoy the viewing of it, but you can't shift hay with it.'

'Correct.'

'Therefore display is crucial. It is as if the painting has no existence unless it is on a wall so people can gaze.'

'I follow.'

'But now we come to the contradiction, the irony, in so much art buying and selling. A large proportion of the works for sale have elements of considerable doubt in their background. The main area of such doubt is to do with possible theft. Has the work – have the works – in question at some point in its – or their – history been stolen, looted, hijacked? Is the apparent owner the true owner? And what does ownership mean here? If someone has bought a painting in good faith, wrongly believing it to have been lawfully acquired by the seller, does ownership rest with the new buyer or with the person or institution the work has been stolen from? The police and courts in different countries vary in their attitudes on this question.

'Because of these kinds of anxieties, the purchased item – or items – although it – they – only exists – exist – to be put on show cannot in many cases safely be *put* on show at present. That's why I referred to stages, Ralph. It might mean a work – works – has to – have to – remain out of sight for a while, even for a very long while, until, perhaps, it – they – is – are – forgotten about or lost in the great crowd of other paintings without impeccable histories. It is because of this contradiction, these contradictions, this irony, these ironies, Ralph, that the facilitator can provide such timely and skilled aid.

'A complicating factor in this is that some paintings, sculptures, figurines are bought – perfectly legally bought and for huge sums – only to disappear, untraceably disappear, perhaps into a billionaire's secure warehouse. They are not displayed, possibly because their owners fear robbery or vandalizing. These are works that seem to defy the generalization I offered just now – that great art has to be seen or it suffers a loss of purpose – that purpose being to get looked at. For instance, Ralph, there is the famous Picasso painting, *Garçon à la Pipe*, completed when Pab was in his twenties, sold to an anonymous buyer for more than one hundred million dollars in New York, but whereabouts now unknown. Likewise pictures by Cézanne, Renoir, Van Gogh. The facilitator can sometimes help in locating even some of these. The collector who pays millions to hide away a work or works will still want to be informed when something interesting is coming up for private sale. So, although ownerships might seem to be anonymous that isn't completely so. Some gallery, some dealer, some facilitator is privy to the supposed secret. The facilitator, above all, hears trade talk, lives among trade talk, and will be able to put the prospective seller in touch with the right kind of prospective buyer.

'You'll ask, what do I mean by "right kind"? But, excuse me, Ralph. You don't like that type of construction – the "you'll ask" construction, regarding it as a presumption, me forecasting your reaction. And that's a reasonable objection, entirely reasonable. Very well then – I'll ask myself. What do I mean by right kind? Paintings on the market carry variable degrees of doubt as to where they've come from, and how. In many deals, therefore, a certain amount of risk is involved. Some buyers will want a particular work so badly that they are ready to accept a high degree of uncertainty as to its background, as long as the price makes allowance for this kind of serious gamble.

'Let's suppose we're talking about a Jackson Pollock. A potential purchaser might have seen a photograph of the work on a well-meant, TV culture programme and found that the dots and swirls and stripes really speak to him or her, in some unexplainable fashion. The fact that it *is* unexplainable is not a deterrent, though. The very opposite! The mysteriousness of his – her – response is what intrigues, what makes the would-be buyer more determined to own it because of this unique, undefinable link.'

Enzyme grew passionate and almost shrill. 'There might be plenty of works with obvious, easily described attractions – light, colour, intensity of portraiture. But that kind of appreciation might come to seem workaday, banal to our collector. The Pollock, on the other hand, unlocks somehow previously unsuspected qualities in the collector's psyche. He – she – thinks that perhaps ownership of the painting and the opportunity to gaze upon it whenever he – she – wishes will constantly reaffirm the presence of something numinous, yes, something profoundly spiritual in her – him. To be elevated in this fashion is judged to be worth almost any level of risk. And from his knowledge of the trade and its people, the facilitator should be able to bring together a suitable pair – buyer and seller – to clinch the deal.

'And, likewise, the facilitator will provide a link for buyers who insist on only a *moderate* amount of risk and are willing to pay for the additional assurance of probable OKness. Plus, of course, the facilitator will know of potential buyers who are interested exclusively in works that have no worrying aspects at all, are clean, exemplary, their market profiles available and righteous, and will fork out accordingly.'

Occasionally, Ralph still wondered if it was out of proportion to decide Basil Gordon Loam would have to go. His offence – offences – was – were – bad, but as bad as that? Although Ember would definitely subsidize Enzyme's family for a while after his death, Ralph recognized that money and income might not be the only consideration. Irene and the children quite possibly felt something for Enz, despite how he was. Ralph began to soften slightly towards him.

And then Gordon Loam suddenly started to make things worse for himself. He'd had a couple of sips of the Armagnac, but he definitely wasn't drunk again. He didn't show any special appreciation of the Kressmann, as if to suggest he routinely drank only the highest quality liquor. That's the kind he was – arrogant, ungrateful, casual. He had to go. He wanted to talk about a foul, sniggering newspaper gossip column published locally under the byline 'I Spy'. It would be picked up by the national media, no question. He obviously thought the writer offered a delicious joke when he – or she – said art was not a usual topic of conversation at The Monty, the hint being that normal conversation in the club was crude, uncivilized, uncultured. Plainly, also, Enz considered it a real hoot when The Monty got the description 'refined'. Enzyme's idea of the club, like 'I Spy's' idea of the club, was the sort of idea Ralph longed to escape from. Basil G.L. was actually in The Monty's precincts now, surrounded by its very texture and ambience, graciously allowed in, contrary to the all-time ban, and yet he could hold this traitorous opinion of it. When moving towards the stairs to the office, they had stepped very close to the actual area of wall space where the paintings would probably hang, totally free now from Worcestershire sauce stains. Gordon Loam's attitude was gross, surely, sickening.

'The "I Spy" is an amusing wink-wink piece, isn't it, Ralph?' he said. '*You* come out of it well: that proud refusal of guilt cash. *I'm* the bad guy.' He spoke this as though many – in fact, most – must find this notion ludicrous. Ralph would have liked to ask how he could come out of it well if his club was mocked and more or less portrayed as a cess pit – the club he loved and cherished and would take forward into new distinction and esteem. Enzyme could not see that Ralph and The Monty were one. Another novel Ralph had read during the Foundation Year was *Wuthering Heights*. The heroine, Cathy, cries out at one point about her soul mate, 'I *am* Heathcliff.' That's how Ember felt about the club. Enzyme would destroy Ralph if allowed to continue, and therefore he must be destroyed.

Enz grew serious. 'But although the "I Spy" squib might be charmingly witty and ironic—'

'Fucking sarky.'

'Well, all right, Ralph, mildly sarcastic.'

'Basely sarcastic.'

'The point is, Ralph, putting aside its tone for a moment – on which you are definitely entitled to hold very personal views – but temporarily forgetting that, there could be certain practical results from the publicity. No, there *will* be certain practical results. The column says you are hoping to buy some paintings. That's the sole point some will take from these paragraphs. They'll discount the irony, tongue-in-cheekness, whimsy. This concentration on a few words will lead to approaches. You are known as someone of weighty financial resource. You would not be in the market for cheapos. You'll want quality. You'll be thinking in terms of at least hundreds of grand, yes, hundreds of grand per pic, at least. That kind of potential sale will be of some interest. You'll get an array of high-price, would-be vendors.'

It struck Ralph that the way Enz's features appeared unfixed on their current sites resembled some famous Pablo Picasso paintings where the eyes, noses and chins of people seemed to be in the wrong places; an eye where you'd expect an elbow, for instance, as if Picasso wanted to assert total artistic freedom by refusing to accept the usual, arbitrary layout of faces. Why should noses be central or an ear on each side of the head and level with the one on the other side? Picasso would probably have to admit that for most people things *were* like that, and he'd expect the women in his life to have their various parts in the customary bodily spots. But an artist, a big fan of the imagination, didn't have to be bound by mere actuality in his or her work. Had Enz ever 'facilitated' one of these paintings and afterwards, still very impressed, tried to imitate it by giving his own various phiz-bits their occasional ticket-of-leave liberty? Enz had mentioned Picasso just now; there was a possible familiarity.

'Main reason I'm here, Ralph – the main reason I bring an apology – is that I recognize – and how, how could I *not* recognize? – I recognize that I've put you in a situation. I concede that the episode with the gun and the Blake and the side-issue of the Worcestershire sauce is not helpful to the club's aura. And it is this aura you so earnestly, indeed, commendably, seek to improve, to perfect, in fact. I acknowledge – have acknowledged already – Basil Gordon Loam's part in putting that purpose at gratuitous risk. These art sales people will also recognize it, Ralph. They'll see through the tact and obliqueness of the "I Spy" joshing. That word "explosive", so early on, plants the idea of cordite, of bang-bangs from the start.

'They'll realize that you, prompted by your inalienable mission to bring The Monty to its full flowering, to its splendid latent potential, will do almost anything to cancel the ill impression caused by the shoot-out – caused, that is, I fear, by myself, though a self essentially different from my true self owing to Jack Danielses. Aware that you believe fine art can help annul the effects of that unseemliness, dealers will come to you with works that might help rectify matters and help also with your glorious, famed aim. But they'll want you to pay a glorious price for it, for them. It's a seller's market.

Art is what they call "currency neutral", meaning it will keep its investment value regardless of fluctuations in the pound or the dollar or the euro or the yen or the rouble. Have a look at prices in the Frieze Art Fair auctions of modern stuff. The world's rich flock to these gaudy sales and fight to get their bids in first. They might ask for a piece to be put on "hold" for an hour while they make up their mind and look at other works. And the gallery will say, "Ten minutes only," because they've got a queue of potential buyers eager for a deal. And – new factor, increasing the rush – a lot of them these days are young. They've made their lot in pop music or IT, or London property, or soccer – as players, managers, owners or agents, especially agents. They're ready to fling the cash about. Art has become not just a juicy investment. Possession of fashionable, super-expensive works is a route to chic social standing – or *more* chic social standing, because some of these people will already have bought their way into select, modish company.

'And in some ways, this is your aim, too, isn't it, Ralph? You'd like to elevate The Monty. Dealers will spot that urgent need. They're experienced at it. They'll try to exploit your admirable ambition. I, conscious of my part in bringing these difficulties on you, Ralph, am here to look for forgiveness and to provide in solid terms a recompense. I can facilitate for you. I can show these predatory, avaricious dealers that you have a clued-up, very motivated ally. I can assist in getting those works you need and getting them at a fair, non-opportunist, non-inflationary price.'

Ralph could admire the ardent, phoney logic of it. Enzyme really did need to be put down, as painlessly as possible, yes, but, in any case, put down. He made a parade of his original gun-craziness, and then said he could engineer everything back to normal, and to normal plus, by middle-manning Ralph's expensive purchases – and, naturally, collecting an unspoken-of commission from the dealers. Enz saw it all so neatly, clearly, egomaniacally. He regarded the appalling treatment of the Blake as a positive step in the furtherance of trade.

'Because of proximity, Ralph, and a precedent set by your old mate, Manse Shale, you'll probably be thinking of Jack

Lamb as provider of the new works.' He went very clipped and absolute. 'OK, but care needed.'

'I haven't thought of anyone.' Bollocks to Enzyme's clairvoyance.

'Wise.'

'But if I *was* thinking, why do I need caution with him?

For a while Enz acted out honest bafflement, held his hands up in a surrender sign, frowned, did a terrifically flamboyant lips-purse. 'Not sure, Ralph. Something, though. That's the talk in London. Rumour at this stage. There's a firm called Cog, part of the art commerce machine. It's possibly something to do with them. George Dinnick. He can be so gentle and polished and vicious. Maybe Cog received a load of stolen stuff and want to flog some of it to Lamb. Cog have a strong connection in Belgium. Ghent. This is very productive. The pics flow from, as well as to. Or it could be a theft raid planned on Lamb's present items. The tale is he's got some nice Dutch school pieces. He maintains his own continental link, maybe Belgium too, but not Ghent. Antwerp.

'Ralph, Lamb's is a sector best treated warily, but certainly a possible. If he is pillaged – well, he's got a pal high in the police, apparently. Harpur? That's the talk. He'd really go after anyone who robbed his chum. But I can cater for that kind of complication. Normally, Lamb wouldn't be able to report a theft to the law because thieved items might have been pre-thieved and criminal. But Harpur is obligated. And he's skilled at doing things his own way on the quiet. Then, above Harpur, there's that supreme froth-gobbed sod, Iles. I'm not saying he's a friend of Lamb as well. But he can be totally vindictive if he thinks big criminality, such as art theft, has taken place on his ground. That's how he talks about it – *his* ground. He's the king, the despot. Well, you've probably met both buggers, so I don't surprise you. They'd make things very tough for anyone who'd had recent dealings with Lamb, suppose his gallery is stripped. I could forestall that as well for you, Ralph.

'Other hazards: OK, perhaps you've bought a couple of works fair and square, as far as you know, but that might be so you could get a look at the rest pre a raid. This is how Iles might think. He's devious and expects deviousness in others. And then there's the matter of provenance. How did Jack get some of these pics? Iles could be very persistent and nosy about that.

'If, for instance, you'd bought one of those Dutch things, it could be very difficult. There's a well known work, *Amelia With Flask*. What's its history before Darien? We need to find out. Perhaps you shouldn't be hanging anything like that in The Monty, Ralph, or the club might go for ever down the chute. Lamb is certainly a possibility for us, but not the only possibility, Ralph, I urge you. I can put you in touch with various commercial interests. My family had exceptionally well-established relations with another London facilitator outfit, "Enduring Arbitrament". I'm very much *persona grata* there, though not actually a member of the firm – yet. As I said – an apprentice. I'm trusted. I hear a lot via "EA", as it used to be known at home in Hampstead. You can count on my and their discretion, Ralph, and my devotion to your cause. I owe you.'

When Enz spoke of his family, he obviously meant his parents and siblings. But the word set Ralph's thoughts going in a different direction – to Basil Gordon Loam's present family: Irene, Dawn, Emily, Jessica. Ember had worked out a method of getting the support cash to them post BGL's death. Obviously, it would be insensitive to roll up at their house with a bag of cash just after the funeral. (Incidentally, he would take care of those funeral costs and ensure things were done decently, exactly as if Enz deserved a proper show. A horse-drawn, glass-walled hearse if they fancied that.) But Ember didn't want it to seem as though he thought only in materialistic terms. That would be narrow and unfeeling. Also, ostentatiously caring behaviour would be taken as a sign that he'd had something to do with the killing. He *would* have had something to do with the killing, would have had *everything* to do with the very justified killing, but this meant he had to be careful not to give any indication that he'd had anything to do with the very justified killing. Most people would surely agree that Enzyme should be shot, but they'd find a victory song-and-dance deeply vulgar.

Ralph thought he'd tell Irene that for years The Monty had offered an unofficial insurance scheme to members, some of whom ran quite risky lives owing to turf battles, and/or *in flagrante* adulteries, and/or attempts to swindle associates in après-job share-outs, and/or prison stabbings and/or kickings. He'd say Enzyme had joined because of general prudence and consideration for the family, not any of those named reasons. He could inform Irene that Enz's contributions had built quite a useful fund, which would now pay out, following the regrettable passing away. Ralph imagined it as a kind of Friendly Society, though there obviously wouldn't have been any friendliness shown towards Enzyme because the verbose, breezily disrespectful, trigger-mad bastard didn't qualify.

'I'm glad we have reached a constructive agreement in our conversation, Ralph,' Enz said.

'Well, yes.'

'I'll be happy to get things under way. No need for you to specify at this point the exact size of investment you're thinking of. I believe I know the likely range. Well, we have already hinted at it, haven't we? You would hardly want slipshod, economy jobs for The Monty. That would negate the whole objective. But now, if I may, I'd like to revert to that meaningful gesture I started with, but postponed because of your reactions then. I have in mind the handing over of the Smith and Wesson as a sign of the changes – wonderfully positive changes – that have taken place since my deplorable, pointlessly vindictive act of aggression against that noble male figure from *The Marriage of Heaven and Hell*. Ralph, I'm aware that another of your hates is the term "symbol", so I won't use it about our little ceremony. Let us just say that this spontaneous surrender of the weapon will have a more profound effect than is immediately evident when I pass the gun to you. May I do that, at this juncture?' Ezn's hand didn't move yet towards the holster. It would be impudent. In any case, an unhurried, ritualistic progress had become *de rigueur*.

Ralph gave a small, permissive nod. Courage garrisoned him now. His body produced no splurts. 'I'll store it in the chiffonier,' he said. Ralph felt this would bring the bullying gun under the control, the mastery of The Monty and its venerable furnishings ending for ever that evil weapon's power to harm the club's supreme Blakeian distinction.

'Thank you,' Enzyme said. He reached up to his left shoulder and Ralph heard the minor, homely, mild sound of an unbuttoning.

Enz produced the black automatic. They both stood, facing each other, so that the procedure kept due dignity, the pace still slow, weighty, significant. Each held an Armagnac glass down stiff-armed at his side. When Ralph took the gun with his free hand he could tell at once from the weight that the piece was fully loaded. This delighted him. He would have liked to kiss the muzzle, but that might be a give-away. If he could kill Enz with his own pistol and his own ammo it would give a charming, tidy completeness to the sequence that had opened with the anti-montage incident. Sow the wind, reap the whirlwind. Ember liked to think of himself as akin to a whirlwind if once aroused, and a slight on The Monty would always arouse him.

Also, many of those in the bar on the night of his insurgent gunplay would remember that Enz used a Smith and Wesson .38, so, if they were brought into an investigation of Enz's end, the police would learn he'd been done with what appeared to be his own weapon. They might decide it was suicide. They wouldn't want to give a lot of time to inquiring into the death of a flitting nobody like Enzyme. Ralph put the S. and W. with elaborate, almost pious care into a drawer and closed it.

Still with their eyes fixed unwaveringly on the other, they raised the Armagnac simultaneously and took small but committed swallows, as if following a time-blessed rite. For Enz, Ralph knew this moment would undoubtedly signal that he'd brilliantly bullshitted Ember into offering him mercy for the Blake abuse, and into dependence for savvy, insider advice on art deals. But for Ralph, rolling the Armagnac around in his mouth, then downing it, this was a kind of silent toast to his scheme for putting at least two rounds into BGL's's heart area soon, most likely .38s.

When Ralph and he went downstairs, the bar staff and some customers looked startled to see the two of them together, both smiling. What had happened to Ralph's rage and the ban? Enz glanced up at the montage. 'So fine,' he said. 'So tasteful and inspiring. Such humanity.' Ralph opened the door on to the street, and they shook hands there with thoroughness and energy, though not for an absurdly prolonged, phoney-looking time. 'Goodbye, Ralph.'

'Goodbye, Basil.'

NINE

That worried Enzyme – the 'Basil.' It meant something, and what it meant, he reckoned, was bad for him. To use his actual first name seemed to Gordon Loam a dirty, distancing trick; precise identification of a target, a sort of map reference for a drone. The goodwill handshake? A mockery. Things had become cold, formal, like execution preliminaries. God, had he been mad to surrender the Smith and Wesson, and to have surrendered it with a full chamber? Ralphy had looked so pleased to get the gun, you'd almost think he'd make love to it. What stopped him sticking a furled tongue intimately up the barrel?

Enz decided he'd better get a replacement piece and fast. It hurt to think of the Smith and Wesson shoved into that mouldy drawer of the chiffonier. Of course, Ralphy was the sort to go for such a far-out, fancy word when what it actually was was a fucking old sideboard. He'd really lingered on the double f sound in chiffonier, hissing like an arched-back cat, just to show he could do the antiques racket trill. People of no class thought use of foreign terms gave them a leg up socially.

Throughout those conversations with Ember, first in the bar, then in his office, BGL had felt there was nothing he could say that would change Ralph's Billy-Blake-based hatred of him. Although Enz had given Ralph nearly all his best insights about facilitators; about the Frieze Fine Art Fair; the new, loaded young bidders; gradations of ownership risk; and art trade routes, a fair bit of it accurate, he didn't think Ralph had been convinced, or even interested. He couldn't, or wouldn't, move away from his infantile fury over the damaged collage and disturbed Worcestershire sauce. It was a kind of obsession. He ought to see a psychiatrist. This type of fixation, on the torn mythscape, the stained pool-table baize and the T-shirt, might be commonplace and a standard treatment easily available, possibly by tablets rather than sessions of electroshock to the brain.

When Enz had spoken warmly about reaching a 'constructive agreement' between them, Ralph replied, 'Well, yes.' To Enzyme that had seemed slippery. Why not simply, 'Yes'? Or, 'Yes, absolutely, Enz,' or, 'Indeed, yes, Enz,' if he wanted to elaborate? Enz was very sensitive to vocabulary and tone. What was the significance of that: 'Well,' spoken in a questioning, challenging fashion? Didn't it show doubt? It was a hesitation word. It was a 'maybe' word. Could it be broken down into, 'Well, yes, if you say so'? – meaning, I'll go along with it for now because I need to lull and fool you, but I'll hang on to my own thoughts, thank you very much, and my own thoughts towards you, Enz, don't have anything to do with a constructive agreement – *de*structive, yes?

Enzyme had come to The Monty very prepared and brought out some of his best jargon and phrasing – 'vindictive act of aggression', Ralph's 'inalienable mission', people who'd 'already bought their way into select, modish company', 'currency neutral', a genuine technical term; and a chunk of flattery referring to Ralph's 'weighty financial resource' – yet Ember hadn't appeared persuaded. Although there'd been a few moments when he'd shown something like friendliness, it was only because he'd realized Enz had a gun and might be on a revenge trip after that humiliating public bawling out from Ember and the for-ever-and-a-day ban. Before this, hadn't he actually told Enzyme to 'bugger off'? Civil? Humane? Enlightened?

One of Ralphy's famous panics had seemed to hit him and, as a result, he'd agreed to talk and even invite Enz into the office. But it had meant nothing – just a ploy to keep himself safe. Once he was in his little comfort-zone throne-room with the chiffonier and all the other historic timber around him, he began to recover from that bad fright interlude. And when the Smith and Wesson was no longer a factor, but had been swallowed up by his decrepit, wormy piece of cherished double ff'd junk, Ralph could shake hands and even smile. There'd been no mention of cancelling the ban in response to all the priceless commercial counselling Enz had provided, though, just that ambiguous and very fucking *un*ambiguous, 'Goodbye, Basil.' There were proper occasions for use of his real name, Basil

Gordon Loam, a name with honour, achievement and excellent tailoring built-in. But a tactical aftermath chat with Panicking Ralphy at his shady club was not such an occasion.

Enz realized there might be difficulties in getting a new pistol. The foul 'I Spy' column in the Press told everyone, without actually telling them – more sly ambiguity that wasn't ambiguous – yes, told everyone who could do a bit of basic translating that Basil Gordon Loam had opened fire on a prime, chichi educational tableau at The Monty club, causing some obvious, grave damage and momentary havoc to members. The natural deduction would be that Basil Gordon Loam was rat-arsed drunk at the time, despite the grandeur of his family background.

People who sold hot guns knew, of course, that they might be used in hot, unlawful jobs. That's why their crooked businesses existed. And that's why the businesses didn't get a place in any city's Chamber of Trade. Secret armourers wanted no trace back from one of these jobs to themselves as accessories. A no-good boyo who got stonkered and blazed away pointlessly in a social club, even a social club like The Monty, was not the sort of client they craved. If someone could shoot their gun off in stupid circumstances, the same someone might also shoot his mouth off in stupid circumstances, including boasts of how and where he got his weaponry.

Guns: Amy and Leyton Harbinger, who'd previously operated from a renowned pub off Cork Street, supplying most of the armaments locally, were locked up for a while because of some carelessness or betrayal or random twirl of fate. The only remaining source hereabouts was Judy Rose Timmins, age forty-sixish, manner chirpy, eyebrows expressive, voice confiding, her legitimate commercial front an infants' playgroup nursery. Enzyme's Smith and Wesson and ammunition had come from her. She'd want to know what had happened to the pistol following that Monty daftness, as code-described in 'I Spy'. Or perhaps she *wouldn't* want to know – would rather not hear anything more of it – or of Enzyme.

Just the same, he rang Judy now from his car and said he was coming over straight away to her Silver Bells And Cockleshells crèche. As he'd expected, she sounded puzzled and unwelcoming. However chirpy she might usually be, Enzyme realized the obvious urgency of his call must trouble her. Removal of the Harbingers had probably increased Judy's trading, but also risk. At the end of their phone conversation, she asked: 'Am I reading the Press right?'

'The Press?'

'William Blake on a plate, a steel plate.'

'Oh, *that* Press!'

'Yes, *that* Press.'

'We can discuss.'

'Yes, we can.'

He noticed the insubordination in her tone, the outright one-upness. He'd said, 'We can discuss,' and she replied, 'Yes, we can.' What this suggested to Enz – what she clearly meant it to suggest – was that as soon as she'd realized why he'd phoned, she'd already decided they should inspect the reasons for his visit, really pick-over the reasons. She didn't require an invitation. As convener, she wanted him to know that she would have charge of any meeting, and he'd better not expect much from it. Enz wondered how his great-great-grandfather, the industrialist and, eventually, Cabinet Minister, Sir Ivan Gordon Loam, would have dealt with this blazing insolence from a suburban childminder. But probably Sir Ivan didn't know any childminder who was also a gunrunner and wouldn't have needed her or him urgently even if he did. And Sir Ivan would have been too sharp to hand over an operational gun to a grudge-bearing dreamer like Ralphy Ember.

TEN

Driving the hire car, Liz Rossol followed Basil Gordon Loam across town in his Audi, trying to manage it so there was always one moderately sized vehicle between her and him for cover, but not more than that, or bigger than that, or she'd lose him. If he spotted the tail she'd probably lose him anyway. Although she'd done some earlier exploring here, he'd know the local roads much better than she did. He'd most likely fashion quick tricks at roundabouts and/or up side streets. In any case, he wouldn't continue to his destination. So, tracking him would have no point. She wanted to know where he was going. Or where he *had* been going before he noticed the constant green Peugeot. That might help her to an explanation of what was happening, might end at least some of her confusion.

It wasn't the first time she'd gumshoed by car. The art business at her level now and then required a spell of crafty mileage and intelligent snooping: hunt the masterpiece. She'd taught herself the skills, but the skills didn't always work. For instance, they couldn't control the size of the vehicle immediately ahead. Sight of the target car might get blocked long-term by a furniture van if plentiful oncoming traffic meant you couldn't overtake. Being so tall was a pain. Too much of her was evident behind the windscreen in a rear-view mirror.

Did Gordon Loam routinely carry a pistol, not just for a collage shoot? Whether or not, she must try to stay with him, unobserved. An info famine had struck. She needed nourishment, however meagre, such as where was he going and why. She liked to find a pattern to things, a shape. So far she saw neither. All she saw was the back of his Audi, and that not all the time.

On the train she'd decided that for her opening move she'd have a look at The Monty club. Last time she was here she hadn't known it existed. The sole focus of her research then had been Jack Lamb's country place, Darien, and its reputation as an art sale centre. What had disturbed her, and still disturbed her, was the possibility of a link between the barmy, fusillade at The Monty and the general local art scene. That kind of publicized event was bound to produce special interest, although the bit of damage to *The Marriage Of Heaven And Hell* wouldn't matter all that much, except perhaps to the named owner, Ralph Ember, if a Blake nut. Obviously, it was only a print and worth next to nothing.

But he had spoken of bringing in costly, original, sought-after, quality stuff to hang in The Monty. That objective had been reported in the 'I Spy' column and could get picked up by media elsewhere. And might Ember be thinking of a purchase from Lamb, a well-known art dealer living in this very area? That must seem convenient and sensible. Even if he had different plans, there was bound to be widespread increased fascination for a while here with pic-'n-sculpt retail. That bothered her. It might jeopardize the proposed Cog operation. It might jeopardize Justin as second-stage pathfinder. Would it be wise in these changed conditions for George Dinnick to send Justin in for a detailed reconnaissance of what Jack Lamb had currently, to judge if a raid were worthwhile?

Because of that almost farcical carry-on at The Monty and its coverage in 'I Spy', Lamb and maybe others would be watchful for any further out-of-the-ordinary developments. Justin at Darien, asking for a squint at what Lamb had there, might be regarded as one of those further out-of-the-ordinary developments. That could put him in danger, although he'd come with a recommendation from one of Liz's brilliantly clean contacts. There were some very rough, not entirely aesthetic, dealers who might themselves see off those they regarded as possible competitors/enemies, or pay a professional heavies firm to do it for them. The huge money potentially involved could breed unlimited violence. In the abnormally excited situation here at the moment, Justin might be suspected at once for what he, in fact, very much was: a competitor/enemy.

Possibly, then, Liz would need to recommend a postponement to George Dinnick, or a switch away from Lamb and his collection, at least for the present. Darien was not the only house with attractive, genuine, potentially available works. Justin's safety had to be paramount, for her. George might understand this. Or he might not. Or he might understand it and hate it.

Earlier today, she'd picked up the hire car at the station and driven to Shield Terrace, then meter-parked at a spot from which she could watch The Monty for a while through the Peugeot's rear window. Because of movie and television cop dramas, people assumed that anyone doing surveillance on a building from a stationary car would be in the front seat and viewing through the windscreen. This could be conspicuous, and especially if you were as tall as Liz. The back was better.

She couldn't have said how better today, though. What did she aim to find by gazing at the facade of this drinking club? It was still before noon, when few, if any, customers would turn up. Even if some did they might mean nothing to Liz. But she'd needed some definite, tangible start location for, admittedly, a very vague, emotionally slanted inquiry. Yes, an info famine. Whatever else it might not be, The Monty at eleven Shield Terrace was tangible, definitely tangible: a passably impressive grey-stone, two-storey building, late Victorian or Edwardian, she'd guess.

A glass-sided, slate-roofed ground-floor porch led to the club's black main door, closed at present. She could see no name board over the porch or anywhere else saying this was The Monty. She thought most big, traditional London clubs would be like that – anonymous, except for those who belonged. You either knew about them or you didn't, and you weren't the sort the clubs wanted to be found by if you didn't know how to find them. They had their own catch twenty-two long before it appeared in book and film form. These clubs favoured discretion. Possibly, Ralph Ember wanted discretion for *his* club, too. He hadn't seen much of that lately. Zooming blobs of Worcestershire sauce didn't rate as discretion. But Ralph's ambition might still exist undimmed. The club stood on a corner of the Terrace, with a tarmacked car park-cum-delivery yard on one side and to the back. The district looked scruffy and due for redevelopment any day or year now, but she thought the handsome Monty building might survive.

She'd been in position for about twenty minutes when she saw the club door open, and two men stepped out into the porch. Almost at once she'd recognized Basil Gordon Loam from the Press picture. She assumed the other must be Ralph Ember, proprietor. The slight hesitation in identifying Gordon Loam had followed from surprise that the pair seemed so amiable with each other, smiling super-chummily as they shook hands. If it *was* Ember, he must be exceptionally forgiving. After all, Gordon Loam had only recently given The Monty the kind of distinction any club owner would detest and strive to avoid. In lurid nightmares, Ember might see advertisements for Monty membership: *Join Now And Play The Ricochet Game*. He'd probably wake up doing a fair imitation of that famous Munch pic, *The Scream*.

She recalled from the newspaper column the description 'El Cid lookalike, Mr Ember', which had puzzled her at the time. Now, though, she could see what was meant. Ember did resemble Charlton Heston, the Hollywood star who had played El Cid so stunningly, a film that still got a showing now and then on one of the movie channels: the long, craggy features, ship's prow nose, epic shoulders, disciplined waist. Ember did have a long, facial scar, though, which Heston had lacked.

Of course, she realized that the lavish enthusiasm of the handshake might be a total deception, each trying to con the other into a belief that they enjoyed hearty comradeliness, even mutual devotion. Just because Ember looked like someone who played the supremely honourable and trustworthy El Cid, it didn't signify Ember had to *be* honourable and trustworthy, especially to someone who'd gone gun-mad in the club.

And then, Gordon Loam. Liz felt again that she might have glimpsed him somewhere in a gallery or auction room or both, and had thought at the time he might have some sort of devious, sly, catch-as-catch-can function in the art business – the kind of devious, sly, catch-as-catch-can function Liz, Justin and George Dinnick had themselves. Today Gordon Loam wore green cord trousers and a brown leather jacket over a scarlet shirt. Perhaps he'd been dressed something like that at this previous encounter? Had she thought it an unnerving mixture of county-set and mildly bohemian style? But she realized she might be manufacturing memories to fit what she could see now.

Gordon Loam had gone to the car park for his Audi, and Liz climbed over into the front seat of the Peugeot and started the engine, ready to tag him. She crouched down in case he came her way. Just before she did this, though, she'd glanced back at Ember, who'd stayed standing in the porch watching Gordon Loam depart. None of the previous geniality remained in his face. He stared at Gordon Loam's back, as if to get familiar with its topography. She heard the Audi pass, waited a couple of seconds with her head below the dashboard, then sat up and got on Gordon Loam's trail.

ELEVEN

Iles said: 'This "I Spy", Col. Not good.'

'In which respect, sir?' Harpur said.

'I have to keep a balance in the city.'

'Few would say you fail on that.'

'Which fucking few?'

'I've heard visitors exclaim in restaurants or The Corval Museum, "This is the most balanced city I've ever come across, and I've been to Toledo *and* Winnipeg." Of course, they don't realize it's thanks to you, because if they're tourists from far off they might, regrettably, never have heard of you. Almost incredible given the global spread of vital information these days, but not impossible. Often I feel like confiding to them, "It's all Assistant Chief Iles's doing. Mr Iles and balance, they are as one."'

'You trying to tell me you go to museums, Harpur?'

'But I know you're not one to want recognition and acclaim for your achievements, much as those achievements deserve recognition and acclaim.'

'We ought to get down to see Ralph Ember,' Iles replied.

'On what account, sir?'

'Urgent, Col. He won't let this rest.'

'What?'

'Why I speak of balance.'

'Right.'

The ACC was in one of his made-to-measure, double-breasted, grey, three-piece suits, with white silk shirt, a silver and crimson tie and Charles Laity black lace-up shoes, the ensemble probably worth well over one thousand pounds, especially if they made him two pairs of trousers to share wear. He said: 'I don't claim to be on my own in bringing that balance and peace to a needy city and, indeed, world. That would be vanity and egomania. Now and then you help, Col, despite everything.'

'Thank you, sir. Despite which everything?'

'Oh, yes,' the ACC answered. '"Despite everything" really sums it up.'

'Sums what up?'

'Oh, yes.'

They were in the ACC's office suite, two rooms linked by folding doors, now open. He could pace a sort of circuit around the full area when under stress or deep into his own prime brand of self-pity. A long conference table and seven straight-backed chairs occupied one room. In the other, where they were now, he had his desk and computer station plus a tall cheval mirror near the corridor door, so he could check his appearance if going out, especially when in uniform. The mirror was fixed at its middle to a mahogany frame, and the glass could be tilted. He kept it swung slightly forward, reflecting only from his shoulders down, because he loathed the shape of his Adam's apple and would be seriously demoralized by glimpsing an image of it. Harpur thought that if Iles designed Assistant Chiefs' uniforms as well as wearing one he'd create a tunic high-necked enough to contain and conceal Adam's apples, like curtains around a hospital bed. Harpur knew the Assistant Chief's contempt for Adam's apples had nothing to do with the Garden of Eden and humanity's fruity tumble into sin. It was the jutting, asymmetrical appearance of his that upset him. 'Why me?' he'd scream sometimes.

Frequently, out of comradely kindness, even pity, Harpur had told him he'd never heard anyone speak hurtfully or disgustedly about the ACC's Adam's apple, even though it did have its repugnant aspects. Iles would not be placated, though. In fact, Harpur *had* heard people comment harshly or jocosely on it, but there was no need to goad the Assistant Chief with repetition of such disrespect. When requisitioning furniture for his rooms, he must have emphasized that he did not want a mirror screwed flush to the wall but one that could be angled for his continued sanity and overall well-being. Harpur knew the ACC did not regard sanity and well-being as qualities that were his simply by nature and entitlement. They had to be worked for, schemed for, as with the cheval. He'd told Harpur he didn't think much of Nature. Hadn't

Nature given him the ghastly fucking Adam's apple? He had another of these cheval mirrors in the bedroom at home – Idylls, in Rougement Place.

Iles said: 'Dear Ralph attempts to bring a little culture into that Shield Terrace shit-pit he runs, and what does he get in response?'

'Well, it's not exactly clear from the Press piece whether—'

'Contumely, Col.'

'Poor Ember.'

'Do you know what it means?'

'In his own way Ralph's quite a progressive thinker,' Harpur replied. 'Yes, in his own way.'

'Contumely – insult, insolence, bullets. Tell me this, Col, would you, please: how do I maintain that balance and peace in the streets if, at no distance from these headquarters, Ralph is getting a load of unprovoked contumely?'

'Some problem, sir!'

Iles had the newspaper page containing the 'I Spy' column in front of him on his desk. He read – reread – it for a moment. 'Who is he?'

'Who?'

'Gordon Loam.'

'The family has slipped down the scale. Fortune in tea, but a long while ago. London mansion then. Gone. Some say an ancestor knew Joseph Stockdale well – the Stockdale Wellington told to "Publish and be damned" when Stockdale threatened to expose Wellington's affair with Harriette Wilson, a court tart. Basil Gordon Loam gets an income from somewhere, though. Maybe an odd-job man in and around the art game. Fixer? Courier? Three daughters at the same private school as Ralph Ember's. Not cheap. He's done some time.'

'How typical of Ralph to refuse compensation payment for the disgraceful damage caused from such a source. Judas money. There is a kind of largeness of mind, a kind of grandeur and nobility to Ralph Ember.'

'Which kind exactly, sir?'

'Yet this large-mindedness, this grandeur, this nobility, does not mean he's a soft touch or will put up with maltreatment.'

'Hardly.'

'Blood will have blood, they say, Col.'

'Who?'

'Who what?'

'Who says blood will have blood?'

'I'm glad you asked that. Same with a beard.' Iles pointed to a line at the bottom of the 'I Spy' column. 'The point is, Col, surely, a beard is very near the head.'

'Many would agree with that, I'm sure, though I've never heard a full debate on it.'

'This is someone pulling out a gun in a drunken fit and rushing to place a couple of shots while the mood is still on him, a slave to impulse, a prisoner of waywardness. Or, perhaps he was so boozed, he feared the collage figure might shoot first. A sort of Gary Cooper *High Noon* situation.'

'I doubt whether *The Marriage Of Heaven And Hell* people had handguns. Doesn't "I Spy" say the target was naked? No holster or bandolier.'

'You're sober and might realize that, but this addled marksman must have been liquored-up and deluded. Perhaps he'd been sampling the Armagnac – Kressmann's – that Ralph himself favours, and which I, personally, will take now and then for a change. How do we know Gordon Loam wasn't aiming to get the figure terminally in its skull or chest, a brazen shoot-to-kill mission? Consider, Col, how a beard is constructed. It hangs from the chin and chops, doesn't it, so if someone is firing from below, as in this instance, he might want the shot to go up *under* the beard, through the neck to the brain. Instead, because he's stewed and not in a proper stance for firing with a pistol, the round is slightly off and takes the beard in error – takes the beard more than once, apparently, he's so blotto. The journalist refers to "rips", not merely "a rip".'

'Probably repairs could be done whether the damage was to the beard, the head or the chest,' Harpur said. 'I'm not certain it makes any difference. We're talking about paper wounds in a paper picture.'

Iles laughed loudly, tolerantly, almost affectionately, for a while, as if this were the sort of moronic answer he'd anticipate from Harpur, or idiots *like* Harpur; but the ACC would be generous and forgiving, as ever. 'The gunfire had an objective, Col. It was to show contempt for Ralph, for the club and for Ralph's efforts to improve the club. All right, we can all recognize that his efforts are loony. The Monty is a hell-hole and will remain a hell-hole. But he will not, cannot, see it like that. He's going to hang pictures there – proper, rated, framed, costly pictures, not some cut-outs from a mag. This is why I say mad large-mindedness, demented grandeur, fractured nobility. And this obnoxious jerk turns up, possibly offended by what he would regard as the over-refinement of the Blakeian motif already installed, and wants to put finale bullets into the head or chest, not the merely affixed beard, of someone who has become a kind of legendary ally in Ralph's wholesome, ramshackle endeavour. Maybe Gordon Loam hates anyone who aims to improve his social status because it reminds him of how far his own lot have slumped. Contumely, Col. I can find no more suitable term.'

'You're known for picking the right one of them, sir.'

'What?'

'Terms.'

Lately, Iles had reverted to the close-cut hair style often favoured by Jean Gabin, the French actor he'd seen and admired in old films on the movie channels. He rubbed his palm slowly over the grey tufts two or three times now. Harpur had realized a while ago that this was compensation: he couldn't allow himself many mirror views of the barbering because it would entail, also, sight of his Adam's apple, so he went for the tactile, safely away from the looking glass. 'I imagine we'd describe the tone of this gossip column as *de haut en bas*, wouldn't we, Harpur?' he asked.

'Most probably.'

'Something from a high point, where Mr or Ms "I Spy" is positioned, looking down to a low point where Ralph and The Monty are. Piss-taking, Col. Sustained satire. Unpleasant hoots. Contempt. Think of Swift's *Modest Proposal* or Pope's *Dunciad*. That insidious description of a Bloody Mary, for instance.'

'Oh? I found it reasonably accurate, sir.'

Iles struck the side of his head mildly with the plump stub of his right hand to signal despair at Harpur's continued thickness. 'Certainly, Col. But isn't it this very accuracy that turns it into a savage tease, claws-out?'

'Right. How?'

'The Bloody Mary, as detailed here, is, as you truly say, exactly, classically, right – vodka, tomato juice, Tabasco, Worcestershire sauce, ice. It represents in that strict form a club bar operating perfectly. But, of course, during the episode we're discussing, the Worcestershire sauce doesn't get to be a standard part of that attractive drink. Instead, in its lone, maverick, fly-by-night activity, it comes to represent the shambolic, deeply disordered conditions at The Monty, the sauce being now on an airborne attack. Also on the attack are sharp, strafing missiles from the broken bottle. This aftermath to *The Marriage Of Heaven And Hell* outrage brings collateral damage to club equipment and a possibly prized garment. It would have been pretty much the same if one of the bullets had hit a bottle of blackcurrant for rum and black. We are talking of utter social breakdown. It happened on Ralph's consecrated, potentially elite, ground. This is why I said he would have to retaliate. Pride. Repute.'

'We don't know there were bullets. "I Spy" didn't say so, might even have been careful *not* to say so.'

Oh, God.' Iles seemed about to give himself another meaningful, impatient thump, but stopped his hand halfway to his temple, as though he'd decided a second performance would be corny. 'Of course there were bullets, Harpur. We have someone – Basil Gordon Loam, as obliquely named in "I Spy" – walking around on our patch with a loaded weapon aboard and ready to fire it in a public place regardless of the peril caused. There are some illegality factors, I think, aren't there, Harpur? Perhaps you see now what I mean by balance.'

'Balance?'

'May I give you an easy to follow narrative, Col? Somebody – Gordon Loam – shoots up The Monty, trashing this dismal prole palace in his ex-upper-crust, arrogant, flamboyant style. Ex-upper-crusts are usually a fraction more haughty and Hunnish than current upper-crusts: there's a violent, subconscious nostalgia element. But the owner sees the club as holy and set to become even holier through his magic. He feels justified in shooting back at a suitable time later; in fact, he feels honour *compels* him to shoot back, or, of course, to do it by knife or garrotte wire. He's unable to pretend – either to himself or to others – that the onslaught on Blake did not much matter because only a beard was ruined, temporarily ruined. He refuses to regard this as sottish waggery. He knows there's nothing *only* about beards. That particular beard has ramifications. Don't you understand this, Col?'

'I'm not at a high enough rank to handle ramifications, sir.'

'Ralph can see beyond the actual – the gunning incident – and discover the real objective. Result? Future vendetta warfare on the streets, maybe. Ralph possibly killed or for ever disabled? The whole tranquil, precious drugs dealing concord – Ralph–Manse Shale – disrupted, maybe permanently destroyed. What chance balance when one scale has been emptied or vastly reduced?'

They drove down to The Monty together, Harpur at the wheel in an unmarked car. Iles said: 'Snotty, snooty, disdainful, those alternative explanations of the "hefty" hoisted girder's purpose in "I Spy": defence or air-conditioning. More crude sarcasm. Likewise the scoffing El Cid remark.' They turned left into Shield Terrace. Iles whistled gently. 'El Cid is there in the porch, Col. He seemed to be staring after somebody, and not fondly, body tense. Don't go into the club car park yet. It would alert him. Let's watch for a minute.' He pointed ahead. 'Look, the green Peugeot is pulling out. There's a metered space. Did I spot a thong-flash as the driver climbed over from the rear into the driving seat?'

'If there was the flash of a thong, I don't know anyone more likely to see it than you, sir,' Harpur replied.

'What was she doing on her own in the back?'

TWELVE

Enzyme had been to Silver Bells And Cockleshells twice previously. He really enjoyed these visits. He loved the bold, bright, friendly decor: vivid wallpaper in blues, reds, yellows and so on, giving picture versions of fairy tales and nursery rhymes. Jack and Jill climbed up a manageable looking mauve hill to fetch the pail of water, but then in the next scene came tumbling down with the spilled grey bucketful dousing them, Jack holding his severely injured head; both were smiling, though, at the arse-over-tit fun of it, so as not to frighten the nursery kids. A cream-coloured, milk-heavy cow flew over a slim, white moon, the cow grinning grandly at this exceptionally unusual lift-off. A big, virtuoso tabby cat, eyes closed in concentration, soloed a violin concerto, standing on its two back legs, the fiddle tucked in professionally under the thick-whiskered chin, an orchestra of other cats in the background on cellos, timpani, brass, woodwind. He had the feeling that their music would be joyful and loud with confidence, probably a Mozart piece. This bucked him up.

The children and Judy's staff at Silver Bells And Cockleshells always seemed happy, too, and this gave Enzyme's spirits an extra boost. For a short time he could stop yearning for the past glistening distinction and wealth of the Gordon Loam dynasty and, instead, enjoy thinking that he could restore all the family's success, even improve on it. That's what a cow jumping over the moon was about – unlikely achievement, brilliant, tuberculin-tested optimism. Of course, he took care not to get physically close to any of the children, or it might look as though he was on paedo sorties. Nurseries did attract crummy interlopers, mostly male. This was the kind of dirty reality the fantasy rhymes and tales provided an escape from.

The first time he'd come it was to tell Judy he fancied the .38 Smith and Wesson and ask whether she could fix him up, plus a tidy packet of ammo. He'd explained that what he needed was a pistol he could rely on to stop, and drop, immediately anyone artistically troublesome within a range of, say, twenty-five metres. An enemy still on his or her feet could fire at you, even if you'd put a good quota of bullets in him or her. To bring about instant collapse they had to be the right kind of terminating bullets and, obviously, in the right parts of his or her body. Smash someone's elbow with a round, fair enough, but he or she would still have the other arm and its trigger finger working OK.

Gordon Loam didn't want a big, lumpy handgun, though,

liable to give a boob-and-bra bulge under his jacket. He required the gun as an essential aid to his career in the Fine Arts. However, because this would be regarded by most as a very cultured and aesthetic job, carrying a pistol – carrying a badly stashed pistol – might seem oafish in the better type of gallery. But, in fact, the pistol was vital equipment, just as much as up-to-date records of auction-house sale prices, or a magnifying glass for signatures; though the gun should be kept hidden, if possible, at least until use.

In this trade, deals of tens of millions of dollars, and even of pounds sterling, had become commonplace; and, as a result, all kinds of international crooks and crookedness had also become commonplace. So had occasional serious gun play. People would die for their art, or for someone else's. Naturally, he'd also asked for a gun offering complete accuracy, in case the person targeted by him was carrying a valuable painting, or paintings, which had to be preserved intact, not riddled. Otherwise, killing the carrier would lose some of its point. Bullet holes in the repro Blake at Ember's Monty didn't matter. Bullet holes in a Manet or Monet *would* matter, could be deal-breakers. You did not see for sale in catalogues a masterpiece 'with perforations'. Monet had done that famous blueish painting of lilies on a lake, and it was so well-known you'd never be able to convince a possible buyer that some of the plant life and canvas under it were torn open as a special new ploy by the artist.

The dignity, beauty and general worthwhileness of art had attracted Enzyme to it as an occupation. He felt that the family history more or less compelled him to enter such a high status vocation – either Art, or the church, or soccer management, or the law. And he needed the .38 automatic to safeguard that esteemed status. In a way, Enzyme regarded this search for quality as comparable with Ralph Ember's ambition for The Monty, although Gordon Loam saw one considerable difference: Ralphy's obsessive wish was hopelessly, pitiably, fucking nuts, whereas Enzyme meant to win through and had the inherited flair, audacity and toughness to win through. Ralph might eventually transform The Monty, and a cow might jump over the moon, and pigs might fly. Enz wondered whether without realizing it at the time, due to drink and bar bravado, he had blasted off at the Blake because he considered Ralph Ember's ridiculous efforts unconsciously caricatured, lampooned, Enzyme's own much sounder purpose.

Judy had told him at their introductory meeting that she didn't have a .38 S. and W. actually in stock, but she'd go to her wholesale source and see what might be available. He hadn't been convinced that she really was without the model he wanted, though. This opening negotiation had struck him as a vetting session where she made a judgement on whether he was what he said he was, and whether it would be sensible and secure to deal with him. That kind of caution he'd entirely understood and sympathized with. He'd had her name, and the Silver Bells And Cockleshells' name, from a couple of hobo-level hangers-on in the pictures and sculpts network. He came to Judy with no solid validation. Enzyme hadn't expected her to produce something at once for this nobody from nowhere. That was how she'd inevitably think of him when he originally turned up. Although Judy might have heard something of the Gordon Loam family's magnificent history, she had to deal with the difficult and dicey present.

Obviously, the crèche was an ideal front for the gun and ammunition business. Parents hoping to make arrangements for their children to be enrolled here would look in to settle things with Judy, and Enzyme might have been one of them; although in reality his daughters were much too old for a nursery. He and she could go to her private office, as if to discuss fees and diets and character foibles of a potential child newcomer. She had a triple-lock safe in there containing the armament, strictly guns and bullets only. She'd emphasized to Enzyme that she never dealt in grenades on account of possible risk to the nursery's little innocents.

On his second call, when some trust had been built between them, and the deal for the .38 completed, she'd said: 'I might accidentally pull a grenade pin, and it would go off, possibly setting all the others off, too, causing the whole sodding shebang to come down on the dear ones. Mothers and fathers trust me with their babes, and I cannot escape that responsibility. It is something central for me. I won't sell the chemical irritant Mace, either – so useful for quelling nuisance people – though

I know a company offering it at a very attractive price. Suppose there were a slip-up and some of it circulated downstairs. It would upset me to see children hawking, spitting, gasping, their eyes inflamed. It's as well you know my limits and principles. I'm an advocate of ethical trading.'

An outsize teddy bear had been fixed to the safe door with cheery, colourful tapes to soften the impression otherwise given by the tall, formidable-looking steel surface. Judy had to lift the plump left leg of the teddy to get at one of the combination dials. Enzyme had found the toy gave a pleasant homely touch. Teddies and all that Winnie the Pooh stuff would probably have been very much features of well-to-do households like the Gordon Loam's in the last century. The bear did suggest, though, another resemblance to Ralph Ember – *The Marriage Of Heaven And Hell* rubbish intended to conceal the real rough-house reason for that thick defensive platter above Ralph Ember's accounting desk at The Monty bar.

On his first visit to the nursery Enzyme had waited below among the children while one of the minders went to find Judy. He'd freighted some tremendous delight into his face as he looked at the cat and the fiddle, the laughing cow and Jack and Jill. He thought that if Judy were studying him from somewhere unobserved she should be able to tell from his crazily exaggerated response to the wallpaper that this was someone laboriously putting on a cover act: not an enquiring parent, but a would-be gun customer.

Today, naturally, there was no need for a repeat of the happy rapture at sight of the spilled bucket, the amusing animals and a dish and spoon, both with long, spindleshank legs and running off together. Judy was waiting, and they went immediately to her office. She closed and locked the door. He said: 'I popped over, Judy, because I thought you might be a trifle perturbed by that rather skittish piece in the "I Spy" column.' He'd decided he had to speak first and set the tone of their tête-à-tête: pre-empt. He wanted a light-hearted, debonair approach to this situation. He was a Gordon Loam, and he didn't fancy being slagged off first by a big-time pusher and slummy club owner, and then by the boss of a dumping ground for pre-school, un-potty-trained young.

He realized he might have sounded very crushed and nervy when he rang half an hour ago. This had to be corrected, and quickly. Gordon Loams did not get crushed and nervy, especially on account of a rather impish, inconsequential carry-on at that unwholesome drinking club. There was surely a hearty tradition of exuberant, unconstrained behaviour by people of some class in plebby dumps like The Monty. 'A rather scapegrace episode, I'll admit, Judy, but once it was over, it's over.'

'So what the fuck are you doing here now?' she replied.

He nodded and chuckled slightly, like someone who recognized he had a case to answer – but *could* answer it with charming ease. 'A fair question,' he said. He felt prepared to be damned gracious. He tried to stay aware that this was a woman with acute sensitivities. She would not do grenades or Mace. 'Yes, utterly fair.'

'So, what's the reply?' she said. 'Do you know how to spot a tail and deal with it?'

'A tail?'

'A car following you.'

'Why would a car follow me?'

'The paper says you fired a pistol in The Monty.'

'Well, no, with respect, Judy, it doesn't exactly say that.' Correct her, but in gentle, civilized, calm style. Undermine her. Diminish her. Let her see she was up against decades of inherited, unshowy poise.

'No, it doesn't exactly say, but definitely. Why would you want to pay for the damage if you hadn't caused it?' she said. 'What are you, a charity? What you did is probably an offence. Having an unlicensed gun is certainly an offence. Some people might wonder where you got it. Some people might watch you. Some people might track you to the Silver Bells And Cockleshells and decide this might be your supplier.'

'You mean police?'

'Think about it.'

'I didn't see anything.'

'That's why I asked if you were used to watching your rear. This would be a vehicle not immediately behind but lurking at, say, one remove. Are you familiar with the tactics?'

'No, but I'm sure, nothing.'

'Well, you don't *sound* sure.'

Gordon Loam thought this cow wouldn't squander her energy by jumping over the moon. Her efforts would go to watching for the nitty-gritty perils she lived with on the ground. Cud was being chewed. Himself.

'You've done some time, haven't you?' she said.

'I've never mentioned that. How do you know?'

'I read in the Press of someone I've supplied goods to banging off at club ornamentation and I'm bound to wonder if what he's banging off with is the article I supplied. So, it would follow I carry out some brisk research on him.'

'I'm not keen on that.'

'No, I don't expect you to be. But perhaps I should have done it a lot earlier, such as before I supplied him with what I supplied him with.'

'Research where?'

'There's a lot of information about if you know where to look for it.'

'But *where* did you look for it?'

'Now, don't make yourself seem even more stupid than you have already. Am I going to disclose my founts to you?'

He decided he'd been wrong to think of her as chirpy. Dogged. Belligerent. Self-protective. He still regarded the eyebrows as expressive, but not friendly-expressive, suspicious-expressive, resentful-expressive. 'Founts?' he asked.

'In this business – the kiddy-care business, I mean, not the armament section – in this caring business it's necessary to do checks on all sorts. There are founts from which info flows.'

'I'm on no sex register.'

'I accept that. But sex isn't the only area they'll dig into if you ask. If you ask and pay.'

'So, you asked?'

'Not until the report of the club escapade. Previously, I'd used my own judgement. As I said, a mistake.'

Someone knocked the door. Judy lowered her voice. 'It will be Fern, one of the helpers. She'll want to discover whether we're shagging in here. It's an interest of hers.'

'What is?'

'Other people having it off. I don't think she gets much

herself. It's envy. I'll tell her you're not on the sex register, shall I?' Judy answered the knock at full voice now. 'Yes?'

'Shall I bring teas?' the woman said.

'Yes, tea would be lovely,' Judy said.

'But the door is locked,' the woman said.

'I'll unlock when you bring it.'

'Milk and sugar? I'd remember better if you opened the door now and told me face to face.'

Judy looked at him.

'Milk and one sugar,' he said.

'Milk and one lump for each of us, Fern. I said lump, not hump, mind.'

The woman gave up.

Gordon Loam wasn't certain of the best way to act. Would Judy take it as a slight if he treated Fern's imaginings as preposterous? The atmosphere was deeply unfavourable to love-making, anyway, but Fern couldn't know that. Gordon Loam got a diversion going: 'Judy, I hate to think I might have made you uneasy. I said to myself, as soon as I saw the "I Spy" gossip, that I must come over to Silver Bells And Cockleshells at once, to explain and apologize.'

'And by coming over to explain and apologize you may have made things worse. Perhaps you've created an obvious link between, on one side, you and the gunman and, on the other, me and the nursery. I don't thank you for that.'

This infuriated him – the quiet, deadly way she phrased it: 'I don't thank you for that.' What she meant was: 'I curse you for that.' But instead of coming out straight with it, she softened things, turned a forthright, no-nonsense positive into a milk-and-water negative. Management-speak. It was how someone in authority, and/or with some class, might tell off a subordinate – say, a duke or pop star to his butler. It was reproof, but reproof a little understated so as not to seem like a rich and/or upper-crust bully; in other words, condescension. It was the kind of patronizing technique his family in the past would have used on their servants: *noblesse oblige* material; a slap-down, but tempered for the shorn lamb.

Because she ran a couple of businesses she thought it OK to behave like a marchioness. She was divorced, and he could understand why. Being alone and in charge had probably changed her from someone acceptable to this. She had a well-looked-after slim body for her age, a strong – maybe overstrong – face and features, and she was dressed in high-grade cling-fit jeans and a roll-top purple sweater. When she'd smashed through the glass ceiling, though, a bit of glass must have sliced off a dollop of feminine sweetness.

'But at least you don't come here carrying that gun,' she said. 'Or not in a shoulder holster, anyway. No giveaway mound.'

'I *couldn't* have brought it.'

'Oh?'

'It's gone.'

'Gone where, for God's sake?'

'Look, Judy, as soon as that foolishness took place at The Monty, I realized there might be results that could threaten you.' He gave this maximum earnestness. 'I realized that perhaps there'd be some means of tracing the weapon to yourself as provider. So, I did what I hope you'd expect me to do as safeguard of your interests. Those interests were my priority.'

'Did what?' she replied.

'Got rid. Gun and remaining rounds.'

'Got rid?'

'Absolutely.'

'How? Where?'

'You're perfectly entitled to ask for details.'

'Yes, I know. How? Where?'

'I drove to the headland at Rondon Point. The load is in about six fathoms of shifting, murky, tumultuous sea and getting pulled and flung by an undertow further and further from land.'

'You're sure?'

'I was alone out there. I could count the splashes. Sad waste of a lovely piece, but necessary, I think.'

She stayed silent a while, then gave what Gordon Loam would classify as a smirk-smile: more arrogance and cheek. She nodded a couple of times, to signal a revelation. 'I see. So, you're without, bereft, disarmed. Does that account for the urgency?'

'The urgency was so I could reassure you as to the immediate precautions I undertook on your behalf. This wasn't something to say over the telephone.' He smiled himself now, a different category of smile, though: frank, wry. 'But, yes, I'm without.'

'And you imagine I'm going to produce again?'

'Absolutely no delay in committing S. and W. and the bullets to the deep. I knew this would weigh with you when I asked for a replacement.'

'It might weigh with me, but it doesn't weigh *enough*.'

Still more of her damn top-notchness. She could make subtle, graded points – yes, she'd admit it weighed, but it didn't weight *enough*. What would she give it, B fucking +?

Fern knocked on the door again. It sounded as though she might be using the corner of a tray. They were sitting in bamboo framed easy chairs. Judy stood. 'Zip up, there's a dear!' she told Gordon Loam, in a voice loud enough to be heard outside. She opened the door. He saw a long-faced woman in her fifties wearing a beige cardigan and black trousers who gave Judy a very close examination first, probably to see whether her clothes had been disturbed, and then gazed around her towards Gordon Loam. He waved. Fern was holding a silver tray with two plain white mugs on it. Judy took the tray. 'Thanks, Fern, we could do with a refresher after all that, I can tell you.' She went and put the tray on her desk. Fern gazed systematically around the room, perhaps in case furniture had been broken during some threshing about. Judy went back to the door. 'Yes, many thanks, Fern,' she said, and closed and locked up again. She handed Gordon Loam a mug, then took the other and sat down.

'I don't want to be fussy this time,' he said. 'I mean, demanding a particular weapon. It would mess you about too much. If you've got a Smith and Wesson .38 I'll take it, of course. But because this is the second call on you – no doubt a nuisance – I'll settle for whatever you have to hand. Cost? You name it. I'll get along to the hole-in-the-wall and fetch cash. It doesn't have to be a new gun. I rather like the prickly cordite smell off a used firearm. Companionable. Mature. Been There, Done That.'

'Do you think I'm fucking mad?' she replied genially.

'How do you mean, Judy?'

'I made a mistake. You want me to repeat it, expect me to repeat it? You really think I would?'

'But I've told you, I recognize that mayhem with the Blake was disgraceful. It can never occur again.'

'You say so now. But I have to think about what happens the next time you're stinko-senseless. We must be clear headed, however painful. I'm afraid you lack control and self discipline, Basil. You shouldn't have a firearm. Now, please don't feel hurt at my saying this. It's well-known there is a certain cohort of people who are psychologically unsuited to guns, sort of allergic. No shame or blame: it's simply Nature imposing an arbitrary mental flaw. It would be irresponsible, even cruel, of me to sell you another pistol.'

His rage soared. She thought she could shove him into a 'certain cohort'. The Gordon Loam family were not made to be members of a 'cohort'. That suggested they were merely part of some afflicted group. The Gordon Loams existed independently of any damn cohort. They had uniqueness and their own special dignity and strength, even if these qualities were temporarily dimmed. Yet he was getting lectured to, told he had a 'mental flaw' by a dreary, fading, harsh old thing with no family history he'd ever heard of, or anyone else had ever heard of, most likely. She was from a backstreet or multi-storey but had somehow wangled her way to a spot where she had a vestige of power. And she would use that power against him, Basil Gordon Loam! She didn't care that he would be left unprotected if she withheld a gun from him. He had deliberately lowered his requirement so as not to give her too much bother. He would have taken any handgun – no insistence on the S. and W. Yet she'd ignored that and shown herself totally inhuman, inflexible, uncaring.

He stood and stepped towards the safe. He didn't know any of the combinations for getting in at the gun hoard, of course, but he felt driven to make some sort of physical gesture, and the safe symbolized the vile brush-off treatment she used on him. He fiercely grabbed the teddy's shoulders with two hands and yanked at it hard so the knots came adrift and the tapes fluttered out behind the bear like colourful streamers from a kite. He wanted to get at the dial and spin it. That wouldn't open the door, and, in any case, there were two others. But it would be a protest, not just to the teddy but to her. If he'd had a gun he might have shot Judy.

'No!' she screamed. 'Stop! I've told you, haven't I – you've no self-control.' She stood, too, now and came to try to pull the bear away from him. 'Stop it, you've no right at all!' She hurled herself at Gordon Loam. They fought, staggering across the room, their arms tight around each other, the bear jammed between them at about chest level, as if two boxers in the ring had turned on the referee. He found it strange, ghastly, to be embraced like this by a woman wearing a purple sweater, not with affection but hate. Would it have felt better if she were younger? They knocked to the ground a red, three-tier, stationery desk tray, scattering papers and a couple of telephone directories. But although his mind registered only revulsion from her terrible,writhing closeness, his body seemed unable to distinguish between very different kinds of intimate contact, and he started to get a hard-on. This perplexed and disgusted him.

He needed another diversion. With his right hand he reached down between them. He took hold of the teddy by one of its ears and pulled it out. In a way, that brought them even more physically entwined, because the bear had operated like an upper-body fender. But he flung the bear across the room. It dislodged a framed picture of a puffin, half a dozen small fish clamped in its beak, which fell to the ground, smashing the glass. As he'd hoped, she wanted to go to the teddy and see it was undamaged. She broke away from him and made for it among the splinters of glass.

'So you turn me down, you refuse me?' he shouted.

'Yes, yes, I refuse.'

A double-fist hammering on the door started. Fern called: 'What's happening? Oh, what's happening? The noise! Breakages! Violence! What's he doing to you, Judy? Refuse him, yes, refuse him. I suspected he was a beast. You're right, they've no self-control, none of them. They're prick-driven. Is he seeking to ravish you on your own child-haven, silver-belled and cockle-shelled premises?'

Gordon Loam bellowed: 'Watch your language, Fern. There are young children out there.'

THIRTEEN

Liz Rossol in the green hired Peugeot had followed Gordon Loam to what she reckoned from her earlier visit would be the smart, north-east end of the town. He'd parked and, as she drew up a little distance away, she saw him leave his car and walk fast, urgently, to a big, three-storey Victorian house on a corner. In the front garden was a large display stand with a sign under glass reading Silver Bells And Cockleshells Nursery and a kind of tree house: no tree, but a small, wooden hut on top of a timber staircase, unoccupied at present. For a moment it reminded Liz of machine-gun guard towers in concentration camp films.

Gordon Loam seemed to knock on the house door and after a couple of minutes disappeared inside. She waited and watched again. Did he have children of nursery age and had come to see them, or discuss something about them? She needed a biog card on him. And, more pressing, did the visit have anything to do with art and Darien and The Monty? How *could* it have anything to do with art and Darien and The Monty*?* Was she straying from her proper job?

This uncertainty made Liz wonder why she was sitting here, gawping at the house and name board. She was supposed to be a fieldworker, for God's sake, an ace fieldworker, and the nursery – *inside* the nursery – was where she should be, not sixty metres away. Or perhaps she should be elsewhere altogether, taking another look at Darien and its surrounds. 'Get going, Liz, you prat,' she muttered to herself. 'Stop skiving on your arse in a safety zone.' She often muttered to herself and was a good listener to what she said. 'I'll take in Darien as soon as I've finished here.'

So, now, Liz concocted in her head what might do as a basic, believable bit of fiction to suit Silver Bells And Cockleshells, got out of the Peugeot and went to knock on the door. A plump, round-faced woman in her late twenties answered.

'I'm trying to find a nursery place for my little daughter, Christine,' Liz said. That 'little' – a mistake? A sign of phoniness in a prepared, overdone spiel? If you came looking for a spot in a nursery for your child, of course the child would be little. It was the only kind nurseries took.

'Please come in,' the woman said. 'I'm Sue.' She led Liz through a mosaic-tiled hall into a large, bright room with vivid, pictorial wallpaper and children's furniture. No Gordon Loam. There were about twenty infants, some watching on a large screen television a children's programme featuring kind-hearted, sweet-tempered alligators, others playing with dolls and plastic toys. Sue showed Liz to a straight-backed adult chair. 'Judy is busy in the office.' She nodded towards stairs at the far end of the room rising to a first-floor landing. 'I don't think she'll be long.'

'Judy?'

'Mrs Judith Timmins.'

'She's in charge?'

'Owner.'

Liz saw a plumpish woman in her fifties, grey hair cropped savagely close, emerge from a shadowy part of the landing, with what seemed to be an empty tray in one hand down at her side. 'Is that Mrs Timmins?' she asked.

Sue smiled. 'No, it's Fern. One of the staff. Like me. She's usually entirely all right. But you know how it is; she gets ideas into her head now and then.'

It sounded like a gentle forewarning that Fern might go ape. Maybe Sue regularly had to red-alert callers about her. 'Gets ideas into her head? Well, I suppose we all do,' Liz said. 'It's one of the things heads are for.'

'Yes, but when I say gets ideas into her head I'm talking about *really* getting ideas into her head. Or *an* idea, to be accurate. One.'

'Right. Which ideas, or idea?' Liz asked.

'She's not too good today. Extra-intense? Marauding? But there's no harm in her or, obviously, Judy wouldn't keep her on. The last thing I'd want is for you to worry. She'll always be fine with the children, absolutely fine. They love her. Your Christine will be very happy with Fern. You might have read about unpleasant cases in the paper involving children, even extremely young children, but that's not the least bit like Fern. It's only with grown-ups that she can get a trifle . . . well, a trifle off-balance. And, of course, the saucy way some grown-ups live is liable to trouble almost anyone. But most people, if they notice bad faults in others, don't say anything, particularly in England, where, of course, we are. There's a sort of tradition of politeness and hushing things up. It might be to do with what's referred to as the "stiff upper-lip", which this country is famed for, meaning silence, regardless. Tact, you could think of it as. Or indifference.

'But Fern, you see, is not like this, and, in my view, she's entitled not to be. There's another phrase, "let it all hang out", and this would cover Fern. If something is bothering her she will speak of it in what could be called a very plain fashion, and often with the volume on sodding max. She's not one to bottle things up. Tact isn't a favourite with Fern. She'd say, "Stuff tact." It's as if some notion, some thought, will take charge of her for a while, like a manacle. The focus is all on that one item. It's not a permanent thing by any means, but during the period it has hold of her she doesn't seem able to think about anything else. It's too powerful.'

'An obsession?' Liz said. 'An *idée fixe*?'

'In that area.'

Liz thought she heard the sound of a thump and then breaking glass from somewhere upstairs. 'And although Mrs Timmins continues to employ her, does she mind about Fern's fits?'

'I wouldn't call them fits. That's too medical.'

'Spasms?'

'Interludes. Nobody would deny they happen here. We've become used to the occasional in-house difficulty. Parents are very good about it. They understand that these moods come and go. Outlandish, certainly, while they last, but nothing worse. Or not outrageously worse. Eccentric – another Brit tradition which can be almost endearing. There's no muzzle-froth or anything similar which might get spattered over some of the children. Hygiene – so important. People regard Fern as quirky, but not in the least bit dangerous. Yes, quirky. Nobody thinks of reporting her to Health and Safety or the police. In a way, it's a lesson to the children in kindliness and tolerance. We could and do try to *teach* them those qualities, but it's much more effective for them to see it in operation with Fern. Obviously, children wouldn't know the word "quirky", but they can tell Fern hasn't always got it all together, and they see that these oddities are humanely put up with by management, no finale fist in her chops.'

As Liz watched, Fern placed the tray on the landing floor and then crouched with her ear against a closed door. It struck Liz that there was something precise and well-practised about Fern's movements, like an actor's in a long-run play. Her face showed the focus Sue had referred to. The right ear, hard on the mahogany, would be exceptionally focused. This was studiousness. Liz thought she heard a male voice shouting something, apparently from the room on the other side of the door, most likely the office. The tone seemed pained and desperate. Liz couldn't make out the words, though, through the solid wood of a Victorian door. It looked as though Fern could. This would come with the focusing.

Liz saw why Fern had put the tray down. She wanted both her hands free. Uncrouched now, she hammered on the door with two fists, like someone belting a punch bag in the gym, and at the same time began to scream-shout: 'What's happening? Oh, what's happening? The noise! Breakages! Violence! What's he doing to you, Judy? Refuse him, yes, refuse him. I suspected he was a beast. You're right, they've no self-control, none of them. They're prick-driven. Is he seeking to ravish you on your own child-haven, silver-belled and cockle-shelled premises?'

The male voice yelled some kind of reply, but Liz still couldn't get the words. They sounded like a reproof this time, possibly about the vocabulary.

'That's the kind of unjolly, raucous thing I mean,' Sue said. None of the children had shown any interest in the door-battering and general din. 'Yes, it's vehement and vigorous, but we have to ask: how could she reasonably have made up her mind so quickly?'

'About what, exactly?'

'Prick-driven beastliness. Fern, it must be admitted, can be rather hasty in slapping labels on when she's into that type of commentating spell. All right, it's not the first time this man has called here, so she might have had opportunities to judge his personality. But what she's saying, isn't it, is that she could tell from the very first visit that he was a beast and prick-driven? She claims she intuited this instantly, no need for any evidence. This conviction has stayed immovably with her, has come to dominate and control her – what you suggested might be an obsession. And so she is always liable to go into one of these outbursts if remarks or events set them off. Today, it must be some sounds she may have heard coming from behind the office door. Wasn't there the noise of breaking glass?'

'Did she expect whatever it was she heard, though? She appeared to be hanging about on the landing waiting for it.'

'What I mean by impressions taking control of her. Or, again, what you termed an obsession.'

'How often has the man been here before?'

'Twice, I think. His family used to be of significance – the Gordon Loams. If you were having a cup of tea at the beginning of last century it would almost certainly be tea shipped in by the Gordon Loams, Indian or Chinese. Mention tea to anyone, and they would automatically think "Gordon Loam". It was that kind of trade dominance. This would be pre tea-bags. Their company didn't adapt quickly enough to changed demands, so I believe he's switched altogether from tea to a career in the artistic line. Some transaction takes place between Judy and him, its nature so far confidential.'

'Interesting. Does he have a child in the nursery?'

'No.'

'But is thinking of bringing a child?' Liz said.

'I suppose it's possible.'

'But you don't believe so?'

'It doesn't usually take three visits.'

'So, might Fern have it right?'

'How?'

'There's a love affair? It's illicit, perhaps, so they have to use the office?'

'It wouldn't be comfortable. No couch or bed. But, all right, there are armchairs and the floor. She does wear those very unbillowy jeans that seem to cosset certain areas, which males would regard as inviting.'

'What else is in the office?'

'A workstation. Bird pictures. A big safe.'

Liz was aware of getting towards outright nosiness. Just the same, she stuck at it. 'A safe for petty cash, perhaps?'

'Perhaps. I've never seen it open. Three combination locks! None of the staff have ever seen it open. We're not given the codes. Security! Plus a teddy bear.'

'Oh?'

'Taped to the safe door.'

'To suggest a nursery flavour?'

'Like that, yes. The safe, so cold and, well, steely, as it usually is with safes. The teddy is to remind her and remind others that although the nursery is a business, the main consideration must always be the happiness and well-being of the gang of spoiled, egomaniac, uncharming kids in our care.' She gave herself a mock slap on the mouth. 'Oh, sorry. I'm sure your Christine's a sweetie. Not all of them are, though. The toy bear helps create the desired atmosphere. Does Christine have a teddy?'

'Oh, yes, dearly loved.'

'She could bring it to the nursery with her, no probs.'

'That's a relief. She's very attached to him.'

'Any attempt by some of these bullying three- or four-year olds to grab it from her will be very heavily negatived by me or, if necessary, a combined troubleshooters staff force.'

'Do quite a number of people come to see Judy in the office?'

'Oh, yes. The formalities.'

'Of arranging for a child to be enrolled?'

'But Fern, with her unique way of treating things at certain periods, will decide occasionally that it's not to do with nursery matters at all. She'll sniff the air. Yes, you'll see her sniff the air, like an animal, and she'll form her own notion as to what's *really* taking place. At these times she suspects Silver Bells And Cockleshells of being a locked-door cover. She apparently picks up an odour indicating this, or indicating it to someone of her analytic bent. This might be sexual, obviously, but once I heard her murmur, "Cordite," as though she detected a firearm with some history, or possibly *wanted* a firearm to deal with some imagined menace.'

'Cover? Cover what?'

'Something not obvious going on.'

Yes. 'How about you, and any other staff?'

'How do you mean "how about"?'

'What do *you* think?'

'Of the locked door?' Sue said. 'And the locked safe?'

'Yes, that kind of thing.'

'I don't want you to be uneasy. That's why I've explained matters so thoroughly. I had an idea Fern might get unpredictable and rancid today. It's the way she puts her head on one side from early a.m., like she wants to see behind what's happening, or what someone's saying, and requires this new viewing angle. Sceptical. A determination to be undeceived. Admirable in many ways. I thought it best if I assured you these moments of unusual carry-on from Fern are *only* moments and are concerned with a limited number of topics, mainly adult matters, in that special, rather unwholesome sense of "adult". Your child and all the other children are totally safe. The cordite aspect I don't see as serious. Cordite should be our servant, not our master or mistress.' She nodded slowly three times. 'Considerable rigour.'

'Considerable rigour in what?' Liz replied.

'Official inspection of nurseries. Certification. These involve considerable rigour and poking about by bloody disgusting professional snoops, "only-doing-my-job" scumbags. They come unannounced. Judy might tell Fern to take the day off, otherwise. So, we just have to hope she's in an unmemorable phase.' Sue suddenly gave her voice grand deference and excitement: 'Well, and here's Mr Gordon Loam now,' she cried.

He came out on to the landing through the door Fern had concentrated on with the blows and discourse. Liz thought he looked angry and somehow deeply deprived. Behind him stood a woman in her mid forties wearing the sort of bodyline, bum-cradling jeans Sue had spoken about and a purple roll-top sweater. She carried a large teddy bear: hugged it strongly to the sweater, as though it had been saved from kidnappers or a flood and would be devotedly protected for ever from now on.

Had Gordon Loam attacked it? Fern was alongside what must be Mrs Timmins. Gordon Loam came hurriedly down the stairs and passed among the children towards the front door, ignoring Sue and Liz. 'For shame, for shame, you dirty, driven dog! Return to your vomit. There's none for you here,' Fern shouted after him. He let himself out.

'Judy, here's a lady who wants to enrol her child, Christine,' Sue said.

'A lovely name,' Fern said. 'She'll have a wonderful time here. A restful, ceaselessly friendly oasis. Oh, I do look forward to meeting your Christine.'

'Come up to the office, will you, please,' Mrs Timmins said to Liz.

'There's been a breakage therein, I believe,' Fern said. 'I heard it. That's always liable to happen. Picture hooks notoriously get metal fatigue. Pictures of birds unfortunately can't fly like birds. But it will all soon be righted.'

Liz and Mrs Timmins went into the office, and Mrs Timmins closed and locked the door. She put the teddy bear on a work station. They sat facing each other in bamboo framed easy chairs. Liz found herself sniffing, but unostentatiously sniffing, for whatever Fern might have sniffed if she'd been in a sniffing mood now. Liz, though, detected nothing. Fern had apparently caught the odour of cordite one day. Liz wasn't sure she'd recognize the smell of cordite, anyway, but she felt pretty sure it wasn't present now. 'I gather from Sue the teddy bear is usually taped to the safe,' Liz said. 'A pleasant touch, and a reminder of what the nursery is all about.'

'The tapes came loose.'

'This is something that can happen to tapes. It's a very formidable looking safe otherwise. But I'm sure necessary. Business papers to do with the nursery? An obvious need for complete confidentiality. So, naturally, under lock and key.'

Mrs Timmins stayed quiet for half a minute, staring without a break at Liz the whole time. 'You're not here about a child, are you?' she replied. 'There's no Christine. You're an observer, aren't you?'

'An observer?'

'Some inspectorate.'

'It all seems in excellent order,' Liz said. 'As your assistant remarked, the puffin picture can soon be repaired and put back.'

'Regrettably, there was something of a mild fracas,' Mrs Timmins said. 'I wouldn't be surprised if you noticed.'

Liz said: 'Now and then we will all run into this kind of thing. The children took it as normal – surely the main point. They are learning a couple of prime lessons: (one) life will not be everlastingly placid and uneventful, and (two) there are occasions when a good, old-fashioned solid wood door is indispensable, rather than one of those frail, modern lightweight ones.'

FOURTEEN

'Col's been grieving about your shamefully violated *Marriage Of Heaven And Hell*, Ralph, and is disgusted by the jocose and flibbertigibbet way this savagery has been treated in the Press,' Iles said. They'd watched while Ralph Ember, in the club porch, seemed to study the traffic and/or the horizon in very concentrated mode. And then, when he gave that up and returned to the bar, they'd followed him in.

During their observation spell in Shield Terrace, Harpur had pushed the car's sun visor around to the side position, giving them some cover. With his gaze fixed hard on Ember, Iles had said: 'I suppose you'll be longing to know my interpretation of what we're seeing, Col.'

'I'm longing to know your interpretation of what we're seeing, sir,' Harpur replied.

'Ralph's had a visitor – someone he wants to make sure he's rid of for now. He feels the club has been polluted, and he intends to guard it from any further insult.'

'Which visitor?'

'We arrived just too late to see. But someone he detests, with possible justification. I deduce this from the cast of his body as he stands there, very upright, very proud, very unforgiving around the tonsils and lower jaw area, buttocks clenched in contemplative rage: they could crack walnuts.'

'I didn't notice that – the tonsils and lower jaw, or the buttocks.'

'Well, you're not the kind who *would* notice, Col.'

'Which kind would, sir?'

'My kind, Harpur.'

'But which kind is that?'

'Mine.'

'This possibly justified detestation and the pollution – you think it was Gordon Loam? But why would he come?'

'Ralph's resolved about something,' Iles replied.

'To do Gordon Loam?'

'Ralph W. Ember is not someone to monkey with. His self-awarded dignity has sublime vastness. This is accompanied by a full-throttle determination to dispose of anyone who damages that dignity.'

'Enzyme?'

'Obviously, you'll be thinking of John Foster Dulles, Col.'

'Astonishing! How did you know, sir?'

'US Secretary of State in the Cold War.'

'Oh, *that* John Foster Dulles!'

'Promised "massive retaliation" if Russia nuked. Likewise Ralphy's response when irritated, for instance by a shot Blake pic.'

Harpur would have regarded these guesses and theories from anyone other than Iles as daft whimsy and consummate crap. But he'd learned that the Assistant Chief's intuitions sometimes turned out spot on. *Often* turned out spot on. He'd told Harpur not long ago that at Staff College he'd been dubbed 'Delphi Desmond' after the town in ancient Greece where, apparently, a Delphic Oracle did top-notch predicting to help prop up the barmy plots of classical tales.

In the club, Iles called delightedly, 'Why, Ralph! What a treat to see you again! How are the family – Margaret and the children, Venetia and Fay? All well? Grand! The Monty's brass fittings and mahogany panels are reassuringly splendid still in this age of three-ply and plastic.' A few lunchtime customers were already in the bar. They went silent for a minute. Iles could have this chilling effect on some Monty members – those who'd been locked up, or were on bail and due to be locked up, or who should have been locked up and knew it and soon might be. The Assistant Chief had this type of impact whether he was in uniform or civvies. 'Nobody shall ever call me dowdy, Col,' he'd told Harpur not long ago.

'I'll be alert in case anyone does, and inform him-her that, on the contrary, you're famous for *non*-dowdiness, *anti*-dowdiness, in fact.'

Ralph ordered drinks, and the three of them went to a table for some privacy. Iles mentioned Harpur's supposed reaction to the club shooting and Press treatment. The ACC continued: 'Naturally, Col had never heard of W. Blake, but he'd picked up from the newspaper column that this guy must be someone important in respectable annals, and so Harpur could feel sorrow at the harm done. Col's a great fan of literature. He doesn't know any, of course, but he gives it genuine, comradely approval in a general way. You speak the word "literature" to him, and a very warm, accommodating smile will brighten his gnarled-before-its-time phiz temporarily, showing he's heard the term before and might even have an idea what it means. Almost definitely I can state he would never do a Goebbels and burn books by the trainload.'

'I don't understand why you're here,' Ralph replied. 'I mean, two people of your rank.'

'There's only one person of *my* rank,' Iles said. 'Me. And then there's Harpur.'

'Mr Iles likes to keep the city peaceful: no blood on the pavements, Ralph,' Harpur said.

'I would certainly endorse that,' Ember said.

Harpur glanced up towards *The Marriage Of Heaven And Hell*. 'So good to see the collage has been repaired,' he said. 'In proper condition it gives the club an ambience.'

'Col's strong on ambiences,' Iles said, 'and no longer mixes them up with ambulances. If he ever got to Staff College, which, plainly, he never fucking will, they'd probably fix "Ambience" on him as a friendly cognomen. Clearly, the club has its own fine, distinguished character which cannot be seriously damaged by a wayward gun-pop incident of that sort, Ralph.

I agree with Col; the salvaged Blake figure relays an additional genial atmos. But The Monty is not only about this lovely interior. It has a place in the wide outside. When we first arrived, Ralph, we saw you in the porch gazing forward in a particularly significant, highly empathic fashion. Probably, you'll want me to point out what, whom, you resembled then – in my opinion.'

'Well, no, I don't think I do,' Ember said.

'The French lieutenant's woman waiting at the end of the sea wall for the French lieutenant to come back in *The French Lieutenant's Woman*,' Iles replied instantly.

'I've heard of him,' Ember said.

'Who?' Iles said.

'The French lieutenant,' Ember said. 'Do we ever find out where he's gone?'

'And do you know what Harpur said to me?' Iles replied.

'Some bollocks,' Ember said.

'He declared: "Ralph is in an act of homage to the city he adores and is so much a pillar of. He revels in its happy, even serene, incessant hum of wholesome activity." Would this be an accurate interpretation of your posture then, Ralph? "Earth has not anything to show more fair." That kind of malarkey?'

Ember said: 'Well, I—'

'Wonderful, Ralph!' Iles cried. 'Harpur might look thuggish and woebegone, but he has this unparalleled perceptive knack. The sight of you in the porch, enjoying the view, and your personal thoughts prompted by that view, would tell Col that you were experiencing a quiet, reflective moment. And, yes, this could be categorized as a spell of homage. I don't think that is to exaggerate.'

Ember said: 'Well—'

'We felt privileged, I and Col, to be part of that grand experience, although from a sizeable distance in our car. Yes, the experience was so strong and authentic that it easily reached us, evidently an experience with legs. We considered it would be a kind of disrespect, a minor sacrilege, to interrupt, just as one would hang back while, say, waiting for a nun to complete her prayers. We delayed until you went into the bar, when our approach would be less disruptive. Col was very firm on that. He's much into decorum.'

'What the hell's this all about?' Ember said.

'Ah! You're one who goes to the core of things, Ralph,' Iles said.

'So much wordage,' Ember replied.

Occasionally, Harpur thought Ralph had part-discovered how to handle the Assistant Chief. It was about time. He'd had some practice.

'This idiot who went on the anti-Blake hunt – did he have a grudge?' Iles said. 'I mean against you, not against Blake or the Romantic Movement, though God knows the Romantic Movement deserves to get blown away by its own sodding wild West Wind.'

'Grudge?' Ralph said.

'The blood on the pavement already mentioned, Ralph,' Harpur said. 'We want to avoid that.'

'Pavements in this city are for pedestrians, going briskly and efficiently about their unthreatened business,' Iles said. 'I, Desmond Iles, exist to achieve and preserve this urban safety.'

Ember said, 'Yes, but—'

'The council is aiming to enter "The City of Culture" competition,' Iles replied. 'We need to be extra careful. Stains everywhere at street level won't help with the application. There's a lot of high-grade snorting goes on among the cultured, Ralph. These are people who believe Charlie, used without stint, increases their appreciation of the arts and straightens out major philosophical glitches. Such heavy users will be drawn here if our city wins the nomination. You won't want to lose that trading opportunity.'

Ember said: 'No, but—'

'Envy,' Iles replied.

'Whose?' Ralph said.

'Think about Basil Gordon Loam, Ralph,' Iles said.

'Think what about him?' Ralph said.

'We take it he was the marksman,' Harpur said.

'It's well-known his family was wholeheartedly, even reverentially, into tea,' Iles said. 'This is what I'm getting at when I say "envy". Tea in a very big way. The Gordon Loams would certainly go along with Cowper.'

'I've heard of him, too,' Ember said.

'Of course,' Iles said. 'You started that mature student degree course, Ralph. Admirable.'

'Suspended because of business pressures,' Ember said.

'Very understandable. Tell me a university course that could put you in touch with six-hundred-thousand-pounds-plus a year, untaxed. You'll know Cowper's another poet,' Iles said. 'He wrote about "the cups that cheer but not inebriate".' Ungrammatical but accurate. You won't see anyone smashed on tea.'

'What's it to do with envy?' Ralph said.

'His family were up there among the importers and promoters of good, innocent cheer, with its particular, noble Brit-honed rituals – warm the pot, water boiling, milk in last, cube or grain sugar if needed,' Iles replied. '*Hombres finos*. But then the slide, the collapse of all that glory and tradition, leaving us with Basil Gordon Loam, someone possessed of an elegant history but not much more than that.'

'And someone who wouldn't be satisfied with a Cowper cuppa,' Harpur said.

'So, in his awful degradation, he notes and resents a present-day equivalent of those formidable ancestors,' Iles said. 'Specifically, he sees The Monty and its remarkable proprietor, Ralph Ember. This is why I spoke of envy. It encompasses him. It roughs him up. He has to work off his jealousy, his hatred of another's distinction and success. He comes to The Monty and delivers his miserable, sick rancour on one of the most public symbols of that distinction and success, the high-floating Blake, like the battlefield flag in *The Red Badge Of Courage*.'

'Mr Iles fears you could feel compelled to hit back, given the special provocative vileness of the attack, Ralph,' Harpur said. 'In that type of conflict, the blood on the pavement might be yours. This is what upsets Mr Iles.'

'Gravely upsets,' Iles said.

'The ACC is very susceptible, Ralph. At Staff College he was—'

'Susceptible to what?' Ember replied.

'As Mr Iles sees it, this city depends on you, Ralph.'

'Not just as *I* see it,' Iles said. 'Many, possibly Harpur included, small-minded, obtuse jerk though he is.'

'Modesty makes Mr Iles reject any claim to uniqueness,' Harpur said. 'He's admired for his humility. At Staff College, I gather, he was known as "Unvainglorious Ilesy".'

'This city exists in a state of equipoise,' Iles said. 'You are vital to that inspiring, yet fragile balance, Ralph. Clearly, your splendid contribution could not be made if you were in the morgue or catastrophically disabled, perhaps a bullet irretrievably lodged in your brain, making logical thought tricky because blocked by metal. You'll ask what I mean by equipoise, as Harpur did when I first used the term way back. But on the third or fourth explanation, aided by graphs and sketches, he came to understand it: patience pays when dealing with Col.

'To summarize: there's you, Ralph, and there's Manse Shale. You provide two stupendously successful firms trading in the recreational commodities, these two firms co-existing peacefully alongside each other without violence, without turf war border disputes, without, in other words, blood on the pavement – not yours, not Manse's, not uninvolved folk's caught in crossfire. This is the major reason I believe in legalization of the merchandise: it would lead to a placid, pleasant commercial scene, one fit to bring up our children in, all three of us here today fathers of daughters.

'But what happens to this happy harmony if, for instance, you get slaughtered in a vendetta-type conflict with someone whose antecedents thrived in bulk tea but who is now mere malign dregs? Suddenly, we lack equipoise, because equipoise demands at least two components. Remove one, and in the resulting lurch the city no longer benefits from those powerful, smooth-running, allied firms. It has been changed into a parcel of disputed, contested ground. Invaders believe there is now an open, available region asking to be grabbed; forcibly, if necessary. Then, Manse Shale feels menaced by such greedy, colonizing incomers on a patch immediately abutting his and decides on pre-emptive resistance. Where there was amity and cooperation there is hugger-mugger; where there was light there is pitch; where there was order there is shit.'

'Mr Iles prefers order,' Harpur said. 'It's a little kink of his.'

More club members arrived. Some, seeing Iles and Harpur there, left at once. Others went into a huddle at the far end of the bar and talked loudly of harmless topics such as the royal family, sport and matchbox collecting. 'Now, Ralph, tell me about Gordon Loam, also called Enzyme, I believe,' Iles said. 'Let's have done with the historical tea and bring things to the present, to now.'

'Tell you about him in which regard?' Ralph said.

'The relationship,' Iles replied.

'What relationship?'

'Or attitude,' Iles said.

'Whose?'

'Yours,' Iles said.

'He's a permanent banee, that's my attitude,' Ember said. 'A vandal and a Hun.'

'What Col has to worry about, Ralph, is: here's a lad with shining forebears, chucked out of The Monty in a public spat and with hurtful, hint-hint Press coverage. He ponders this humiliation. His suffering is increased because he knows that in previous times if his ancestors did any pondering it would have been high-powered, positive and wealth-backed, probably to do with possible purchase of another couple of expensive tea-trade fast clipper ships, called "clippers" because they clipped hours, even days, off the import voyage. Presumably, he has a loaded .38 pistol still on his person, short of only the rounds used against *The Marriage Of Heaven And Hell*, and these perhaps replaced. Harpur frets about you, Ralph. You're dear to us.'

'We wondered if you'd seen anything of Enzyme since the Worcestershire sauce night, Ralph,' Harpur said.

'Why should I want to see him?' Ember replied.

'But *he* might want to see *you*,' Iles said.

'Hardly,' Ember said.

'I could have Gordon Loam pulled in for possession of a firearm, of course,' Harpur said. 'But we'd like to get him for something meatier than that.'

'He might come to apologize,' Iles said.

'He apologized at the time,' Ember said. 'I could not accept that apology and would not now, if it were offered. His barbarism was practised not just against The Monty, myself and William Blake, but against the very character and prestige of this city.'

'A kind of treason?' Iles asked.

'Betrayal,' Ember said.

'Or he might have come about your interest in art,' Iles said. 'Col tells me Enzyme has links in that realm.'

'Does he?' Ralph replied.

'The mix of prestige cultural and spiritual values and lavish commercial gain might appeal to him, as with that famous expert and critic a while ago, where he might have favoured his own pocket in some deals he handled for others,' Harpur said.

'What?' Iles said. 'What? Which famous expert and critic? Who have you been talking to, Col? How the hell would you have heard of Bernard Berenson?'

'I don't know anything about Gordon Loam except that he is an ex-member of the club, for ever ex,' Ember replied.

'Cast into outer darkness? You're hard, Ralph,' Harpur said.

'In the cause of good, decent standards we all have to be, surely,' Ember said.

'So true, Ralph, so true,' Iles replied. 'Unwavering. Adamantine. There are times when I think of The Monty, with its strict moral nature and brilliant scrupulousness, as like a cathedral rather than a mere club, no matter how elite that club might be.'

Harpur drove again when they returned to headquarters in the unmarked Ford. He felt a kind of respect, even admiration, for Ralph's entrenched, noble, farcical love of The Monty. Iles had mocked him about this just now. But Harpur knew the ACC, too, regarded Ember with some genuine warmth, and not just because he was crucial to Iles's strategy for decent civic orderliness. He liked Ralph simply as Ralph. His cooperation in the maintenance of peace came as an extra, though a massive extra: it helped Iles demonstrate that properly controlled toleration of drugs trading could bring big benefits.

Alongside Harpur, the ACC said: 'I've been giving some thought to the green Peugeot, Col – the woman climbing over urgently from the rear seat, apparently in a frantic hurry to move the car off.'

'And offering the thong-flash?'

'Yes, *that* woman.'

'Did you recognize it, sir?'

'The Peugeot?'

'The thong.'

'Shall I give you a scenario, Col?' Iles replied.

'This will be a treat, sir.'

'We move from fact to speculation, but speculation based on fact. It's known as extrapolation, Col, but don't you get in a sweat about complicated words. I'm confident you could manage a dictionary and realize things are laid out there alphabetically.'

'Thank you, sir.'

'Thuswise then: Ralph stands in The Monty porch, apparently intent on watching someone depart, most probably in a vehicle. I speculate – speculate from his posture, Col—'

'From his body language.'

'I'd rather you didn't reduce everything to cliché, Harpur. That all right with you? I speculate from Ralph's posture that he is taking leave of a visitor for whom he feels no respect or comradeship. The reverse. Vast enmity.'

'Possibly Basil Gordon Loam, you'd say, though Ralph denies this? More or less denies it. Evades the questions.'

'Now, additional but vital, new, raw speculation, Col: the woman in the Peugeot – has she *also* seen a vehicle depart from the club yard and therefore rushes to get after it, gumshoe it, for some reason?'

'The woman? You consider her as involved?'

'I'm tying two apparently separate events together: the behaviour of Ralph, and the behaviour of the woman, eagerly joining the Shield Terrace traffic.'

'Yes, I think I got that.'

'What I'm creating is termed "a synthesis", a merging, Harpur. This is the kind of mental process that those with overarching intellects will often exercise. I don't use that term – overarching – out of crude vanity, Col. It is merely a description. Such people see connections many would miss. They draw together the apparently totally dissimilar. You'll say, "Like the metaphysical poets' imagery, such as where John Donne compares a grubby flea-bite to the glories of coitus."'

'Like the metaphysical poets' imagery, such as where John Donne compares a grubby flea bite to the glories of coitus,' Harpur replied.

'It is a flair, and possibly more than a flair.'

'Up your street, sir. I've heard people say after meeting you, "That Mr Iles, though, he's a synthesis man, no question, the sort who can see a fuck and a flea bite as more or less the same, if we discount the possibility of pregnancy, though not from the flea bite."'

'Talking of coitus, I ask myself, in the typically relentless, dogged fashion I often use when confronting a problem, what was she doing in the back of the parked car?' Iles said. 'This is broad daylight, a.m., on a busy bit of road, pedestrians who might be peeping into the Peugeot, and numerous vehicles passing close. Indecency surely couldn't be contemplated. So public!'

'Much more obvious than a flea bite,' Harpur said.

'In any case, there was nobody else in the back, as far as I could see. I suppose he might have rolled down to the floor, attempting concealment, as part of this abrupt change of programme. But wouldn't I have spotted him, Col?'

'Plus, there's her thong.'

'In which respect? What's your point, Harpur?'

'As you can testify, it was still very much in place. That might not have been so if she wasn't alone in the back but suddenly decided she had to break things off, as it were, and hurry to fix herself on someone's tail. As I see things, sir, the need to restore a basic piece of clothing would not be a priority then. She could get herself shipshape at her leisure in private later. For the moment we don't know where that will be.'

Iles mulled this analysis for some while. Glancing at him in the passenger seat, Harpur saw the Assistant Chief nod a couple of times, clearly impressed by Harpur's thong logic. Then Iles said: 'So, we're mystified as to why she was in the back alone, Col, but maybe that's not a pressing question. There are several of those: first, who is she; second, who is she tailing; third, why; fourth, what, if any, is her connection with Ralphy?'

'I wondered if she knew a bit about surveillance from a car, sir. She might be a fieldworker for some outfit. A professional pathfinder who's learned the skills? Maybe she's even heard that police are trained to use the rear seat of the car sometimes when doing a watch, instead of posing viewable, very blatant and snoopy, in the front. Perhaps she's had leg-over training in how to get fast from her viewing position to behind the wheel, regardless of normal modesty – the end justifies the flash.'

'You wondered, Col? When, Harpur?'

'While it was happening.'

'You mean you were ahead of me in reading the situation?'

'I wouldn't say that, sir.'

'Why wouldn't you?'

'I felt you were preoccupied. Quite reasonably preoccupied. The Peugeot presented certain unusual activity requiring your full-out attention. This was very much an all-round situation. You took one aspect, me another. I have the Peugeot number.'

'You *have* the Peugeot number? Where do you have the Peugeot number?'

'In my head, sir. It seemed the obvious thing to do, to remember it. The computer might be able to give us an identity from the reg.'

'It seemed obvious, did it, Col? If it seemed the obvious thing to do, why didn't I do it? Is that what you're sodding saying in your roundabout, furtive way, Harpur?'

'Very much a two-man operation, sir. You can't be expected to do everything.'

'Who can't expect me to do everything? *Why* can't he or she or they expect me to do everything?'

'At that stage – the pre-synthesis stage, before you over-arched – we didn't assume the Peugeot and Ralph in the porch might be linked, sir,' Harpur replied. 'We made a double-pronged approach – you with your admittedly special area of interest, I with mine; yours to do with the woman's brisk, completely-dressed hurdling, mine with clandestine observation techniques.'

Iles said: 'She'd read about Ralph in the "I Spy" column.

She decides to get down to Shield Terrace and case the club. That's what a fieldworker might do, isn't it, if you're right and she's a fieldworker? She'd need actuality.'

'It could be that, yes.'

'Thank you, Harpur. To do with art?'

'It could be, yes.'

'Enzyme's in that kind of game, yes?'

'On the edge.'

'"I Spy" mentions art, doesn't it?'

'Ralph's Monty rebirth plan.'

'She to do with art?'

'It could be, yes.'

'Thanks, Harpur. I've managed to get you to see clearly.'

'That's another of your flairs, sir.'

FIFTEEN

When those two had left, Ralph went at once into The Monty cloakroom and methodically and with no panicky rush – no Panicking rush – studied himself in a wall mirror. The matter was serious, though not an all-out crisis, at least for now. He would meet it unflinchingly. He saw himself as that kind of man – determined, stalwart, practical – surely the total reverse of Panicking.

Ralph loved this men's cloakroom, and it always irritated him badly to hear any member refer to it as 'the bog' or 'the pisshole'. Although he didn't regard that kind of arrant coarseness as bad enough to deserve a life ban, or even suspension – except on persistent repetition – he'd tell the member very plainly he was out of order, should adopt some decent delicacy and refinement of language, and to watch his fucking gutter gob.

Before Ralph bought The Monty, it had been a club for local businessmen and professionals – lawyers, university staff, dentists, gambling machine purveyors, journalists, vets, hairdressers, surgeons: the kind of people who would very reasonably feel entitled to proper facilities because they'd never been on Welfare. Ralph knew that most people believed humanity was at its least dignified when using this kind of depot for one or more bodily discharges, and therefore, to compensate, he felt the location should be brilliant and touched by overt prestige. The magnificent male cloakroom was a clincher when Ralph had wondered whether or not to buy the club. He kept it in the same state as the previous proprietors had created, accepting this as a precious obligation.

The cloakroom was large, well lit, spotless, the five cubicles with glinting push-button flushes – the buttons as large and handsome as two-pound coins, a kind of proclamation about the importance of hygiene; bright shining metal paper-holders in the cubicles, always adequately stocked with arse-friendly wipes; plus elegant mahogany doors. The radiantly white urinals had very substantial high sides, like angels' wings, Ralph thought, to ensure considerable dick privacy for those who wanted it. Ralph also thought he detected a pride element in the plump, marble smoothness of their construction. It was as if the urinals declared, 'We are urinals, content, and more than content, with this designation, and not to be mistaken for anything *but* urinals.' He didn't ever hang about long with this fancy: a talking urinal must be near the top limit of as ifness.

Although Ralph abhorred crude slang in speaking of the cloakroom, he regarded the Americans as stupidly squeamish about such things. 'I have to go to the bathroom,' Michael Corleone says in *The Godfather*. Go *where*? Have you got your shower hat? He's in Louis' restaurant, for God's sake, with two men he's going to shoot dead, using a gun secretly hidden behind the lavatory cistern for him. A restaurant might supply a gun. It wouldn't supply a bath. Ralph couldn't remember even seeing a washbasin. And then there was that Woody Allen film where the sister of the man he's playing finds she has agency-dated a relieve-himself pervert. Explaining, she says, 'He went to the bathroom over me.' Such daintiness! Yet Americans invented the term 'motherfucker' because 'fucker' had come to be regarded as tepid. That brand of contrast tickled Ralph, made him wonder at the oddities in language and in the human beings who used it. He often went in for wide thoughts about the nature of existence.

In the middle of The Monty's cloakroom floor was a battery of hangers on a metal frame set around a radiator for drying out raincoats when necessary. Not many present Monty members used the hangers because of theft or wilful wrecking and abuse of a hated colleague's garment; but Ralph kept the sets of hooks for when he had improved the club's aura and membership quality. He would bet that in, say, The Athenaeum club, Pall Mall, London, they didn't have many instances of members' topcoats getting chiv-shredded in the cloakroom and/or their pockets stuffed with dead tabby kittens; and it was a club like The Athenaeum that Ralph dearly wanted as model for the new Monty.

Despite this kind of problem, Ralph considered the club cloakroom to be an ideal area for someone wishing to do some careful, confidential scrutiny of his features in a big, clear looking-glass: somewhere he'd read that the term 'looking-glass' had more class than 'mirror', and he preferred this when describing his own, vital and extremely well-justified sessions in front of it. He did listen carefully for any approaching footsteps, though. He wouldn't want to be seen like this, apparently obsessively self-focused, sort of ego fixated. He could imagine the demeaning, malicious gossip that might go around:

'*I found Ralph in an act of sacred worship at his own holy altar.*'

'*Where?*'

'*The Monty crapper.*'

'*Sacredly worshipping who?*'

'*Ralph.*'

Wrong. Utterly wrong. Utterly cruel. But nobody could know the real reason for Ralph's fierce, immediate need to check on the eminent integrity of his face. It incensed him that Iles had compared his appearance to a woman's – that woman waiting at the seashore for the French lieutenant. This wasn't *just* a woman, but a woman abandoned, desolated, crushed. Of course, Iles probably knew the suggestion would shatter Ralph, ruin his self-esteem; it was why slimy Iles concocted it. Most likely he didn't really believe Ember resembled that pathetic figure.

But Iles was the sort who'd doggedly search his brutal mind for a remark aimed to give maximum, enduring pain, and he'd find one, no question. He kept a hoard of them, perhaps alphabetically filed, poised to be called on, and added to daily as he dreamed up and polished more abuse.

Ember had considered pointing out quietly yet forcefully to Iles that many people – intelligent, unbiased people – saw a similarity not between Ralph's looks and those of a blighted, hopeless woman staring out into nowhere, but with Charlton Heston's, the late major Hollywood star's, when at his career peak as a hero in epic film roles: Ben-Hur, El Cid, Moses. Ember had known something poisonous would come from Iles when he asked if Ralph wanted to hear about the supposed degrading, cross-gender likeness he'd noticed. Naturally, Ralph said at once he did not want to hear. And, also naturally, Iles ignored the reply. He ignored anything that didn't suit him, and plenty didn't suit him. What suited him were items as malevolent as he was, and the world could supply only a limited number of these.

Ralph had reckoned that if he answered this malevolence by referring to his very obvious and widely acknowledged link with Chuck Heston it would only prove to Iles that he'd done the sweet degree of damage he intended, forcing Ember desperately to protest, using the Charlton comparison. Undoubtedly, this would give Iles a fine, filthy inward chuckle of triumph, the taunting sod. Ralph had to avoid appearing hurt and riled and defensive. That reaction would spell weakness, and Iles was sure to exploit it with some further Association of Chief Police Officers' intensively cherished yobbishness.

In any case, although Ralph knew of his reputation as a Heston *doppelgänger*, he never spoke of this himself. It would have seemed grossly boastful, and anything like that he loathed. Modesty he prized. Ember always put on a wholly convincing show of surprise if anyone mentioned the vivid, honourable Chuck cloneship, as though this were the first time he'd heard the compliment and couldn't take it seriously. 'I'm just Ralph W. Ember,' he'd say in a charming, humble-type, take-me-as-I-am plea, 'not, I fear, an icon of the Cinemascope scene and screen.' He could tell that some saw this as the screen's loss, not his.

He got himself sideways on to the cloakroom looking-glass and became completely still, to confirm that the rugged, solidly masculine Chuck profile remained intact, nothing like the profile of any woman, French lieutenant's or not. This was no easy manoeuvre, but, undaunted, he went at it, undauntedness being another quality he prized. He wanted to get the full impact of his mirrored profile which, naturally, entailed looking straight ahead, not at the glass, because that would offer only an angled, imperfect version, part profile, part full-on. Solution? He had to keep his head rigid as if gazing straight in front but swivelling his eyes, and *only* his eyes, as far as they could go to the left, in this way catching the reflected profile to perfection, exactly as would a stranger standing close on one side of Ralph in a room or the street and staring in sudden, delighted amazement at the Chuck replica. It was a tricky exercise for him now, yes, but feasible. He had to confirm his heritage. Although he had always declined to have music relayed to the cloakrooms, feeling this would trivialize things, he wished today that his efforts at the looking-glass were accompanied by some of the magnificently epic background score to *El Cid*. He felt this would have helped resoundingly confirm the glorious identity links between him and Heston.

He possessed DVDs of all the main Chuck movies. The sight of Moses in *The Ten Commandments*, struggling to bring those tablets of stone down from Mount Sinai, always thrilled and heartened Ralph. This was gloriously applied effort ending in success, and he felt he had the same kind of prolonged, immensely worthwhile task with The Monty upgrade, getting the whole club to the select amenity level of the cloakrooms. Ralph considered that if Moses had been brought in to do an inspection of The Monty, he'd very quickly spot the shortcomings. He wouldn't leave matters there, though. He was, above all, a positive figure, possibly needing to prove that being found as a baby in a basket among the bulrushes hadn't in the least stunted him psychologically. Moses would propose drastic but manageable remedies for The Monty's defects, all in line with Ralph's own objectives. This thought pleased and fortified

Ralph. He detected a kind of heartfelt bonding across the centuries between Moses and him.

Ember admired the terse definiteness of all those 'Thou shalts' and 'Thou shalt nots' of the commandments inscribed on the stones. Obviously, he couldn't go along with every one of the bans or life would become very narrow, tame and unsatisfying, but he approved their clarity. He thought jokingly that he would have liked to see one commandment saying: 'Thou shalt not use the word "bathroom" in phrases such as "go to the bathroom", "went to the bathroom", to mean something else.' Ralph could cite stretches of El Cid's noble talk in another Chuck film, but would do so only to himself in private. Although El Cid was a mighty leader, he would never be the sort to go around screaming for attention, recognition, adoration. They came automatically, and Ralph liked to think this would also happen in his own case. On the whole, he regarded humility as quite a satisfactory state.

Ralph left the cloakroom, more or less reassured about the unchanged coherence of his nose, jaw/chin, cheekbones, mouth/lips, and went back to the table he'd sat at with those two constabulary louts. Several more members had arrived and were standing at the bar. Ralph greeted them heartily, unhesitatingly, each by his correct name and with separate, personalized smiles. Although they might be entirely without distinction or even wholesomeness, as club owner he was their host and had certain standard duties, including a show of friendliness, and of knowing which customer was which:

'Royston, grand to see you out and about again absolutely untagged.'

'Caspar, the teeth look almost wholly natural despite everything; a fine reconstruction.'

By inventorying his features, Ralph felt he had neutralized Iles's foul slur and now could do an examination of the rest of what had been said during the recent meeting. He signalled for a Kressmann Armagnac refill to help with concentration. The barman cleared the other glasses. In one sense, of course, Ember could have savoured a concealed smirk at what Harpur and Iles discussed with him. Ralph's knowledge was one very considerable step up on theirs. They believed Enzyme to be out there with the same, loaded .38 pistol, whereas, in fact, it lay snugly not at all far from them in the chiffonier drawer upstairs.

Harpur had spoken of not getting Enzyme pulled in for illegal possession of a firearm because they wanted to do him for something bigger. But, although he certainly had been in possession when the Blake got hit – in lunatic, show-off possession – he wasn't in possession any longer. There had been that crazily solemn handing-over ceremony of the guilt-ridden Smith and Wesson by Enzyme to Ralph, as a token of regret and future good fellowship; plus, perhaps, reinstatement at the club – as Enz would imagine. Mistakenly. Very mistakenly. 'Unwavering.' 'Adamantine.' Those had been Iles's words about Ralph's refusal, meant by Iles as over-the-top mockery of Ember's toughness. But, in Ralph's opinion, they were completely to the point.

But, although Gordon Loam would not be handed back his membership, Ember thought he might uncontroversially allow a traditional Monty après-funeral send-off party for him. The club was a community institution, and Enz, regardless of his blatant status as a right imperial prick, thoroughly belonged to that community. This could be fully, respectfully, emphatically, affectionately acknowledged once Ralph had wiped the fucker out. Clearly, Enzyme could not physically be present at the party, but his spirit might be pervasive there. Ralph didn't mind Enzyme's spirit. That could pervade as much as it wanted to. It was the rest of him Ember couldn't stand.

The club would offer free drinks for the first, measured, half hour of the knees-up, as a gesture recognizing the esteem and fondness folk might have regarded Enz with, if only he hadn't been such a committed, tireless, right imperial prick: forget, briefly, the shooting and eternal gab about his cut-above, tea-trafficking far-back family. As well as the overall foulness, Enzyme might have had a couple of marginally OK qualities, and Ralph would go along with any efforts to inflate these after his death and make him seem more or less acceptable, as long as it *was* after his death, Gordon Loam definitely out of the way for keeps and not having in fact to be accepted. RIP, Enz: you deserve it. Nobody Ralph could think of deserved it more.

But, as it sometimes did, the Armagnac seemed to sharpen

Ralph's brain a fair bit. *In Kressmann veritas*. He'd had a couple. He began to see some unfavourable, hazardous elements in what Harpur and Iles had been saying beneath the seemingly harmless, rambling, inane chatter. Combined, this pair had hit on the two crucial themes in the Enz story: (i) they thought there might be terminal vendetta stuff between Ralph and Gordon Loam following the Blake atrocity and feared the spread of disorder this might bring, endangering a unique, fragile, civic tranquillity built by Iles. (ii) Harpur had suggested there could be an art connection, with Gordon Loam interested in Ember's plans for picture buying.

This was the smart-arse thing about Harpur and Iles: they jibed and wandered and drifted, but always there would be a dirty purpose, and always some acute, inspired, very meaningful, probably vindictive observation disguised by the fooling about. On the Foundation Year university course, undergrads looked at *Hamlet*, and Ralph adjusted one of the play's best known lines: Deviousness, thy name is Iles. And/or Harpur.

Occasionally, it did take Ralph a Kressmann or two to get the hidden message or messages. He didn't think this marked him as stupid, no. But Ralph liked to bring a touch of decency and fair play to life, and he expected others to feel the same. In periods of clarity brought on by the Armagnac he would realize that to centre this hope on two high-rank police, one of them Iles, ONE OF THEM ILES!, was pathetically optimistic. Iles – decency, fair play? Some joke that! The barman had left the bottle, and by now Ralph was starting his third double-plus.

If Iles and Harpur fretted that there might be blood on the pavement, they would know where to look immediately once there *was* blood on the pavement, or somewhere equivalent, after Ralph had dealt with Gordon Loam. They'd see the motive, of course. In fact, they'd more or less *expect* Ralph to go tit-for-tatting because of the bar assault on Blake – barbaric, base bar assault – leading to the perilous Worcestershire sauce bottle transformed into unguided missiles. This wasn't just a case of the rampant genie getting out of the bottle, but of bottle bits themselves becoming rampant. Gordon Loam killed meant Ralph the chief suspect, Ralph probably arrested,

Ralph probably charged, and Ralph probably convicted and sent down for years. Where would his glittering plans for The Monty be then? To put himself at risk would be a self-indulgent betrayal of the club and its quality cloakrooms. Also, he had his family to think of.

Discovering that Ember had used the gifted gun to see off the giver of it – Enz – might puzzle Iles and Harpur and their bullet-matching forensic specialists for a while, but they'd sort that out eventually. The Armagnac bluntly, awkwardly, asked: could it be wise, could it be safe, could it be *sane* for Ralph to plan Gordon Loam's death and after-funeral remembrance drink-up? Casualness. Brazenness.

And then came (ii), Harpur's art reference. If Gordon Loam, in these new circumstances, was allowed to stay alive, at least for a while, and brought pictures for Ralph and The Monty, would the police suspect that, because they came via a supremely dubious bugger like Enz, they might have very uncertain origin? Iles or Harpur would possibly put their expert arty detectives on to checking what Ralph knew was called the work's 'provenance': its genuine, total history. Stolen? Manufactured as a copy in someone's box room? Used as currency by crooks to buy weaponry, and/or wholesale drugs for subsequent street, pub, disco, college trading, and/or jewellery for their women, and/or a bolt-hole villa on an Algarve golf ranch?

Ralph considered it a kind of irony that, although the Kressmann's helped produce these disturbing questions, it also kept him buoyed up. He'd look for answers to those questions. He thought he should push ahead now with some of his plans, even if the removal of Enz might need to be shelved. He went to the office and telephoned Jack Lamb's place, Darien. Ralph considered it unusual for someone like Lamb to be in the directory. Perhaps he hoped this would prove his business was entirely honest and open, nothing suspect and needing secrecy. Nice one, Jack – his own type of brazenness. But the rumours still went around. He'd run into Lamb a few times, once at a successful meeting called to resist plans for a big wind farm on rural land near Lamb's and Ralph's properties.

It wasn't Jack who answered the call now. A perky-voiced, mature-sounding woman with a mixed Brit-American accent and phrase-pattern said: 'This is the Lamb residence. Mrs Lamb speaking. Can I help you in some respect?'

'I wondered if I could have a word with Mr Jack Lamb, please.'

'I'm his ma.'

'Nice to talk to you, Mrs Lamb.'

'On a short visit from the USA.'

'I'm sure it will be very enjoyable.'

'I chose to become Lamb again after an absurd remarriage in the States. I see the return to this name not as defeatism but as self-cleansing, as morale therapy, as morals therapy. Probably something to do with all those lamb mentions in the Scriptures. I have in mind, especially, Revelation. But I don't say any of those Bible references are specifically to me or Jack!'

Ralph offered a merry, miniature laugh. 'No, I shouldn't think so, Mrs Lamb. But I seem to run into Bible matters quite often.' He'd heard Iles claim that a previous Chief Constable here, Mark Lane, driven three-quarters mad by Iles, used to scour Revelation, scared he'd find prophetic mentions of his name and rank and the cosmic mess-ups he thought he'd perpetrated, because Iles apparently kept telling him he had. Ralph said: 'I'm a kind of neighbour, I know Jack.'

'A neighbour? One of the farms?'

'Not exactly.'

'Well, it must be Low Pastures, with all the chimneys. Georgian plus Victorian additions? Bigwigs lived there? A Lord Lieutenant etcetera?'

'Right.'

'Have you got a sweep on the permanent staff? It's Mr Ember, yes? Jack's spoken to me about you. "No Windfarms Here!" Windy Nimby, he was called, I believe, taking the initial letters of "Not In My Back Yard". A rather extensive backyard, as it happens, but I expect you can match it over at LP. Paddocks? Yes, I think Jack mentioned paddocks. Your daughters, riding fine ponies? Probably gymkhanas? It's all the apparatus of what some would call the *nouveau riche*, the jumped-up. Used in Britain, those terms would not be complimentary. But what I've learned Stateside is that *nouveau riche* can be regarded as a very desirable state, and much better than being *nouveau* skint, as can happen. And "jumped-up" is a jump in the right direction – up – and much preferable to "fallen flat".'

'We have to look after the countryside,' Ember said. 'We are, willy-nilly, its custodians. Yes, I'm very much a fan of the environment in its many forms. Point a finger this way or that, it's all environment. Whenever I hear that sublime word, a rush of other words is released automatically in my brain – "protect it", "guard it", "maintain it", "revere it".'

'A wind farm would have put a blight on both your glossy properties, I guess, maybe knocked a nought off the value. What did the two of you do – terrorize the planning inspector? Or money passed? Like, "Have a little drink on us, pray do, sir, to celebrate due rejection of this disgraceful proposal." Gun to his head as extra? But I mustn't speculate. This is an open line. Remember that give-away voice on the phone near the end of *The Great Gatsby*?'

'Is Jack at home, Mrs Lamb?' Ralph replied.

'You've got some club down the town, yes?'

'Well, yes.'

'What kind of club would that be then, Mr Ember?'

'Of a social nature.'

'I suppose most clubs are. Guns bought and sold *sotto voce*? Also recreational aids? I think of usages like "club together" – suggesting an harmonious group. Or someone can be described as "clubbable", meaning he fits in to the company – not that he can be head-banged. Jack doesn't go to your club?'

'I'm making some changes, some major adjustments of tone, much beyond fine-tuning, which would not be adequate. Important to evolve rather than remain stalled, as it were, in formaldehyde. A thrilling prospect.'

'This second hubby I had, American, he'd never go anywhere without one and a half thousand dollars cash on him in case of trouble,' Mrs Lamb replied. 'He believed money in a fair quantity could smooth away rages – others' rages. That's the sort he was. Is. Kind of unimpetuous? Have you come across the type? But perhaps we shouldn't make fun. No question, people are very various. Think of Mother Theresa, sure, but think also of Heinrich Himmler. Quite a personality gap, wouldn't you say, yet the same breeding process for each?'

'I have no trouble at The Monty, thank heaven. As a matter of fact, it's about the club that I wanted to talk to Jack. And art.'

'Which art?'

'Generally.'

'I expect you're in favour of it.'

'What?'

'Art in general. Your expressions – they have that air, like they'd look very good framed and with under-base lighting.'

'Yes. Art – it's *so* worthwhile.'

'Same as the countryside.'

'Art can be an enhancing element,' Ralph replied.

'Me, I can take it or leave it alone. That's a quote from somewhere. Thurber?'

'Is Jack about?'

'Jack,' she yelled. 'It's your environmental buddy from Low Pastures. I gather he looks like Charlton Heston, real name Charlie Carter, used to look. Topic, art – art in general, art that enhances.' He could tell she'd taken the receiver from her ear and was holding it low on one side. Now she brought it back to her ear and mouth. 'I don't know whether an artist would like to hear the term,"generally" about his, her art, Mr Ember.'

'Please, it's Ralph.'

'Alice. The thing with art is it's one person in front of an easel, trying to slap on to the canvas colours and shapes special to that individual artist, not to art "generally", which would diminish the artist, make him or her feel like just one of a bunch, a production-line operative. Painting by numbers. Or by government edict, like those old Soviet posters proclaiming the glory of hard work for the state and showing proletarian Russians with very strong Stakhanovite jaws, the sun rising encouragingly behind them. Jack's got a picture here, *Amelia With Flask*.' She bellowed again. 'Jack! A visitor. Your rural accomplice. In favour of the environment. Ralphy.'

'They like that.'

'Who?' Alice Lamb replied.

'Artists.'

'Like what?'

'"So and so *with* something", as title of a work. It could be a flask. Or a whippet or a lute. It gives the portrait a connection with the ordinary things of that time. Known as hinterland, or sort of props, like in the theatre. Now it would be an electric toothbrush or pit-bull. Ephemera.'

'There's some very valuable stuff here, yet not a protective gun in the house, as far as I know. Of course, Charlton was big on guns. Believed in them for home owners – a constitutional right, a near blessed right, as he presented it.'

'That's an American thing, too, I think.'

'Don't dismiss it, Mr Ember. Some items have to be guarded. *Amelia With Flask*, for instance. Not cheap. Why? Because it appeals. It appeals on two levels. Somehow, the artist has to get the universal side of that flask over to the viewer, as an emblem of life-giving water carried with her in what might be a scorching and scorched country, even desert; but, at the same time, Ralph, it has to be a flask unique to Amelia, who is also herself unique, of course. Yes, the flask is in one sense "general", but in another not general at all, important simply for its blatant flaskiness as a flask, without deeper significance.

'The artist would say to Amelia at the start of a sitting, "Hello, my dear, I want you to nurse this flask while posing, Am." She'd take it. The flask would be no odds to her, just a flask. It wouldn't be for her to query his instruction, she not being an artist with an artist's sensibility. Or, if the artist was known for pranks, she might feel sort of cagey, suspecting it was actually a kind of fart cushion, liable to go off with a rude rasp if she hugged it to herself too hard for a moment, causing the artist to laugh helplessly, bent over his palette while daubing, possibly even to stagger about in the grip of successive, tumultuous, ever-been-had-Am guffaws, liable to knock the whole caboodle to the ground, easel, paints, the canvas. She wouldn't have any idea of the coding and implications behind that flask. It's what's known as semiotics – like a sign or a symbol of something, while at the same time being simply a flask. This duality is what the greatest artists can do every time via a flask or wheat field or old-style warship, namely *The Fighting Temeraire*. Incidentally, you probably know that the ancient

Proto-Indo-European civilization from which most modern languages derive had separate words for two different kinds of fart, actual, not jokey mock-up.'

'No, I may have missed that.'

'Sophistication. Precision. But if this comes as news, I expect you'll ask, which two kinds?'

'I wondered if Jack might be about,' Ember replied.

'Yet this was thousands of years B.C.'

'Certain pressures and requirements are timeless. Possible high-fibre veggie diet. The people I bought the club from installed magnificent cloakroom facilities, especially the men's, which I'm very keen to preserve, and even improve on.'

'Here he is, Ralph. I'm going to hand you over to Jack, now.'

SIXTEEN

Iles said: 'I'll interpret what you've told me, shall, I, Col?'

'That would be a treat, sir.' What Harpur had told him was that the Peugeot had been hired locally from J. and R. Simmonds Ltd. on Valencia Esplanade the day before, by a woman in her twenties called Elizabeth May Rossol. He did not recognize the name. It would be genuine. The hire documents had to square with her licence and payment card. He'd called in at Simmonds' to look at the paperwork and, if possible, get a description of the hirer.

'She's late twenties, I gather, sir,' Harpur had told the ACC, 'fair-to-mousy-haired, rather than outright blonde; tall, slim, squarish faced, cheerful looking; pricey jeans; pricey woollen three-quarter-length dark-blue top coat; pricey silver and gold silk scarf worn dangling both sides – unfettered elegance not winter-warm wrap-around; pricey, perhaps man's, open-necked shirt – blue background multicoloured stripes; pricey half-heel black shoes. Evidently comfortable in her own thong. Signature bold and biggish: "Liz Rossol."

'The young bloke who did the formalities with her at Simmonds' was impressed going on bewitched; might have tried some flirt talk but got nowhere. He thought London poise, London money, London accent, meaning metropolitan-aloof and cool, not cockney. No rings, marriage, engagement, signet or decorative, plumpish lips. Deposit covered on American Express, in the due Elizabeth May Rossol name. I have the details. She said it would be a two or three day hiring for short hops around the city and its outskirts, no big mileage.'

Iles said: 'But before I give you my deductions, Col, there's a formality.' He picked up the phone, dialled and velveted his voice. 'Tomasina,' he said, 'how invigorating to hear you again, as ever. Elizabeth May Rossol – R, O, double S, O, L – under thirty, fashionable, moneyed, probably single. Has someone so christened and describable ever wandered into your bailiwick, or you into hers? Possibly art-related. Well, obviously, or I wouldn't be calling you, delightful as such a call might be.'

He listened for several minutes and made a pencilled note or two. They were in the ACC's suite at headquarters. Iles had been pacing while they talked. This was a habit. He'd apparently read that Churchill often walked about when dictating to typists. 'Some of us don't like to seem desk-bound, desk-tamed, Col,' he'd said. 'Hemingway, novelist, but also vigorous outdoor marlin-angling man, wrote standing at a kind of lectern.' Because Iles had two large, adjoining rooms, he could build up quite a good pace on strolls. But he'd stopped and sat down to make the telephone call. He was in uniform today, dark-blue trousers and a short-sleeved white shirt. His tunic hung draped over the back of a chair. He looked slight, wiry, lithe, with no visible tattoos. He hated his mother and possibly had something to that effect, perhaps with threats, on a covered part of his body.

'Did you say "Cog", Tomasina?' he asked. 'Spelled like it sounds, as in a machine? What's that? A kind of modesty, you think? Yes, I suppose so. Part of something much bigger. Harpur, one of the officers here, is very similar – part of something so much bigger that he becomes more or less unnoticeable. That, of course, could be a great asset for a detective. I do my best to make him feel of some worth – poor Col.'

When Iles put the phone down he said: 'Tomasina, Harpur, a stalwart and quietly incisive chum from way back, now with the Arts and Antiques squad at Scotland Yard. She says Rossol is part of the outfit I mentioned, Cog. No convictions yet for her or the firm, but that's more luck than innocence. Tomasina confirms the high-powered sexiness and audacious fashion sense. Tommo has both of these herself, so her judgement is not negligible. She mentioned uncued that Rossol's lips are, indeed, plump, but naturally plump, not from a beautician's puff-up pout treatment to stoke men's dreams of a very snug, accommodating mouth. Tomasina also confirms the cheeriness of Rossol's face, and I get the feeling, Col, that this pisses Tommo off because it means Liz is still free with a fine cash-flow and prized by other Coggers, including George Dinnick, the sometimes violent bossman. Nothing sexual in that, just professional, at least from her side, Tomasina says. Liz has something nice going with another Coggy, Justin Benoit, about her age, who's on the very active, gallery-level side of the business. He has the knowledge – can spot the difference, straight off, between a matchstick-man job by Lowry and Sir Joshua Reynolds's portrait of his auntie. Cog will conduct quite lawful transactions now and then, or even oftener, but Tomasina and colleagues believe that when it's something dubious, Liz does a pre-reconnoitre, and if this is OK then Justin will arrive, run through his own preliminaries and get the operation properly under way. Oh, yes, you'd guessed things were like that, Harpur, but I didn't tell Tommo. It would make her feel redundant and prone to the obvious. I'm one who likes to look after people's morale, Col, and general well-being.'

'What about mine?'

'You'll ask me what I visualize now, given this new information, Harpur,' Iles replied.

'What do you visualize now, given this new information, sir?'

'Your questions are always very much to the point, Col.'

'Thank you, sir.'

'"Reconnoitre", Col.'

'Who, me, sir? Where?'

'"Reconnoitre", Harpur. That's what I see as the key term.'

'Rossol reconnoitres? Reconnoitres at The Monty*?* But why?'

'A beginning. She had picked up the name from the Press. She told Simmonds' "short hops about the city". Right? The Monty was one of the short hops, part of a planned pattern, an itinerary item, Harpur. It led her to another, I expect. We missed that. But we saw the urgency. Somewhere not very far.'

And then, Harpur recalled, she'd spoken also of 'the outskirts'. Jack Lamb in Darien would rate as a rural outskirt. If Rossol were reconnoitring art connections, Jack might be on her list – that itinerary. Harpur didn't speak of this to Iles, though. Harpur was never certain how much the Assistant Chief knew about that 'arrangement' between him and Jack Lamb. This was like Iles: he knew a lot but didn't necessarily show what he knew. He could deliver rough shocks when it suited him to.

Harpur grew anxious about Jack. He recalled – of course he recalled – that vision of him with his throat cut, infringing on *Amelia With Flask*. There always existed the fear that someone just out of jail would come looking for the secret voice that put him there: secret, but not secret enough. And now Lamb might get reconnoitred by Elizabeth May Rossol of Cog, and anyone who came as follow-up, if Rossol put in a positive assessment to George Dinnick for onward reference to Justin Benoit, as Harpur recalled the names.

He gave the Peugeot registration and a description to the Traffic and Rapid Response people and ordered a general call for any sightings of the vehicle, probably still with one woman driver. He stressed he wanted sightings only, no contact to be made by the patrol if she and the car were located. The aim had to be discreet surveillance at this stage because, at this stage, he didn't really know what he was looking for and needed the green Peugeot and the lady from Cog to offer him a clue. Then he might be able to get to the next stage, supposing there was one.

SEVENTEEN

'Excuse me,' he said, 'I saw you in there and waited for you to come out.'

'Yes?' she said.

'I hope that's OK. I wanted a word, that's all.'

'Yes?'

'I had a feeling you'd understand.'

'No,' she said. 'Not yet.' Or, possibly, yes. Liz Rossol had left Silver Bells And Cockleshells and was walking towards the Peugeot when Gordon Loam appeared from somewhere ahead of her – the bus shelter? One of the shop doorways? A planned interception, at any rate. He said so and offered the greeting with a very nicely worked, reassuring smile. He must reckon that, if you were going to accost a woman on the street, you'd need to do it with a disarming, neutered smile or it might seem you'd mistaken her for a whore. He appeared to have recovered from the rage that had so vividly invaded his chops when he stormed from the nursery not long ago.

'I was in there, too,' he said. 'As you know, of course.'

'Well, yes, I *had* noticed.'

'To be frank, I wondered why you'd called,' he said.

'But why would you wonder that?' she said. 'I'm sure lots of people visit – the children's parents and so on.'

'I don't see you in that kind of role.' He lowered his voice, and the words came confidingly, came as a compliment: she wasn't a mere run-of-the-mill parent; she was her special, enigmatic self, worth hanging about for and aiming some gauche charm at.

'But *why* don't you see me in that kind of role?' she said.

'It's a feeling I have, a kind of instinct.' His voice reverted to full-pitch now. She sensed a big-time sprawling spiel starting. Nerves? Salesmanship? 'I believe wholeheartedly in instinct,' he told Liz, not in the tone of, say, 'I believe wholeheartedly in God,' or, 'I believe wholeheartedly in colonic irrigation,' but more combatively, more defiantly. 'Perhaps it's an inherited thing,' he said. 'My family were big in commerce, you see, and they'd be used to following impulse, perhaps with no actual data or other evidence to back their decisions, but something in their very blood pushing them irresistibly towards a new positive venture. Fractions of that virtually clairvoyant attitude come to me as a happy legacy, perhaps.'

'There seemed to be a little trouble for you in the nursery,' Liz replied.

'Trouble? Oh, Fern! Moods.' He had a small, tolerant laugh. 'She can become disturbed and aggressive for no apparent reason.'

'Instinct?' Liz said.

'She has her own problems that we know nothing of, I expect. Occasionally, they'll burst out, affecting her general behaviour. One learns to accept these unpleasant moments for what they are – unpleasant, yes, but of the moment only. I feel no enmity towards her. Absolutely none . . . none . . . none.' His face and neck became flushed. His tone sharpened suddenly. He seemed to have ditched tolerance. There was quite a pause between each 'none', as if he had methodically to recheck his attitude to Fern before all three announcements. He said: 'To retaliate would confer a significance on Fern that the ludicrous, unstable, ugly cow in no way merits. One is forced to wonder whether it's wise to have her in contact with children. Well, I gather she doesn't actually foam over them. But she should take her screams and yells to where they might be regarded as normal – e.g., a madhouse. How can someone like Fern understand the sort of respect due to a family such as the Loams? I trust I do not speak boastfully, but I'm the product of a lineage that cannot be gainsaid or discounted.'

'You visit Silver Bells often, do you, and sometimes Fern's unbonkers, sometimes super-bonkers?'

'I wouldn't say often, but occasionally.' This came as more or less a snarl. It indicated: topic closed. Then he went ingratiating again. 'Do you know what I thought when I saw you waiting there today, and not looking at all like a parent or some sort of inspector? I noted those stylish clothes – and this is going to sound silly – but your face didn't seem right for either of those roles: the cheeriness, and something about your mouth and lips. Taken together, these points made me fix on another explanation for your presence.'

'You could read my lips, could you? Didn't some American politician say that?' She felt an increasing absurdity about this conversation – about this situation, standing face-to-face in the street mid-morning, chatting away intently near the Peugeot. What would people think, glancing at them as they passed the pair on foot, or in their cars or lorries or on a bus? Did he and Liz look as if they might be friends, bumping into each other after a long absence, both eager to bring things up to date? Or even like ex-lovers, maybe even an ex-married couple? Perhaps such spectators would have time to notice the abrupt changes of emotion on Gordon Loam's snub features and wonder whether they were watching the start of a quarrel. Or a reconciliation.

Although they were *not* friends, of course, or otherwise linked, ex-linked, she felt fairly sure now that she *had* seen Gordon Loam around in galleries and/or auctions. Her memory of him was vague and possibly imagined, possibly, in fact, false, but she thought he'd been in small-time, fringe jobs on those days. Didn't she recall the dark hair worn long over his ears and the blue-black eyes and blobby nose? Did he recognize her, too? Was some sort of game being played out here? If so, which sort? She couldn't answer this, but she wanted it to continue, badly needed it to continue: somehow, he might offer a route into the sort of conditions she was here to investigate – and, so far, the *only* route.

'Do you know the lady chief well?' he said.

'Which?'

'Of Silver Bells. Judy.'

'Do *you*?'

'Judy can be a bit variable.'

'Like Fern.'

'Have you noticed it with Judy?'

'I suppose we're all a bit various from time to time,' Liz replied.

'Woman to woman, though, it might be easier.'

'What might be?'

'She can be illogical, hasty. Negative.'

'In what way?'

'Yes, hasty. A woman might have a better chance of leading her back to good sense. What could seem like bullying from a man would be simply well-intentioned advice from a sympathetic, close female acquaintance.'

'You're assuming I'm a sympathetic, close female acquaintance, aren't you?' Liz had the notion that he wanted her to intercede for him about something or other with Judy. But what something or other? There'd been that obvious all-round hostility towards him at the nursery, and he seemed to think she might be able to talk to Judy, plead for him. And talk to Fern, also? But he'd said he considered Fern and her moods and loudness didn't really matter. Liz felt that something was under discussion between them here which could not be defined, as if to speak openly, clearly about it would be tactless, or even dangerous. Perhaps he knew what it was. Of course he did. Liz didn't. He seemed to take for granted that she did and was acting ignorant, *only* acting. This would probably exasperate him eventually. She couldn't see how to avoid that. 'I don't have any cause to fall out with Judy,' Liz said.

'No, naturally not. That's what I mean.'

'What is what you mean?'

The clever-clever, mock-awkward, would-be-witty use of his own words against him seemed to speed up his fury. She realized she'd been stupid. He lost any sign of a smile. His voice fell and grew gruff. 'Look,' he said, 'when I saw you I had two thoughts of *why* you were there, and I've said that doesn't include being a parent or a look-about official. No, I thought you'd come with the same objective as mine. Or, you'd followed me.'

'But I don't know your objective.'

'Don't you? *Don't you?*'

'Followed you? How could I have followed you?' she replied.

'Why not? You're in a car, aren't you? Is the Peugeot you?' He nodded towards it. 'Where did you pick me up? The Monty? What were you doing there?'

'Are you talking about tailing in traffic?' Liz replied. 'That's a tremendously high skill.'

'You might have it,' he said. 'I didn't notice anything. Dozy of me. You're not police, are you? Not in gear like that.'

'Police? Why would police tail you?'

'Why do you answer every question with a fucking question?'

'Do I?' she replied.

He shrugged. She saw he was giving up. Had she won a victory of sorts, she wondered. Which sort, though? Verbal and inane. She'd lost him and whatever she might have learned from him about the scene here. So, sodding Pyrrhic! He turned and walked away towards his Audi. She decided she wouldn't try to tail him again. He'd be alert to that now, and he'd know he was looking for a green Peugeot in his mirror.

EIGHTEEN

Harpur had a call from Rapid Response saying the Peugeot was parked at a permitted one-hour spot in Brendan Street between the Silver Bells And Cockleshells children's nursery and an Oxfam charity shop. As an additional map reference, the message mentioned a tree house in the nursery's front garden, a wholly carpentered tree house with a timber staircase, no tree. The vehicle seemed unoccupied, but a woman and a man were talking on the pavement near it, the woman, tall, probably in her twenties, three-quarter-length dark-blue woollen top coat, the man older, perhaps late thirties, brown leather jacket. Someone in the RR car had half recognized Gordon Loam, and the sighting report suggested the man might be that gun-toter who'd had recent publicity, including a picture, following the shoot-bang-fire Blake incident at the Monty club in Shield Terrace: Basil Gordon Loam, art world connections. The conversation looked animated: maybe a quarrel, maybe just a happy, unexpected re-encounter.

Harpur realized the descriptions had to be very brief. The RR crew would have to behave as if they just happened to be cruising in Brendan Street – no pause, no obvious eyeballing of the pair on the pavement. RR vehicles were conspicuously coloured, easily identified, jam-sandwich police cars, so they could get fast through traffic. Officers were uniformed. This patrol could not hang about as if interested in the chatting pair because Harpur's instructions said to keep things distant and non-involved; or as distant and non-involved as possible. This was a start-point only. Cameras banned.

He took the unmarked VW Golf from the pool and drove over at once to Brendan Street. More or less as he arrived, the two finished talking. The man walked away quickly, no formal leave-taking, no looking back. Harpur thought he seemed very offended, his footfalls heavy and reproachful. He strode with his shoulders hunched forward, as if to cradle and protect his anger for further development, like a mother kangaroo with its pouched joey. The RR guess appeared correct, and this *was*, in fact, Gordon Loam. The woman gazed after him for a while, perhaps revealing some regret. Maybe she admired him for loosing off at *The Marriage Of Heaven And Hell* – found it audacious, amusing, unconventional. Gordon Loam went to a black Audi saloon parked in another timed space and started the engine. Harpur once more noted a registration number. He had pulled in on double yellows, and the Audi passed him and also passed the Peugeot. Gordon Loam seemed to ignore both it and Elizabeth May Rossol. Gordon Loam apparently had big-wheel ancestors. A portion of hoity-toitiness might lurk in his genes, liable to show itself if he felt someone had bugged him. But bugged him how, if she had? Harpur put the VW into the space left by the Audi.

So, Cog – or, at least, Cog as represented in Elizabeth May Rossol – had a connection with blaze-away Gordon Loam. What connection, other than a street interlude? And how had this pavement conference come about? A fluke, as hinted at in the RR account? *Well, fancy bumping into you!* Or did she follow him after hurriedly quitting that other parking spot near Ralph's Monty? Harpur had no reliable answers. And additional mysteries came his way now.

Rossol was about to get into the Peugeot when something seemed to stop her. She stood with the key in her hand, ready to open the driver's door, but turned and stared towards the nursery, as though she'd heard a call, or some other important sound. Harpur stared there, too. A woman was with a couple of infants on the stairs of the tree house, apparently supervising their little clamber-climb; the woman in her fifties, chubby-faced, thick necked, grey hair cut savagely short, perhaps self-done with a kitchen knife as a wager or sponsored charity stunt.

She had started waving wildly to Rossol and was obviously shouting something. Rossol smiled and waved back, the car door key still in her hand, as though to announce that her arm-wags in reply were only interim – moments of mere, basic politeness – and she'd be buggering off very soon. In profile, her face looked neat but questing. Harpur lowered the driver's window in the Golf and listened.

The woman and the two children had reached the top of the tree house. She continued to wave and yell. There were no solid side walls to the square garret where they stood now, only a lattice of wooden safety struts. It made Harpur think of guard towers with their machine guns and searchlights above the barbed wire in prison camp movies. He wondered whether Rossol saw it like that. She didn't seem uneasy.

The woman's voice reached Harpur very clearly, and would reach Rossol clearly, too, the tone desperate, commanding, inexhaustible, slightly unhinged. 'Come back, oh, do come back,' the woman cried. 'Leave not in such circs, please. Oh, please. So much to say. We never spoke. Do, do come back. I have so much to comment on about him and other matters. Yes, him and other matters. Who are you? Who *really* are you? Is there truly a prospective Christine?'

To Harpur, her monologue sounded like something in the trailer for a super-intense, soul-searching TV drama. Rossol waved again, but Harpur saw immediately that this was a farewell gesture, not a greeting. She obviously didn't fancy discussing with someone sporting a butchered coiffure in a pseudo tree house whether prospective Christine truly was or wasn't at all. Rossol pointed the key at the Peugeot and pressed the unlock button, then gave one final wave and one more smile before driving off. Harpur followed. It hadn't quite been a: 'Get lost,' reply to the woman from Rossol. No, more a: 'Sorry, I have to move on,' reply. The woman stood open-mouthed up there, but silent now, obviously hurt and dismayed that Rossol had ignored her invitation.

Harpur hadn't waved to the woman. He'd felt he was outside this relationship, whatever it amounted to. Which 'him' did the woman mean – 'so much to comment on about him'? Gordon Loam? Had he and Rossol been together in Silver Bells And Cockleshells, though without speaking? Why? Who was the prospective Christine, if she existed? Prospective where, how? Sometimes, when working alone and hopelessly stymied, Harpur would wish Iles and his clairvoyant, leaping, telepathic, vindictive brain were with him and willing to help – that last bit not at all certain. One of those moments had arrived. Harpur always felt ashamed to be stricken like this – to be so dependent and feeble – but he had to recognize that it did happen now and then. Yes, now.

He couldn't tell whether Rossol knew he was lurking behind the Peugeot. He had to drive as if she didn't. This would give the most promising possibilities, so he mustn't fuck it up by carelessness. He needed to keep one, or two – two maximum – vehicles between her and him for cover, but not a vehicle, or vehicles, big enough to kill his view of the target car: no furniture vans, no army tanks on low-loaders, even, ideally, no four by fours.

In a short while, though, he was forced to recognize that she definitely did know he was there, and that she did know, too, one of the standard methods for shaking off a motorized stalker – also one of the most simple, most geographically subtle, and most potentially head-on risky. Harpur thought of it as originating from some Portuguese Academy of Advanced Motoring, where the basic taught principle was the opposite of what prevailed in most sane countries. That is, an over-taker had precedence over oncoming vehicles, which should get out of the sodding way. 'I'M POWERING THROUGH!' Given some luck, some extensive luck, the car would pass one or even two vehicles immediately in front of it and squeeze past the approaching curse-flinging, horn-screaming, lights flashing stream. The tail would not be able to follow for at least a few minutes because of safety considerations, which had been brilliantly junked by the target.

This manoeuvre operated most effectively where the main road on which they were travelling had side streets off; what Harpur meant by 'geographically subtle'. The escaping vehicle had to get into that maze of minor routes and capitalize on the series of corners, service lanes, and junctions there, so that by the time the tail could enter this network, the fugitive had disappeared, leaving no indication for the tracker to know which of many turnings to take. The target might well get back on to the main drag from another exit point eventually and either resume its journey untroubled, or go home and make the trip on another, safer, unattended day.

Rossol and Harpur played out this episode of road theatre now, Harpur, at the end, infuriated by the simplicity of it, and the predictability of it, but not simple and predictable enough for him to cope and keep a hold on her. If Iles had been here he . . . But bollocks to Iles! Iles definitely was *not* here. Harpur had to handle the situation solo, just him and a pool Golf. The Peugeot had one vehicle immediately ahead, the white van of a green grocery firm. Harpur had been two small cars back from her – a Clio and a Mini – with a satisfactory view of the Peugeot, chuntering at a comfortable built-up area speed just above thirty mph.

But suddenly the Peugeot accelerated and brazenly started to go around the grocer's van, not actually ignoring oncoming items – a silver Merc estate and another van, workaday grey, in the lead – but discounting them, signalling to them that they were not entitled to the slice of roadway fancied by the Peugeot.

Well, of course, of course, the Peugeot did all that. Harpur knew he ought to have anticipated it. But this woman was a surprise. Should she have been, though? Rossol went around the grocer's van, forcing the Merc to swerve and brake and the grey van to skid and finish across both traffic lanes. The Peugeot nicely avoided these new, temporary obstructions, edged its way neatly between them and turned at mad speed into the mouth of a side street. For a couple of minutes Harpur and the Golf were blocked in by the Mercedes and the grey van. Neither was damaged, both still mobile, and slowly they picked their way back on to their proper route. Foot-down, Harpur put the Golf into the minor road and, as he'd expected, saw nothing of the Peugeot. He kept going at his own mad speed, turned right and right again. Still nothing. He felt as if he'd been on a training exercise with an instructor who'd done this kind of gifted ritual so often that error for her was unimaginable. Art fieldwork seemed to involve special skills, not all of them obviously to do with painting and sculpture. This had shocked and flummoxed Harpur. Would it have shocked and flummoxed Iles? Bollocks to Iles.

NINETEEN

Near the fag end of his jinxed search, Harpur found himself driving along a short street of late-Georgian houses that always delighted him with their elegance and muted charm. He loved the narrow glazing bars of the neat windows, and the rendered facades in gentle pastel shades – ochre, turquoise, pink, light blue; no fucking use to him today, of course. Green. He wanted the green Peugeot.

A healthy looking middle-aged woman, with forcefully auburned hair, and wearing a kind of multicoloured sarong and tan hiking boots, had come out of a pink-themed house and stood on the pavement watching Harpur and the Golf, her eyes big, placid, brown. He drew in near her and lowered the driver's window again, as he had at the nursery to hear the tree house pleas. He asked the woman here if she'd seen the Peugeot and, if so, whether she'd noticed which way it turned, right or left, at the next junction.

'Who are you?' she replied in a large, conservation-area voice.

'There would be one occupant, a young woman,' Harpur said, 'full of filthy driving tricks, a contempt for the normal rules of motoring.'

'Who are you?'

'As I say, the car was probably shifting, at some pace,' Harpur replied.

'Who are you?'

'It's a personal matter, between her and me, as you'd expect, I expect – oh, dear, much expecting!' Harpur replied. 'No need to embroil others in the least, except to ask very basic guidance.'

'*What* is a personal matter? Who are you?' she said.

'As a matter of fact I've heard someone else ask that lately,' Harpur replied.

'What?'

'"Who are you?"

'Well, and what's the answer?' she asked.

'To what?'

'Who are *you*?'

'In my own case, you mean?' Harpur replied.

'Why not?'

'These personal matters can get very pressing, because . . . well, because they're personal,' he said. 'This is widely recognized. Identity is so intriguing, isn't it?'

'Personal in which respect?'

'Yes, personal,' Harpur replied.

'You might not believe it, but we get all sorts coming down this street,' she said. 'However, perhaps that's in the nature of an urban setting. Not wishing to be rude, but you now are one of those "all sorts" using the street.'

'I'm after one particular vehicle,' Harpur said. 'A good deal after by now.'

'With what intent are you "after" it, to use your rather baroque phrase?'

'Personal.'

'That tells me sweet fanny-all,' she replied.

'True,' Harpur said. 'It's what's known as a summarizing term.'

'That would be fine if we knew what it was summarizing,' she replied.

'Fair comment.'

'There's one thing I hate to see,' she replied. 'You'll wish to know what it is.'

'Is it to do with unplumped up cushions? Or possibly safari park animals in Kenya?' Harpur asked.

'I hate to see someone male, regardless of age, in a VW.'

'The name Volkswagen means "the people's car". That's all people, no matter what gender or height.'

'Just the same.'

'You're against *all* VWs?'

'I don't distinguish.'

'A kind of allergy? Like some people with peanuts? Look, next time I come this way I'll make sure it's in a different vehicle. That's easily arranged. I can choose from several.'

'It's not much to ask, is it?' she said.

'Minimal,' Harpur said. 'I'm not boasting about car ownership. Where I work there's a pool.'

'Now and then if I'm feeling in need of a bit of burnishing, a bit of stimulation, I mock up a crisis with the electric light or water heater,' she replied. She spoke confidently, as if certain Harpur would sympathize. 'I'll ring the local firm, and they'll send someone out. They have several slim, very intelligent lads there, totally spruce, despite having to deal with wiring under floorboards and in cubby holes day in day out. They naturally get intimations when they find there's nothing really wrong with the electric at all. In due course they'll invoice me for something minor, but in a house as old as these you have to expect repair bills.'

'Do they come quickly?' Harpur asked.

'What? *What?*'

'When you ring.'

'I've never seen one of them in a VW of any shade or marque,' she replied. 'So, you'll appreciate my present position.'

'I don't know whether proper research has been done on that,' Harpur said.

'What?'

'Reliable data about the use, or absence of use, of VWs by on-the-job electrical engineers. Are you on the lookout now for other spruce lads?'

'Adolf was behind the Volkswagen project, wasn't he? That's another reason to have reservations about the model, models,' she replied.

'I suppose since the EU we are all volk now,' Harpur said.

'I have the feeling that you and I are on very similar, interweaving wavelengths. I'm wondering if you'd like to come in. I don't want to seem inhospitable and starchy.'

'You're the least starchy person I've ever had a conversation with through a Golf window. Your invitation is kind, but I'm hopeless with electricity. I might fuse everything. And I have to do some tracing.'

'All you can think of is that damn green Peugeot, your face scrunched up in concentration.'

'Did you see it?'

'A woman driving – no passengers?'

'She'd be wearing a thong,' Harpur replied.

'Exceeding the speed limit.'

'Which way did she go?'

'I wasn't interested.'

'You didn't notice whether she went left or right?'

'Of what possible significance might that be to me?' she said.

'You mean, the Peugeot could offer no burnishing or stimulation?'

'How could it?' she asked.

'Would this be the same for *all* Peugeots, as with the VWs? Do the electrical boys ever come in a Peugeot?'

'Just don't drive down this damn street in a VW again,' she answered.

'I'm going to try left.'

'Why not?'

'Even if you did return at some time, there's no guarantee I'd be here like this. My temperament has its . . . well, temperamental aspects. Moods are not set in stone. And I go hill walking. These boots have taken me safely across many a non-urban escarpment.'

'I'll have to risk the disappointment of not bumping into you again. But I'll remember the house – its pinkness – and the tumult of tints in the sarong.'

'That small-scale VW is the kind of car plain-clothes police would pick – anonymous. And your clothes are definitely plain.'

'Often I try to keep them on in working hours.'

'Goodbye, then. Continue your damn chase,' she said. 'Yes, the Peugeot went left.'

'Thanks.' He went left, too, but didn't find the Peugeot. There'd been too much chat, too much lost time. Or perhaps she resented his attitude and had deliberately lied as retaliation. She might have preferred to give him a kicking with the fell boots, but that was impossible. Harpur drove back to the Silver Bells And Cockleshells district and found another timed spot to park in near the charity shop. He felt that the only way he could get insights on Rossol now was to talk to the woman who'd been in the machine gun tower with those two children, and who seemed to know Rossol from a visit to the nursery

– seemed to know something about Gordon Loam, also, from a visit to the nursery.

Harpur would wait for her. Best not call there and start questioning. If he did that he'd be more or less obliged to say he was the police, even if the people there couldn't deduce it from the plainness of his plain clothes. He'd prefer not to cause alerts at present. That could mess up future inquiries. He was not investigating any offence and wouldn't be able to explain why he'd become interested in Silver Bells And Cockleshells. He saw nobody in the tree house now.

Harpur was growing fond of this stretch of ground – the well-ordered parking facilities, a good-cause Oxfam store, a busy bank, the handsome nursery. This healthy thriving mixture surely typified how a city's essence should be. After about ten minutes he noticed a shirt-sleeved, burly looking man of about fifty watching him from inside the Oxfam shop, over the top of an attractive blue and white kitchen crockery front-window display: A TENNER THE LOT INCLUDING CONDIMENT HOLDERS. Harpur gave him a friendly half-smile, adequate for a lumpish charity worker, he thought. The man withdrew, as if unhappy at being spotted, but in a little while appeared at the window again, this time with a slightly older, skinnier, balder man, and they both stared at Harpur. He didn't bother with giving further smiles, in case they assumed he was interested in the plates and so on, but looked ahead at the nursery. He had the Golf head-on to Silver Bells. There hadn't seemed any need to disguise surveillance by observing from the rear.

He glanced back to Oxfam and saw the two men had come out from the shop and were approaching the VW. They looked purposeful. Did they have a down on VWs, like the sarong woman, though caused differently? The thin man carried an American baseball bat, a much longer and weightier item than the bats used in British baseball. He didn't look the sort who would buy that kind of thing, even with a charity-shop price cut, and there were no local American baseball teams, anyway, of course. He thought these two must be volunteer assistants at the shop, and the bat might be kept handy to clobber anyone trying to mug the cashier.

The burly man bent down and pulled open the driver's door

of the Golf. It was not a friendly or helpful pull. Hostile. Combative. 'Who are you?' he said, his tone virtually a snarl, sounding as though whatever Harpur answered the man wouldn't like it, or believe it.

'I'm always getting asked that,' Harpur replied genially. Sitting behind the wheel he felt constricted, disadvantaged for any fight.

'Who the fuck are you?' the man said.

'Who the fuck are *you*?' Harpur said.

'You're a damn paedo, aren't you?' he said.

'Yes, a damn wanker paedophile,' the thinner one said. 'Hanging around to gawp at the Silver Bells nursery kids, and maybe worse than gawp. We've had your sort here before, eyeing, lusting, breathing the little ones' innocent air. And today, you've been around twice. We noticed.'

'As a matter of act, I'm moving off now,' Harpur replied. He'd seen the woman from the guard-tower leave by the nursery front door and walk quickly away in the opposite direction from where Harpur waited. 'Shut the door, will you, chum? You can get back to your ethical commerce.'

'Moving off? *Moving off?* Hark at him, Albert. So smooth and brass-necked. Don't "chum" me, you pervert! You're not going any sodding where, sonny,' the burly one said.

'I thought you were to do with charity,' Harpur replied. 'What about "the greatest of these is charity" – First Corinthians, New Testament – meaning the greatest virtue is love and consideration, so shut the door, will you, or I'll break your fucking arm?'

'We've called the police,' Albert said. 'And we'll keep you here till they come. It is a moral duty upon us. Your sort can't be allowed licence to roam and pleasure yourself on a public highway in a modest, harmless-looking car.'

'I know someone who sees only evil in VWs,' Harpur replied. He leaned forward, aiming to grab the handle and pull the door shut. 'I *am* the police,' he said.

The burly one guffawed, the kind of total vastly-tickled guffaw he might have used viewing some tripey gift for the charity shop. 'Oh, falsely claiming to be an officer now!' he said. 'Making things worse for himself! What are you hanging about here for if you're police, panting with your tongue hanging out like on heat? And in a little Golf. Who ever heard of police in a Golf?'

'Anonymous,' Harpur replied.

'He's got an answer for everything, Vernon,' Albert said.

Vernon was crouched and part into the car. He had hold of the front of Harpur's jacket and shirt, with both hands, trying to pull him out through the open door. Albert had stepped back and raised the baseball bat. He could manage it all right, although so spindly. It appeared to be a rehearsed two-prong attack: Vernon to drag Harpur clear of the Golf, Albert to cosh him. Harpur felt very conscious that the back of his head would be totally exposed – realized he might not be very conscious of anything shortly.

Harpur bent his face downwards and was about to give one of Vernon's hands holding him a deep, possibly infected bite – Harpur understood human bites out-contaminated all others – when he heard a car arrive with a big roar and hard braking somewhere near, and then running, urgent footsteps, the shoes sounding very high-grade, probably good leather throughout, uppers as well as sole. Harpur felt slightly disappointed at this interruption. He would have liked to get his teeth into that creep, Vernon. Harpur didn't mind the taste of blood if it was in a good cause. But he sensed now that, in possibly changing conditions, biting would not be acceptable.

Side-vision, he saw Albert suddenly hit backwards in some sort of ferocious rugby tackle, his rubbish physique seeming almost snapped in half as he dropped. There was a terrible preponderance of bony elbows and knees. The baseball bat fell to the floor and rolled into the gutter. Iles shouted, enraged, 'What the hell do you two think you're doing to Col?' He'd landed on what there was of Albert during the assault, but quickly got back to his feet, feet accustomed to the quality shoes identified by Harpur a minute or two ago. Iles had his Charles Laity footwear individually crafted for him on a personal last.

He was in full Assistant Chief's uniform, including cap. Albert lay on the pavement, probably not concussed or spine-damaged, but winded and badly shocked. He began to weep, though not loudly, and Harpur felt relieved about this. It always upset him to hear a man blubbing on the ground, like a child tipped from its scooter. Vernon had released Harpur, and he turned and straightened up alongside the Golf to defend himself. Of course, he would have seen the ACC's uniform, with its gaudy epaulettes, and realized he was police. But Vernon would most likely realize, too, that Iles was not the kind of police he wanted, or, in fact, the kind of police who would normally be in the police at all.

Iles gave him a single, middle-power punch on the right ear. The ACC did sometimes show what was known in politics and the law as 'proportionality' – that is, any violence coming from him would be at the required force, and only at the required force. It would be meticulously in proportion to the danger and/or stroppiness of the target. Vernon fell to the ground like the baseball bat, then rolled into the gutter like the baseball bat, though still partly conscious. This had been a very nicely judged right-hand jab to Vernon, and shoulder charge to Albert, only moderate interference from the Assistant Chief, civilized, more or less kindly. His cap had remained in place throughout. He would have loathed to see it spin from his head during the bother and bounce about farcically on the pavement, like a symbol of disorder and insurgency, and liable to bedecking in dog shit.

'They called up the Control Room and gave the car make and number, Harpur,' Iles said, 'and the inspector recognized it as ours. She's a smart one; sensed it might be important and told me. I checked with the pool and found you'd taken it. I guessed this was your sort of disgusting street-level trouble and came myself, Col. We don't want everyone at headquarters to know what a twat you are, do we?'

'Guessed how?'

'Oh, yes, guessed,' the ACC replied. 'And I saw the siting report from Rapid Response saying the Peugeot had been hereabouts. What's with the charity shop, then – these gentry attempting a hard sell?'

'This is something very ongoing,' Harpur said.

'Yes, I thought so. What, though?'

'Yes, ongoing, sir.'

Iles went and helped Albert to stand. The ACC took a brilliantly white, carefully folded handkerchief from his pocket and extremely caringly wiped the tears from Albert's face. 'Bear up,' Iles said. 'There will always be hazards on the Oxfam front line.' The ACC wouldn't want the used handkerchief near his body, especially not in a trousers pocket abutting his balls, and once the Albert clean-up finished he held the square of cotton at arm's length and dropped it into a nearby litter bin. 'I'm not going to proceed with charges for carrying an offensive weapon, viz., a Joe DiMaggio,' he said. 'I admire those who give their time freely to Oxfam for its work in Africa and Sydney, Australia, and for clothing Harpur fashionably throughout his life, if we take "fashionably" to mean "clownishly".

'But the thing about charity is it begins at home, you know. There's a maxim to that effect. Think of myself and Col as looking after you and your home as part of our constant remit. The law exists to protect folk like you, and it is vital that application of the law should be "in good hands", as an old-time thinker put it. Where, then, do we find those "good hands"? May I point you both towards Detective Chief Superintendent Colin Harpur? In return, he surely deserves better treatment than what you were offering, don't you think? He is your standby, and you should stand by him in gratitude. And if ever you're feeling down and would like a reassuring hour or two's chat, why don't you call on Col at a hundred and twenty-six Arthur Street? He'd be only too delighted to welcome you, wouldn't you, Col? Delighted. That's his admirable nature. There'd probably be *petits fours*.'

Harpur climbed out of the VW. It took him and Iles, on an arm each, to get Vernon off the ground. 'He *is* police, then, is he?' Vernon asked Iles.

'Who?' Iles said.

'Him. The VW.'

'We use that kind of vehicle sometimes,' Iles said.

'Anonymous,' Harpur said.

'But why's he watching Silver Bells?' Vernon asked.

'Silver Bells?' Iles replied.

'The nursery,' Vernon said. 'That building with the tree house out front.'

'Ah, you think he's interested in the nursery, not your shop?' Iles said.

'Why would he be interested in the shop?' Vernon said.

'Why would he be interested in the nursery?' Iles asked.

'Kids,' Albert said.

'Kids?' Iles replied.

'Like – you know – under-age abuse,' Albert said.

'Harpur prefers them grown up,' Iles said. 'Don't you, Col?'

For a moment, Harpur thought the ACC was going to slide into one of those occasional loud fits about his wife's affair with Harpur a long while ago. But that would have sounded like a compliment now – a denial that Harpur went for children, the proof Mrs Sarah Iles. Harpur could see this step-by-step reasoning canter across the Assistant Chief's face. He'd stay quiet about Sarah.

'Col will have some explanation,' Iles said.

'Will he tell you?' Vernon said.

'Probably not,' Iles replied. 'Or not at this juncture.'

'Which?' Albert said, recovering quickly now.

'Which what?' Iles said.

'Juncture,' Albert said.

'This one,' Iles said. 'There have been others where I've had to dash with urgent help for Col.[5] On the whole he's worth it.'

Harpur picked up the baseball bat and returned it to Albert.

'We must be getting along now, lads,' Iles told him and Vernon.

TWENTY

After that little escapade with the Golf tagging her – attempting to – Liz knew many would say she should remain out of sight for a while, adopt some low-profiling, or no profiling at all. 'OK, Liz, you've done a fine job getting clear, so be thankful and *stay* clear, stay hidden somewhere, yourself and motor.' That's how the chinwag would go, intelligent, well-meant, cautious.

[5] See *Disclosures.*

She thought this would be a stupid response, though. Always she trusted her own brain, her own thinking. Almost always. Her school, Marlborough, had encouraged that kind of mental sturdiness, and it stayed with her through Oxford. Plus, she was a fieldworker and that's what workers in the field did: they saw situations whole, say, as farmers saw the seasons, not fragmented. They never acted on impulse. They despised catch-as-catch-can stunts. Occasionally, this kind of solid independent stance might even put her into conflict with George Dinnick, founder and potentate of the Cog corporation, who didn't much care where his people went to school. She had the idea he'd been at somewhere quite pricey and non-State himself, but he never spoke about that, never spoke at all about his background. He was Cog incarnate. He'd obviously decided to reveal nothing more.

Defiance of George could be very dangerous, but she didn't know how to change, or want to, not as yet, anyway: George had never gone full-out unpleasant and/or threatening towards her. If this *did* happen one day, Liz realized she might have to accept some adjusting, some trimming. Her splendid, cocky independence had boundaries, like everyone's. Marlborough had been a powerful influence, but Marlborough was only a school, and quite a while ago. Now, there was Cog, and minor cogs in the general Cog machinery. She figured as one of them.

The Peugeot had become an obvious liability. She couldn't tell who knew about it, but plainly the Golf driver did, and possibly those who sent the Golf driver, and/or those who were passengers in the car. From very brief, imperfect mirror glimpses of the VW she believed that the driver was a man – a biggish, heavily made, fair-haired, blunt featured man, late thirties – and that he was alone. Perhaps. He might be the man they had on film, also in an oldish Golf.

Eventually, the Peugeot would be a give-away, no matter how long she remained inconspicuous. There might be a general call out to report sightings of the car. Instead of hiding, she decided she would finish her fieldwork now, today, immediately, while the Golf was somewhere trounced, hopeless, all wrong, temporarily neutered, then return the Peugeot and disappear back to London on a late-afternoon train. Not that she'd discovered much. Things might still change, though. She drove out towards Jack Lamb's home, Darien.

On the way, of course, she tried to guess who exactly the Golf driver might be. Police? They were trained to get two non-bulky vehicles between tail and target. This absolutely matched the Golf's tactics. The police often used small, unmarked, anonymous vehicles as cover – not always a smart ruse, because some big-built drivers looked so cramped that nobody could believe they'd buy that model. Although she'd managed to shuffle off the Golf, it hadn't been easy. The driver seemed to have learned the motorized stalking routines, but was simply unprepared for a non-cop to apply evasion skills so expertly and ruthlessly. She'd taught herself these tricks early on in her fieldwork career – had foreseen a possible need now and then for that type of sudden four-wheeled disappearance. Neither Marlborough nor Oxford had taught such slick procedures, and she'd had to improvise a personal instruction course. She'd used them twice before, but never in such risky circumstances as today's.

Liz reckoned those skills were only very good, not faultless. She thought she might have made herself noticeable by bolting too fast through suburban side-roads, and particularly in that Georgian terrace where, from outside a dinky pink-painted house, the strange woman in hiking boots and a lurid sarong had seemed to be watching every passing vehicle, hope and avid need in her body language and possibly eyes, though Liz had gone by too fast for a full inspection. If the Golf followed into this street, and stopped to ask for directions, she might have let them know the Peugeot went right at the crossroads ahead. Liz kept her eyes on the mirror but saw no resumed adhesive company.

Assuming the Golf *was* the police, she knew they'd quickly trace the Peugeot to the hirer and obtain Liz's name and details. But, so what? She'd committed no offence, except, possibly, the speeding and wild driving when leaving the main road. They'd have no first-hand evidence for either, though. She couldn't understand, in fact, why the police should be interested in her at all: interested enough to put her under close observation?

Liz did realize she could be absurdly wrong to assume police. The Golf driver might have been Basil Gordon Loam in a changed car, or an associate of his. Or – another or – it was perhaps someone connected to Silver Bells And Cockleshells. That seemed improbable. But, then, a hell of a lot seemed improbable. Why not this extra? She wanted to take into account all the possibles and consider every contact she'd made in the city on this visit. That's how she was. If a job had to be done, it had to be done exhaustively, nothing discounted because *prima facie* it looked unlikely. No skimping. She might make that the title of her autobiography, if she lived long enough to do one.

She continued to watch for the Golf but became confident after a few more miles that she was safely solo, alone in the fieldworker's field. Perhaps the sarong woman didn't care for the police and had told them left out of the street, not right. People said the middle classes didn't always support the police these days. Given the adventurous gear and that Georgian byway, she'd be middle class and perhaps trendily anti-law, until her charming, beautifully preserved house got burgled. '*Yes, go left, Mr Golf, and you may yet find her.*' And then a brief, private, interior chuckle at her shameless mischief-making and bolshy behaviour, pinko to chime with the property.

Liz drove at modest pace now around the countryside setting of Darien, checking that approach roads, getaway roads, farm traffic, general traffic and gated railway level crossings were all pretty much as they had been on her previous reconnaissance visits. She had her self-made maps and detailed guidance notes on local conditions in an A4-size ring binder open for reference on the passenger seat. She systematically covered all that ground, re-familiarizing herself and making sure there had been no major alterations – no land slips, bridges down, flooding, diversions. She'd amend her A4 stuff where necessary.

Although Liz remained proud of her professional zing and thoroughness, she had begun to wonder seriously whether the planned hit on Lamb and Darien would ever happen. *Could* ever happen. The idea was very nice, but didn't it look exceptionally prone to all sorts of possible catastrophic snags? Although George had some good information, from herself and other sources, weren't there too many unexplained factors about this scheme, starting with the gunfire and talk of art-purchasing at The Monty club; then the sight of Gordon Loam leaving The Monty, seemingly on friendly terms with Ralph, despite the Blake victimization; an utterly mysterious call at the Silver Bells nursery; the pavement encounter with Gordon Loam near it; and, from there, the Golf hounding her until she sweetly gave it the elbow?

Liz had experienced too many conundrums, too much vagueness, too much outright blankness, in fact. No matter how dogged and inspired she might be in her researches, there were areas she did not understand, knew she did not come anywhere close to understanding, and would not be able to help George Dinnick and/or Justin to understand. It was as if the situation said to her: 'So, you're a fieldworker. Gee! Well, fuck fieldworking, you'll get no harvest from *this* field.'

For Liz, Justin was the essence of it all. As she felt so far, she could not back a plot that put him into positions full of bewildering complexities and unknowns. These might add up to a stack of lethal dangers. This was Liz trying to do one of her wide, deep, unflinching surveys. But she feared George would listen to her story of doubts and obscurities and decide she had become pitifully, contemptibly, overcautious and nervy because she and Justin had a hot love affair on the go. Dinnick might suspect she would do all she could to keep him from risk by calculatedly exaggerating the difficulties with the Darien job, her aim to get the operation killed off, in her view a considerably better development than Justin killed off. Maybe – maybe – George would have it part right. She'd admit this to herself. Would she be so opposed if she were scouting the locations ahead of somebody other than Justin?

She had a feeling George would regard her objections as selfish, cowardly, treacherous. George could turn very rough. George could become very determined. Her scheme was to show by the rigorousness of all her fieldwork, including careful update revisions, that she took a totally sensible, businesslike attitude to the Darien project and that her inescapable anxieties about some aspects of it should be respected – should be regarded regretfully – yes, regretfully – as an irresistible case for abandonment. At times, fieldwork could produce a negative, a firm, wise, powerfully valid negative. That could be as good a contribution as to OK a go-ahead. Live to pillage another day. Would George see it like this, though? There was some big money stuff at Lamb's place. These opportunities didn't come all that often. He might feel *carpe* fucking *diem* – seize the nearest day, not another day. Seize the day and the paintings, soonest.

She couldn't get too near Darien in her tour. That was the trouble with a country house, or perhaps the advantage: there came a stage where the road led only to that property; nothing else around. A strange car would raise alerts. She took a narrow hill route up towards Chase woods, a straggling collection of ash, beech and willow. She stopped on the edge of the wood and got out of the car with a pair of field glasses. From here she could look down on all but the far side of Darien. A couple of miles to the east she could just about make out another manor house, rich in chimneys. She'd looked up Darien on the Internet before her previous visit. It was sixteenth century, with additions and alterations of later years, but maintaining the basic, Elizabethan serene style. Apparently, the house had been a stronghold for Royalist forces in the seventeenth-century Civil War.

She fancied that period of British history. You had clear opposites – the king and the decapitators. Politics were so wishy-washy now. She'd never thought much of a famous poem about the execution of Charles I at that time: 'He nothing common did or mean, Upon that memorable scene.' For the sake of a cheap rhyme the poet turned this into a 'scene' – a bit of harmless theatre starring 'the royal actor' – instead of the actuality of an axe hacking the best way it could through flesh, sinew and divine-right bone. But that's what the arts, and art, were all about, weren't they – turning reality into something that could be represented in a poem or a largo or a frame? After all, 'picturesque' meant fit to be put into a picture, a picture possibly priced at something very tidy and therefore worth nabbing. Someone had suggested there should be the term 'literatesque'. Her life story? Maybe one day.

As before, she could identity in her overview of Darien what would be stables, barns, an outdoor swimming pool, staff bungalows, two garages, flagstone terraces to the front and rear. She had not much interest in the rear of the house. If that became important it could only mean the operation had foundered and crisis ways of escape were needed. This should be a coup where the works were lifted, brought out through the front door to their vehicle, a fast departure down the larch-hemmed, gravelled drive and on to one of the double-checked getaway roads.

Alarms and pursuit were unlikely because most probably some or all of the works in Lamb's gallery had a crooked history, and he would not want full-scale involvement in his business by the police. '*So, just for the record, tell us how you came by these works that have been stolen, Mr Lamb, would you, please?*' The Cog trawl, if it did take place, would be a hijack in the proper, original sense of the word – theft of items that had previously been thieved, or got by similar special methods. What she hadn't been able to discover on her previous surveys, and couldn't discover now, was the number of people normally around in Darien; impossible to tell whether all three of what she assumed were staff bungalows had occupants, nor what kind of occupants. Did Jack keep a live-in private security contingent? If so, how many? Armed? Round-the-clock rotas? The only way to count personnel in a place like this would be to watch non-stop for hours, perhaps days, and chart the comings and goings, see how many rooms and buildings were lit up at night. Liz could give only a couple of hours. She'd stick by her plan to leave for London later today. She saw no comings or goings of any kind at the house or in the grounds now.

She did, though, hear from behind her in the wood women's voices, having what seemed a sporadic, relaxed conversation, and the sound of one or two horses' footfalls, hoof-falls, approaching slowly. Quickly, she opened the Peugeot rear door, put the field glasses on the back seat and covered them with a coat. She leaned over to the front and flipped closed the ring binder on the passenger seat. Then she gently, noiselessly shut the car door.

She turned. Two women in riding gear, and on very classy, tall, chestnut horses, had come out from the wood and were moving at walking pace towards her and the car. She recognized them, of course, from her previous reconnaissance trip – presumably Jack Lamb's girlfriend, and his mother from the USA. The women were of very different ages, the older one probably in her sixties, the other maybe twenty-two or twenty-three. If Liz hadn't carried out that earlier identification she might have thought mother and daughter. But Liz saw no physical resemblance – not facially, nor in figure, the 'mother' long legged, long bodied, aquiline featured, very upright in the saddle; formidable, Liz thought. Her nag would know who the boss was – no maverick, unauthorized gallops, no rearing and melodramatic snorting. They stopped, and the younger woman dismounted, in a smooth, easy movement. She was pale skinned, wiry, mid-height, some blonde wisps of hair trailing from under her black helmet. She wore jeans, tucked into brown boots, and a tweed jacket. The older woman had on proper jodhpurs, boots, a similar tweed jacket and black helmet.

'Well, hi!' the older one said. 'You're enjoying the view, I see. We're not crowding you, I hope.'

'It's so lovely,' Liz said. She gave the words a degree of thrum, but nothing goofy or madly lavish. 'I just had to get out of the car and pinch a little time. From a hillside like this one can see so much of the country. And there's what I take to be a manor house – lots of chimneys – over there.' She pointed into the distance. 'Plus, in fact, one just below us here. But I expect you know this, are familiar with the scenery and so on.'

'Well, yes,' the older woman said. 'Helen and I, we come out here quite a deal, as it happens.' Her accent seemed part local, but with a kind of American intonation now and then. Her horse bent its neck and foraged in the grass. She let it.

'You're so lucky,' Liz said, 'if all this is on your doorstep.'

'Are you just visiting these parts – passing through?'

'Yes, a visit,' Liz said.

'In a way that's like Alice,' Helen said, her voice cheerful, amiable, utterly local, nothing Yank about it. 'She's over for her regular hols from the States.' So, Liz had done a good inventory – Helen, the girlfriend; Alice, almost certainly Lamb's mother.

'And the USA is fine, fine,' Alice said. 'I live in a desirable spot near my daughter and her husband on the edge of San Francisco. But it's important for me to come back here, stoke up my Britishness for another year, check on the national mood and make sure Nature is still doing its wholesome best.'

These days some people did call a parent by her/his first name, but Liz got the feeling now that the pair were not mother and daughter. Alice spoke of 'my daughter', as if Helen were something else.

Alice said: 'When I praise Nature and its beauty, I don't want you to think I'm opposed to all advancement.'

'Alice is not against wind farms, for instance,' Helen said.

'Consider Van Gogh,' Alice replied.

'Van Gogh?' Liz said.

'Alice means windmills,' Helen said.

'What are some of Van Gogh's most cherished paintings of?' Alice said.

'Are you interested in art?' Liz said.

'There are three or four Van Gogh windmills that are among his most esteemed and valuable canvases,' Alice replied. 'People speak of their vibrancy and quiet power. Does this put you in mind of anything?'

'She means wind farms,' Helen said. She sounded apologetic, as if Alice preached vandalism. 'Vibrancy. Power.'

'*Quiet* power,' Alice said.

'Some living near them say they're not so quiet,' Helen said.

'You know a lot about art, do you, Alice?' Liz said.

'Think of coal-driven power stations,' Alice replied. 'Huge, noisy lorries and trains delivering constant new supplies. None of that with wind farms. Helen's young, touched by sentimentality, wants these hillocks preserved undeveloped, left as they have ever been, which is admittedly glorious. But this terrain and its gales and breezes should surely contribute something more than mere appearance and weather. Oh, forgive, that might be the US side of me talking now – a bold determination to exploit – in the best sense – to put land and its conditions to profitable use.'

While Alice spoke, Helen, holding her mount's rein near the bit, was moving about with the horse, as though to get a better view of the landscape, but giving the Peugeot quite a stare, outside and in, Liz thought.

'Let me put it like this,' Alice said. 'I was married for a while in the States. These things happen. One can't be eternally clear-headed. My husband would never go out with less than one and a half thousand dollars on him, small and large denomination notes. Various pockets. What do I make of that, you'll ask. What I make of it is money brings power – power, in his case, to buy himself out of trouble, the mixed value bills from multiple nooks about his person giving him scope to negotiate a skin price – his – depending on the measure of the mugger's scare factor. But the reverse also is true – power is money. A wind farm on these hills would help light half a city. This is gain, this is enterprise. This is what they call over there "another dollar".'

'A company wanted to put a wind farm here,' Helen said, 'Planning permission was refused, though.'

'And you're pleased, aren't you, Helen?' Alice said. 'Well, I guess you're entitled. But that's not the same as being right.'

Helen got into the saddle again, and they said goodbye.

It was the omissions in this splurge of quaint, rural talk that registered most with Liz. There'd been no mention by them of Darien, lying nearby, though Liz had referred to it, half implied it was their 'doorstep'. Hardly any indication of where these two had come from was given. San Francisco had been the only geography. They hadn't asked Liz her name, as though they didn't want to show they might be curious about her, put her on guard. They'd decided, had they, that she was 'passing through', was simply 'visiting'? Passing through from where to where? That, apparently, didn't concern them. Or did it concern them a lot, but they hadn't wanted her to realize it concerned them a lot because, if she was up to something – and they'd very probably guessed that she *was* up to something other than counting chimneys on a distant manor house – yes, if she was up to something, they would like to surprise her by being very ready to blitz whatever it was she was up to when she tried to reach the next bit of what she was up to, perhaps the crunch bit and ultimate reason for the 'visit'? And would this be centred somehow on Darien, which they'd seemingly ignored, because that's where the terminal surprise would kick in and they didn't want her forewarned? Solution: have some fanciful, mad discourse about wind farms and Van Gogh.

But Liz did feel forewarned, thanks to their attempt not to forewarn her. This was the kind of subtle, contrary mind she assumed she'd been born with and which she constantly worked hard to improve. When Alice said 'San Francisco', in an utterly surplus statement about her home-life, Liz had speculated that Alice's purpose was to take the focus off the immediate locality – up the hill from Darien – and, instead, on to almost anywhere else that was far off, such as the Pacific side of the USA, though still a long way from the original Darien. That monumentally irrelevant chat about her ex-husband's money fetish was to direct the subject matter from the here and now and on to something foreign and emphatically yonder, the dollar: fifteen *hundred* dollars.

Oh, yeah, there was the San Francisco mention, but also there was the scrutiny of something much nearer, i.e., the Peugeot and its contents, though the contents wouldn't tell much because of Liz's scampered precautions. But, of course, they might apply similar obverse logic to that of Liz: if the contents didn't reveal anything it must be because those contents had something to reveal but had been given the treatment so they couldn't – a closed ring binder, a coat over something significant.

Maybe they'd go back home, and Alice would say to Lamb, 'A woman casing the property, Jack. She didn't hear our approach until a little too late, and we saw her hide field glasses and shut a ring binder in a rush, then close the door with super-quietness so as not to draw attention to what she'd just done. A Peugeot. We've got the number. Possibly, you have a salaried chum in the DVLC who'll handle the tracing?'

Helen might say: 'Alice did her stuff to make them think she must be dim and radiantly harmless – someone who'd marry a mugger-obsessed idiot, and someone who didn't quite understand the difference between a windmill and a wind farm. Madam Peugeot would imagine she'd successfully fooled this pair of horse-borne twerps.'

Liz got back into the car and opened the ring binder. She read her previous notes on Darien and Jack Lamb. They were slightly more speculative than her knowledge now, but not bad, all the same. Anyway, this hillside encounter confirmed what Liz had already begun to suspect – that the Darien project was menaced from a bevy of directions and too hazardous for anyone to attempt, but especially for Justin to attempt, on her say-so. She and he had discussed the Darien project several times privately, of course, most recently at his place one evening a while ago now. He'd axed some logs from the thick branches of a lopped tree in the garden of the apartment block, and they'd sat comfortable and content in front of the wood-burning stove talking Darien, and talking Darien very positively, very confidently. That was before she'd been confronted by this tangle of possible hazards, though. She was a pathfinder, and she'd found the path impenetrably overgrown.

TWENTY-ONE

When Jack Lamb had something especially confidential and salty to tell Harpur they'd meet at a downtown launderette and talk quietly while watching through the glass front panel of the washing machine as the items rotated, whirled or lay like doggo, momentarily at rest in a programme pause. Harpur greatly liked those periods of stillness: after the seemingly random, haphazard jostling and plunging, there would come this imposed stoppage. It demonstrated, didn't it, that, despite so much apparently ungoverned, frantic activity, there was, in fact, a carefully timed, systematic procedure under way: no chaos of soaked garments and linen, but an immaculately organized progress towards cleansing, towards renewal. Harpur considered that policing must achieve something similar, even policing graced by someone like Iles. Good order should be established and devotedly maintained where there would otherwise have been very sketchy order or none at all.

Jack had declared recently that he'd come to feel tainted, degraded, by this informing arrangement and it must end. But he'd rung today saying he'd come across something so bad, he had to speak of it. They should meet once more.

There was a launderette ritual, and it took over again now. They'd each bring a bag of washing with them. The launderette cycle for cleaning and drying lasted well over an hour, which gave Jack plenty of time to spill. Perhaps too much. He could be terse. On some visits they'd sat silent for most of the session, lulled by viewing the spells of bubbles and frothy splashes in the drum. Perhaps because this occasion was such a breach of Jack's terminating decision, he seemed to start quite nervously – chatty and off centre. 'There's a splendid Western film with Henry Fonda that comes on to one or other of the movie channels regularly, Colin, *The Ox-Bow Incident*.'

'I don't get on with Westerns. All those damn lariats.'

'What I wanted to discuss today, Colin, is not the ox-*bow* incident but the Ox*fam* incident,' Lamb replied. 'Venom. Vigilantes. A baseball bat. Accusations of lusting for the considerably under-aged. Iles. Violence – that is to be expected if Iles shows up, and he did, at, I gather, a gallop, and with silver-leaf cap on.'

Under the previous system, the launderette had not been their only secret dialogue spot. Sometimes they'd choose – or, rather, Jack would choose – an ancient concrete defence post on the foreshore, left over from the war; and, alternatively, there were, not far from this, the remains of what had once been an anti-aircraft battery site in the 1940s. It had an approach road, still usable; the gun emplacements; and brick foundations of a barracks hut for the crews, this demolished a couple of decades ago. Jack loved these military spots and what he referred to as their 'overtones'. To enhance this mood he'd usually come to the pill box or anti-aircraft area wearing army surplus garments from the forces of any or several combatant nations – Britain, France, Germany, Italy, the United States, Russia. He preferred these two locations for their evening or night get-togethers. Jack heard the overtones loudest in the dark – could visualize through a loophole the enemy trying to sneak ashore in the shadows, or imagine the ack-ack ordnance banging away at blitz Heinkels or Dorniers. The present conference was an early afternoon, daylight rendezvous, and so the launderette.

'That pavement fracas – you in a Golf, I believe – came to my notice, Colin.'

'Came to your notice how?' It was the kind of question no informant would ever answer, but also the kind of question Harpur generally did ask: a tic.

'Oh, yes, came to my notice, as you'd expect, Colin. This city speaks to me. If it didn't, I'd have been of no assistance to you, would I? People whisper to me, and I sometimes whispered to you.'

'When it, the city, spoke to you, what did it say?'

'It said what I've mentioned, Colin: the Oxfam environs and staff, vigilantes, mayhem, a misunderstanding, Des-Ilesian instinctive thuggery. All in very plain view, after all. I'm certain about the misunderstanding being a misunderstanding. I don't believe you'd go after infants, regardless.'

'Regardless of what?'

'Oh, yes, regardless, Colin.'

'Thanks, Jack.' In a way, Harpur had always found the undercover rigmarole absurd, whether here, in the launderette, or at one of those ex-army installations. After all, he would openly visit Jack in Darien now and then, and Jack had once come to Harpur's house in Arthur Street and would also phone there. But Jack had seemed to like these occasional episodes of fleeting subterfuge. Perhaps they excited him, as well as giving him two-out-of-three chances to get warrior kit on. Whatever his motives, Harpur had gone along with Lamb's wishes. The information that came from Jack was often crucial, indispensable. Possibly, he'd savoured these hideaway powwows because the need for such furtiveness would remind Harpur of the risks Jack took for him. But Harpur didn't need reminders. Although Lamb always argued that he informed only about matters he regarded as disgusting and/or deeply antisocial, Harpur knew this kind of explanation wouldn't save him if he were ever found out. Among the people Jack might have to deal with then, a grass was a grass until the grass was under grass, not necessarily in one piece. No launderette could get the stain out of narking. No wonder Harpur could hallucinate awful damage to him.

'But what we have to ask, Colin, or what *I* have to ask, anyway, is whether the Oxfam connection is really a connection at all,' Jack said. 'Because something occurs *near* a certain point – a certain shop, in this case – it doesn't mean that this point-stroke-shop is integral, does it?'

'Integral to what?'

'Integral to what is taking place *near* the Oxfam shop but not necessarily anything to do with it, except that two thickos on duty that day helping the charity come out with the baseball bat because they're in the grip of what I've called a "misunderstanding".'

'Oxfam does very fine work abroad,' Harpur replied. 'No dispute.'

'But as to connections, links, Colin, perhaps after all there are some, and not based on mere local geography.'

'Connections, links, between whom and what?'

'Or who and whom? Let's consider what these two Oxfam louts appear to have been thinking when they began their foolish attack. They believed you were on the lurk, waiting to get filthy satisfaction from the sight of toddlers close at hand. I'm told they actually spelled out this indictment.'

'Told by whom?'

'Now, we have to inquire, Colin, how that piece of pavement outside Oxfam comes to offer a vantage point for paedo glances – for, at the least, glances,' Jack replied. 'Answer? More or less next door to Oxfam is, I learn, a children's nursery, namely Silver Bells And Cockleshells.'

'Learn from whom?'

'Bingo! We have the connection, the link, haven't we, Colin?' Lamb replied. 'Timed parking spaces for shoppers. So convenient. So ostensibly ordinary. You could have been sitting there waiting for the missus to come back with the groceries. As we know, the Oxfam pair put a different interpretation on it, but they are a special, benighted case. One or both of these phoned the police, we assume.'

'Which we?'

'They meant to detain you there until officers arrived, if necessary by clobbering you cold with the bat. Of course, they don't get any old cop. For reasons we haven't discovered, their call goes to the Assistant Chief, and he delightedly spots there could be interesting scope for brutality. He decides to handle the situation personally, perhaps hurriedly, privately, gluing the cap to his head so as to indicate, when it remains fixed, that law and order will always prevail, and prevail without much sweat and with no loss of daintiness.'

'Mr Iles likes to feel he symbolizes rectitude. It's always best to behave towards him as if he really might,' Harpur said. 'This response is an act of civility and goodwill. No harm is caused.'

They basketed their stuff and then transferred it to the dryers. They returned to their seats. Lamb said: 'So, we have dismissed Oxfam and pederasty as reasons for your Golf sojourn. What other reason could there be?'

An elderly woman in a kind of plaid cape sitting behind them seemed to have caught some of Lamb's words. She leaned forward and whispered: 'My God, it's into Oxfam now, is it? And golfers? Not just celebrities, so called.'

'What is?' Jack said.

'That peder-what-you-call you mentioned – the kids thing, abuse, and that.'

'Don't worry, madam,' Lamb said. 'We have it in hand.'

She nodded and drew back again. 'Good on you.'

'Thanks,' Jack said. He spoke more quietly to Harpur now: 'I'm not going to ask what you were doing there in Brendan Street.'

'I'm grateful, Jack.'

'Because I know you wouldn't tell me. Info flows only one way in our arrangement, doesn't it?' As ever, he sounded matter-of-fact, unbitter.

Harpur said: 'I can tell you quite straight it was part of an investigation, Jack.'

'Well, fine. I think I might have guessed that.'

'Yes, an investigation.'

'But which? What kind?'

'Yes, an investigation,' Harpur said.

Lamb smiled, a tolerant, forgiving smile. This troubled Harpur. It was as if Jack didn't mind being brick-walled. Harpur thought that might mean Jack knew something Harpur didn't, something to outstrip easily whatever he could have told Jack. Such situations between Lamb and him had happened frequently, though Jack wouldn't usually smile-smirk about them. Naturally, an informant knew things his/her detective didn't or there'd be no need for the informant. Perhaps, though, what Jack had called the one-way flow of confidential stuff under their 'arrangement' had struck him as exceptionally hurtful today, and he felt angry. Or perhaps he smiled – genuinely smiled, no smirk component at all – yes, smiled because he had something brilliant for Harpur and took healthy, comradely delight in it. Harpur would prefer to think this was the reason. Of course he would.

'I don't know whether you understand properly how these things work, Colin.' Jack was speaking at normal volume again now.

'Which things?'

'Discovery. Revelation. As implemented by me.'

'It works, Jack, that's what matters.'

'We have to ask *why* it works, though, don't we?'

'Do we?'

'When I refer to discovery and revelation, these do not come to me suddenly out of nowhere. I'm not Saul, soon to be Paul, on the road to Damascus.'

The woman bent forward again. 'That Damascus is a different kettle of fish today, isn't it, because of the war in Syria,' she said.

'Saul is advised to stop kicking against the pricks,' Jack replied.

'These days it's sometimes hard to know which ones *are* the pricks and which are the others.' Her drying finished, and she took it and left.

Lamb said: 'Let's look at my role, Colin, shall we? It's like this. I hear of a street disturbance and the details. Certain folk know I'm in the market for such material.'

'Which certain folk exactly?'

'But then I have to move into the following, more challenging phase,' Lamb replied. 'How to assess and interpret this material. For instance, I discard Oxfam and fix my thinking on the Silver Bells And Cockleshells nursery. I have to ask – to ask myself – I have to ask, what is the real nature of this nursery? There is, of course, an *apparent* simple answer to this: it is an established facility in a pleasant street and occupying a handsome building. You'll notice that I've emphasized the word "apparent", Colin. I have to try to get behind that mere appearance and seek out its essence – seek out the reason it is under observation by you. And I am aware that if you know the true answer to this you will probably not tell me – a professional reticence, which I can more or less entirely sympathize with. But what I have to consider, also, is that you might not know the hidden function of that nursery yourself. I sense this to be probable. Hence, I go to certain folk – not necessarily the same certain folk who drew my attention to the street disturbance. I go to certain folk and ask them to look "in depth", as it might be termed, at SBAC.'

'So which are these different "certain folk", Jack?'

'A very determined, comprehensive yet discreet scan takes place,' Lamb said. 'Does the name Harbinger resonate with you?'

Yes, the name Harbinger did resonate with Harpur, or rather the names Harbinger, plural, though not linked to SBAC, as far as he knew. But, then, how far about all this *did* he know, as Lamb had suggested? 'Amy and Leyton Harbinger,' Harpur said. 'They kept a pub, Cork Street area. A talking parrot in the bar. On the walls, framed photos of boxers and bouts.'

'They *did* keep a pub. It *did* have a talking parrot and pug pics, including one of Rocky Marciano, undefeated heavyweight world champ, whom some say you look like, Colin, except you're fair-haired. But none of this is what you remember them for, is it?'

'I think they're both in jail.'

'They *are* both in jail and will be for at least another year, I gather. Not for keeping a pub, though.'

'Didn't they run an under-the-bar gun business?'

'Congratulations! Yes, they ran a deeply illegal, nice little arms shop on the quiet there, Amy the main figure. A small back-room to do the private deals in. At a price they could supply any type of handgun, given a couple of days' notice, payment in cash only. Leyton got the stuff from undisclosed sources, Amy managed the actual face-to-face selling side, with no inquiries from her about the articles' possible use: a kind of positive, intensively cultivated, "I-don't-want-to-know" ignorance. This was a beautifully organized, smooth-running enterprise, gradually polished and perfected over the years. But then tragedy: some of this weaponry was traced back to them after a considerable turf war shoot-out with casualties, including a couple of deaths.'

Their drying ended. As they loaded it into the bags, Jack said: 'You see the significance now, do you, Colin?'

Yes, Harpur thought he saw the significance, but the significance was damned hard to accept. 'Of the Harbingers?' he asked. It would have been lame-brained if he'd meant it.

'Obliquely of the Harbingers. Their absence. However, that's the past. We have a thriving go-ahead city here. Quite abruptly, arbitrarily, it has lost one of its major amenities, hasn't it? Not the Harbingers' pub. A new landlord could soon be drafted in. But the pub is only one aspect of the trade previously done there, and probably not the most profitable aspect. A very handy, homely, concealed armoury has been lost. I've heard of people temporarily stunned by grief as a result. Gun customers used for yonks to dealing with the Harbingers find themselves bereft. These are customers who don't like to retain a weapon for too long in case it can tell a story – tell a story to someone like you and your Forensic boys and girls. They crave change. They adore newness. For them it amounts to a kind of hygiene. Substantial projects might be in the planning stage, and fresh accessories will be needed, but none are available. How can this be remedied, Colin, for remedied it must be?'

'God, Jack,' Harpur replied.

'Quite. Were you drawn somehow to Brendan Street, possibly without knowing exactly why?'

'You're saying SBAC, a toddlers' nursery, is a replacement for the Harbinger pub?'

'There is a small back-room at the nursery, I'm told – the proprietor's office, equivalent to the Harbingers' tucked-away arbour for Amy and her dealing.'

'So near the children!'

'It's the monstrousness of this, Colin, that leads me to speak – the devilish exploitation of a nursery's innocence and harmlessness. As you appreciate, I do not bring you information willy-nilly. It must have a moral core. This situation does, I think you'll concede. It is exceptionally exceptional – why I have ditched my embargo for this once.' Jack picked up his bag of laundry and moved towards the door. 'Farewell, Colin.'

TWENTY-TWO

Basil Gordon Loam realized he would have to go back to The Monty and try to get his .38 Smith and Wesson returned. That refusal by Judy Rose Timmins, the flinty cow, to come up with something for him at the nursery had really shaken Enzyme. It seemed disgracefully in restraint of trade, an arrogant defiance of normal commercial principles recognized and abided by worldwide. He had the means to pay for the items – pistol and bullets – yet she would not permit the transaction; actually physically fought with him to prevent the sale, a teddy bear jammed between them. Yet on the other side of that office door and down the stairs dear little children, trustfully left at SBAC by their parents or parent, played and wandered, only metres from the mixed-gender violence and glaring misuse of a teddy.

Plainly, Timmins was not entitled to dictate how he should employ his money, or *not* employ it, in this case. It was an unforgivable infringement of his personal status and dignity, and therefore upon the reputation of his family, despite the widely recognized, triumphant way they had long ago established themselves in tea. If a previous Gordon Loam had wanted a replacement sidearm it would have been a simple, open purchase, the armourer proud to have such an eminent customer. Enzyme felt humiliated, and the fact that this appalling behaviour by Timmins had taken place in a nursery made it definitely worse, definitely more degrading – as if he were a child having controls imposed on what he might and might not do.

And then, outside in Brendan Street, he'd intercepted, in an entirely civil, polite fashion, the other cow, the green Peugeot woman, who'd pretended – cow, cow, brazen cow – that she was simply a parent earnestly seeking a kiddie haven, and not just someone like himself with a terrifically different purpose, such as acquiring a piece. It would be unusual for a woman to come looking for a gun, but possible. She might have been there to get a shooter for someone else – a lover, partner, husband, brother, boss – who led a dodgy, maybe crooked, life, and who didn't want the risk of attending Silver Bells And Cockleshells in blatant search for a weapon. It could be rather like drugs traffickers using innocent-looking women as 'mules' to smuggle commodities through airport security.

Or the Peugeot lady herself might be in some kind of work that brought dangers and threats so she needed means to defend herself. There were small 'purse' pistols sold in the United States and probably obtainable on order via SBAC. Peugeot woman must surely have been able to see he needed immediate support, but didn't offer to help change the cruelly negative mind of Judy Timmins for him. Enz knew why Judy's attitude had shocked him so deeply. On previous visits he'd thought she'd shown some intelligent deference, realizing he came from a clan with quite a distinguished name and history, substantially helping to make British tea drinking a major national foible. He did not claim that without Loams there would have been no tea habit in Britain, but it might not have been on such a scale and at such an early date. On one of his first visits Timmins had personally prepared cups of tea for both of them – no Fern involvement then – and he'd pointed out to her the pleasant fitness of this. She had readily concurred with a charming smile.

But, God, on that very recent session, she had become so reproachful and heavy about a couple of shots at some fucking ancient beardie in the Blake. Yet, surely the point was, at the time when the poet and artist was doing all his works, including *Tyger, Tyger*, Loam's ancestral family must have been around and already a considerable entity on account of the bulk tea? So nobody should expect Gordon Loam to show a kind of silly reverence for that illustration; *some* respect, possibly – and he'd admit it broke down momentarily during the salvo – yes, proper respect, but not quaking idolatry, for heaven's sake. Ember's *Marriage Of Heaven And Hell* wasn't an original, was it – just a print? You could probably buy such copies by the hundredweight.

Anyone would think from Judy's tut-tuttiness that he'd massacred half The Monty membership. OK, there was damage – though very treatable damage – to the William Blake print, print, fucking mere print, and ricochets causing glass splinters to zoom very briefly. But nobody was actually hit and hurt. Did anyone lose an eye or even a tooth? No. Did any woman member need to have Worcestershire sauce bottle shrapnel dug out of her tits under general anaesthetic? No, again.

Although some Worcestershire sauce got freed from the bottle, it smeared only one T-shirt and the surface of a pool table. It was not even in use at the time, so no players had been put off their strokes by the sudden arrival of sauce. This wasn't the London blitz. And the Worcestershire sauce concerned was not some special, precious vintage from the cellar dating back decades. Ralph could simply order another bottle from the club's supplier, as with the print, print, print. Enz had more or less at once promised to pay for any replacement Worcestershire sauce – possibly even a larger bottle than the one hit – and all repairs and cleaning.

Also, he would have met the cost for complete new pool-table baize if Ember considered that necessary, though he hadn't said so. He would be too vain and snotty to accept compo. Most likely he came from a nothing family, yet he seemed to think *arriviste* ownership of a manor house, Low Pastures, and his moth-eaten club, transformed him into quality: *Squire Ember; Milord Monty*. Gordon Loam had done some research on Ralph's genealogy and found only low-grade clerking and shopkeeping Embers. As far as Gordon Loam knew, Worcestershire sauce caused no actual chemical damage to baize, shrivelling it up, for instance, like acid flung on a face. There wouldn't be much research data on this by pool table manufacturers. The staining might be unsightly, but would not prevent normal playing of a game. A slight stickiness would perhaps slow the balls until the sauce dried, but that could provide an interesting extra challenge when cueing. Despite the insignificant damage, Enz had said he'd gladly cough up for that total renewal.

Didn't Timmins understand that the kind of playful, exuberant, jolly larkiness at the club was commonplace among high spirited – high octane – folk with notable backgrounds? Trashing of pubs or hotel rooms or restaurants – that sort of unfettered, merry carry-on – was more or less a rite of passage for some select people. They needed to show they were not cowed by rules and/or boring, restrictive conventions. These were for lesser folk. Enzyme thought of those roistering, classy, boon companions who would fling their excellent quality champagne flutes to shatter against the wall when they'd downed enough drink: the expensiveness of the glassware was vital; it made their point about freedom from customary, banal, penny-pinching cares. The damage and breakages, along with a wry apology, would be routinely seen to when the fine wine effects had worn off.

Enz regarded the assault on Blake and, inadvertently, the Worcestershire sauce bottle, as that type of uninhibited, impulsive, alcohol-aided, entirely excusable gambit. In a way, this brand of roughish behaviour linked the upper classes and the Marxists: both displayed a contempt for ownership of property, theirs and other people's. Also, it linked races. Wasn't Louis Armstrong, the great black jazz trumpeter, sent on a special correction course as a boy after he'd excitedly, harmlessly, fired a pistol into the air at New Year's Eve celebrations? This festive trigger-happiness had been just his way of saying then, 'What a wonderful world!', a genial thought he would repeat in a song later, entirely without gunfire.

But someone like Timmins probably had too narrow and drab an upbringing to recognize that a bit of fun was *only* a bit of fun, not arrant destruction and chaos. It functioned beyond her paltry understanding. Hell, though, Enzyme wished the Harbingers still operated. True, they didn't have much class about them, either, but if he'd gone to Amy H. for a replacement piece and ammo there'd be no insolent poking about into the recent past, no uncouth interrogation, no primness, no questioning his reliability merely on account of a naughty prank. The deal in the small back-room at their pub would have been swiftly completed and with a kindly smile from her as she counted the twenties – no fifties, because of forgery risks – and he checked the action of the gun and the number of rounds. He'd go back into the bar to finish his drink, the gun shoulder holstered, chamber full, the rest of the ammunition spread around his pockets. The parrot might croak a question: 'All ship shape and Bristol fashion, my grand lad?' There was nothing friendly and amusing like that at Silver Bells last time, only the trite teddy bear and Fern, an insulting loudmouth. The parrot would most likely come out ahead of Fern in a Mensa intelligence test.

But the Harbingers and the parrot were gone and would never resume: they'd be watched non-stop in future. Things for them could no longer be all shipshape and Bristol fashion. There'd be no more harbingering. This meant Timmins had a monopoly in the trade, and monopolies inevitably, and always, worked against public well-being. They could screw customers because customers had nowhere else to take their custom, like the old 'Tommy Shops', run by pit owners, where miners were forced to buy overpriced goods out of their poor pay. All right, Loam would admit his own family probably exercised a tea monopoly at one time. It would be foolish not to acknowledge this. Regrettably, that's how business was and still was. Enz had a lot of self-awareness and could be unsparing in examining his own and his forebears' lives.

But now it wasn't a question of being fleeced by SBAC. Timmins wouldn't sell to him, not at any price. Blockade. Ban. There might be other armourer firms in the city, but Gordon Loam didn't know where, and he was afraid that, even if he did find an alternative to Timmins, he would run against the same sort of measly, yellow, scaredy-cat un-cooperativeness. It was as though they insisted their weapons should go to a good home, like someone selling puppies. He was not regarded as a good home because he shot Blake. That matter had become too well known and not helpful. These dealers were so fucking cagey. They fussed about their 'reputation'! Crooks fussing about their reputation! They were all like Timmins, unable to appreciate a light-hearted joke.

So, Enz thought he'd go to talk with Ralph again at the club. He'd explain to Ember that when he handed over the .38 as an entirely meaningful gesture, that's what it was, a gesture. It spoke of regret and of an assurance that he would never get unruly in the club again. The gesture had been graphically, emphatically, made in the handing over of the .38 during that little, dignified private ceremony. Gordon Loam's 'gifting' of the pistol then did not need to be a permanent transfer, though. Once the offering had been made and accepted, the thing was done, the apology conveyed – conveyed once more. Ralph had no obligation to retain the gun indefinitely. He would surely know that if he returned the .38, Enz would never blast off at Blake with it again, or any successor to Blake. There might be one. Enz knew – in fact, everyone knew – Ralph Ember liked to show he had an education. Loved to. He had started a degree course at the university up the road from The Monty. But Enz had heard Ralph was forced to put that on hold mid-course for the present because he needed to give full attention to his several businesses, especially the sustained, heart-warming upsurge in Charlie use. After Blake, he might want to stick a different picture on the floating rampart at the club – a picture to demonstrate once more what a learned prat he was, such as Julius Caesar or Rudolf Valentino.

Ralph would also know that if Enz began looking for paintings on his behalf to improve the image of The Monty, there might be some dangers, and it would be in his own and Enzyme's interests for Enz to safeguard himself adequately. Possibly safeguard some paintings intended for Ralph adequately. So, *could I have my gun back, please?*

Did that argument stand up OK, he wondered. This was more courageous self-scrutiny. Yes, Enz could be tough on himself and his thinking, and his wife, Irene, could be tougher. He'd consult her. She was sharp-brained, for ever calm and practical, from what Enz considered only a lower-middle-class background with no big-time monopolists in her lineage, but confident and perky just the same. He would never go on at her about a total lack of breeding. That would be uncharitable and snobbish. No need for it at all. He'd find that kind of thing appallingly distasteful. She could not be blamed in the least for this patent deficiency. In his opinion, to a remarkable extent, she'd triumphed over it.

They'd met at evening cookery classes way back. She was thirty-three, dark-haired, slightly dreamy looking, but not in the least dreamy, just above mid-height, slim, quietly beautiful. Enzyme told her everything about his work and about everything else. When he had a problem, as he did now, he'd describe it to her in detail and listen intently to her advice. At times she'd make fun of what she called his 'obsession' with the grand, 'char-blessed' history of his forefathers and mothers. That term, 'char-based' – 'char' the army slang name for tea – showed she wanted to trivialize, make slightly comic, the success of Enzyme's predecessors. It was a kind of retaliation. He did not resent it. He understood. She wanted equality, and he would not do or say anything to suggest this was impossible. He remembered her quoting some American woman writer to him who'd said dwelling too much on the past was 'one of the most disastrous forms of unrequited love'. Slick. A lot of those bookish American women liked to sound-off.

But, as to love, Irene had married him, never mind his affection for old times, and she accepted without objection the dubious, unglittering, present-day way of life he had chosen for her and the children in place of that famed, epic tea-mongering. If Irene had been with him at The Monty before he shot the bulwark, she would have sensed something ridiculous was likely to happen and moved smartly to stop him. Irene had remarkable instincts. She knew the whole story of the incident, naturally, and considered he'd been showy, vulgar, and barmy, but nothing worse. She'd called him 'a juvenile jerk' when she first heard about it. Now, Enz wanted to know what she thought about attempting to reclaim the gun from Ralphy, and about the Peugeot driver. He'd described to Irene the whole nursery saga, including the cow Timmins' foul, degenerate rejection.

It was late in the evening, the children asleep upstairs. A television culture programme was on the screen, sound switched off, and they had armchairs facing each other, she with a glass of Rioja, he a vodka and tonic. 'You really consider the Peugeot dame was at Silver Bells for a piece – a woman, young, you say,' Irene said, 'but looking to buy an illegal firearm?'

Enzyme produced his two possible explanations: she was there on someone's behalf, 'muling'; or she was in some sort of dark, dangerous job and might need self-defence. He saw Irene didn't think much of either. He hadn't really expected her to: stand by for some lateral-fucking-thinking, as her kind of far-out ideas were called. But, he'd admit, sometimes they worked. Of course they did, or he wouldn't be so eager to consult her.

'How about: Peugeot lady followed you to the nursery?' Irene said.

He'd suggested that to the woman, hadn't he, but he played dismissive now. He wanted to see where this line took them. 'Not possible,' he said.

'Why?'

'Where would she have got behind my car?'

'You told me you'd just been to The Monty to redeem yourself by donating the gun – rather like an old-time defeated general sadly, symbolically surrendering his sabre.'

She knew how to take the piss. She knew how to get a special sting through alliteration of those damn hissing, pissing, 's' sounds. 'So?' he replied. God, he was helping her with them!

'Couldn't she have picked you up there?'

'How would she know about The Monty*?* How would she know I'd be there?'

'Maybe she didn't know you'd be there. But she *could* know about the club, couldn't she? It's been publicized – the Blake farce in the "I Spy" column.'

'I wouldn't call it a farce.'

'What would you call it?'

'An unwise jape, maybe.'

'It's been publicized – the Blake unwise jape that turned to farce,' she replied. 'Let's proceed. If she's something to do with the art game here, she might like to have a look at The Monty. It's a kind of landmark, prominent in the gossip column. More than prominent: central. And she gets lucky. You're there, and you leave while she's watching. This she immediately recognizes as super-important. She changes her objective – not Ralph and The Monty. You. She could have seen your picture in the newspaper. She's an opportunist. She knows how to adapt fast to a new situation. You're it, Bas.'

'I'm sure there was no green Peugeot in the club car park.' He noted the daft feebleness of this as he spoke it. But he mustn't let her completely commandeer the talk. Say *something*, idiocy or not.

'Of course there wasn't a green Peugeot in the club car park.

She's cleverer than that. She's not going to announce her presence. She was doing a bit of clandestine surveillance. She'd most probably be parked on the road. No green Peugeot in the car park, naturally, but try to remember, Bas, did you get a green Peugeot in your mirror on the trip to Silver Bells?'

He objected to that 'try to remember'. He wasn't senile, nor a dim kid. 'But I wouldn't be watching for a green Peugeot,' he said.

'I didn't ask whether you'd be watching for it. I asked whether you'd seen it. Somewhere behind. Not immediately on your tail, but staying with you for the whole journey, possibly hidden for part of the time by intervening vehicles, like in TV cop dramas.'

'But why do you say she's in the art game?' he replied.

'Not as precise as that. I suggested she might be. It's a guess.'

'Based on what, though, Irene?'

'You're to do with art. Ember is apparently thinking about art for the club. These could be pointers, couldn't they? She might be from one of those "facilitator" art firms, mightn't she? Same as yourself. Have you seen her at auctions, in galleries?'

Had he? Did her question put the notion into his head that, yes, maybe he *had* seen someone like her? But he couldn't have said when or where. And why had it taken Irene to bring the memory out from him? While Peugeot woman had actually been on view – in the nursery, or on the pavement afterwards – he hadn't even for a moment thought he recognized her.

Irene said: 'What does she look like? Is she striking, memorable?'

He felt he'd better be careful answering this. It might irritate Irene if he'd thought Peugeot woman striking, memorable. 'I'd remember her, supposing she were memorable, wouldn't I, Irene? She's tall, hair somewhere between fair and brown, squarish face.'

'Friendly?'

'Not that I noticed.'

'Lively? Animated? Vivacious?'

'Which?'

'Boobs?'

'Probably.'

'Age?'

'About thirty, or late twenties.'

'Which?'

'Difficult.'

'It's important. Ask any woman.'

'Can't help.'

'Ring? Rings?'

'Couldn't say.'

'Accent?'

'Not local.'

'London?'

'Not cockney.'

'Refined? Educated?'

'Possibly.'

'Smart? Good clothes?'

Pricey, low-slung jeans, blue shirt, hip-length navy jacket. Fairly striking. But he said: 'I didn't notice. I was more interested in the conversation, although, as we know, it turned out dud.'

'Did she seem to know you? I mean, by sight?' Irene asked.

'I don't think so.'

'She's thorough. She's daring. To follow you into Silver Bells for a possible glimpse of what you were up to would need some boldness, some professional acumen. She could be a fieldworker, accustomed to go doggedly after what she needs to find out. When you spoke to her, did you get the feeling it wasn't really the nursery that interested her? Did you suspect *you* might be her target? If I'm right, and she's a real operator, she'd know by training and practice, not just TV, how to road-tail you undetected. Conceivably, she had a gun on her from the nursery when you intercepted her afterwards.'

Enz had heard Irene do this before – build a narrative, a plausible narrative, even where there was a bundle of uncertainties. And he saw a bundle here. Who was the woman? Had she learned of The Monty and the Blake stupidity? Did these interest her enough to make her determined to see the club? If so, *why* did they interest her? Had she been outside The Monty, watching it when he left? Did she follow him to the nursery and actually *into* the nursery? Did the conversation on the pavement show he believed she'd been after a gun? Did she, in fact, have a gun on her when they spoke?

Irene's version took in several of these questions – the main ones – and provided answers. Reasonable answers? Well, pretty reasonable, and she knew how to spell out her points with force and shape. Yes, that confidence and perkiness he'd listed among her qualities earlier, remarkable and very wonderful in someone with absolutely no memorable figures among her forerunners.

'I suppose, Bas,' she said, 'that what we need to decide first is which was the bigger mistake – putting the bullets into Blake, or feeling so guilty about putting the bullets into Blake that you give up the gun to Ember.'

No, Enz would have liked to reply, but didn't, *that isn't the priority. It's intellectual fucking flimflam and philosophizing. The immediate need is to guess, and guess right, whether it would be a doomed mission for me to go and ask Ember to return the Smith and Wesson.* Another refusal after Timmins would really clobber his morale. He said: 'Ember's a moody sod.'

People on the telly seemed to be getting very steamed about clips from a French film. Enz switched off vision also. And then, as he should have expected, Irene quit the waffle area and went very practical. 'In a way, it's sadly ironic, isn't it?'

That was one of her favourite chichi words – ironic, meaning contradictory, as diagnosed by those with acute sensitivity. 'What is?'

'Well, one of the reasons you felt so compelled to make a big thing of your apology was you wanted Ember to reverse his ban on you. Yet the place is a total, undeniable dump, isn't it? Should anyone care about being banned, especially you?'

Enz had thought of this, naturally, but he'd tried not to think of it too much. Male members of his family in the past would have been elected to top-notch London clubs – The Reform or even Boodle's. Now, here was their descendant fretting about expulsion from The Monty, eleven, Shield Terrace. Not a cheerful idea. Yes, he wanted to hold on to what he had, or what he used to have: The Monty, and the business that The Monty might put his way if things between Ralph and him were smoothed. Giving back the pistol to Enz would prove things had been smoothed.

'Why are you so keen to get the gun, anyway?' Irene said.

'There's activity. I can smell it.'

'What sort?'

'Not sure.'

'Peugeot woman a part of it?'

'You thought that yourself, didn't you, Irene? You cited the art connection via "I Spy", Ralph, me. I might need some protection – self-protection.'

Irene looked alarmed, but, of course, she would have realized that if he needed a gun he must feel threatened. To hear him speak the thought, though, as something matter-of-fact, something obvious, seemed to make it more actual for her. She nodded a couple of times, hurriedly, as if wanting urgently to put distance between what she felt now and her previous cool brusqueness. 'So, yes, perhaps you should try Ember.' She stood and came and bent to put her arms around him in his chair. 'Meanwhile,' she said, 'you're at home, with no notable art on the walls, but safe. I think we should go to bed now.'

TWENTY-THREE

Ralph had a visitor at the club early in the evening. At the time he was busy with his rampart. He'd had this brought down from its usual spot near the ceiling and laid across the seats of three straight-backed chairs, as if taking a due rest after its long vigilance at altitude and its vulnerability to mad gunfire. Pulleys and ropes lay behind it when the slab was on station, and a barman had brought a ladder and gone up to fix the descent.

Although *The Marriage Of Heaven And Hell* illustration had been very skilfully repaired after the shooting, Ralph thought he detected a hint of a join where bullet holes in the beard had been worked on and the treated surface then restuck; *only* a hint, but enough to trouble Ralph. He'd noticed this from ground level while the steel rectangle was still in place above, and it had been brought down temporarily so that he could look more closely at the spot. He was afraid the heated atmosphere of the club when crowded would cause curling of the join's edges, giving a dilapidated look to the picture, like some old, untended placard. Also, the loosened, drooping segments might become unpleasantly discoloured.

This was the very opposite effect he craved from the Blake, of course. Its purpose was to bring distinction and elegance to The Monty, not scruffiness. He'd admit that the picture was only decor. The equipment's chief function was to stop Ralph getting his head blown apart while sitting behind the bar at his little accounting desk. The painting had no real relevance to this. It was the metal, not the print, that gave Ember protection. But appearance did matter. It had to contribute positively to The Monty's aura and image. Several Monty members might have heard of William Blake, owing to *Jerusalem* and the stuff about building on the green belt. They'd know he was near the top of the pile with some of the greatest poetic names, and they'd feel, as Ralph did, that The Monty garnered some of that quality by having *The Marriage Of Heaven And Hell* so prominent. Although Ember intended to bring The Monty up to the social standard of the best London clubs, he realized that, say, The Athenaeum would have neither the elevated rampart nor the Blake illustration in its bar. They would be regarded as unnecessary and non-metropolitan. But, for the present, The Monty had problems that would not affect The Athenaeum, and Ralph needed to devise special precautions for his club and for himself.

He knew he could easily get a new copy of *The Marriage Of Heaven And Hell*, but he'd been keen to show that the damage caused by that prick Enzyme would be righted *in*, as it were, *situ*. *The Marriage Of Heaven And Hell* rebuilt was a demonstration that appalling behaviour like Enzyme's could be effectively countered. It was a kind of home-grown, resourceful triumph over gross malevolence. Sending away for a new copy would be like a defeat, Ralph thought; an admission that outside aid was needed as an answer to Enz. Also, there would be a delay because the book illustration of the Blake needed considerable enlargement for use on the bastion, and this would require high-grade photographic handling, by a separate firm.

He saw now that he was correct. Although the reconstruction of the beard had been carried out with brilliant care and delicacy, to someone with the kind of uncompromising, scrutinizing eye of Ralph, it was still palpably a mend. Something of a small revelation came to him then: did he need to confine his thinking to *The Marriage Of Heaven And Hell*, or even to Blake? Certainly, Blake was important, but not unique when it came to prettying up a defensive length of steel. Ralph asked himself: why shouldn't he win something positive from the situation and scrap the impaired pic? Forget about ordering a new copy and, instead, get an utterly fresh topic by a completely different artist? This would help demonstrate, wouldn't it, that The Monty's proprietor had range, as well as taste; was not confined to some isolated bit of knowledge he might have picked up by fluke, such as *The Marriage Of Heaven And Hell*, but had a magnificently broad outlook which would almost certainly lead ultimately to transformation of The Monty?

Ralph wondered whether there was a picture somewhere of Spartan women leaving some babies out in filthy weather on cliffs or mountainsides so they would either toughen up for the wars or snuff it. He liked classical references. That kind of illustration – coloured, or black and white – was bound to bring a very intriguing aspect to the barrier. A pity Enzyme's mother hadn't left him out as an infant for too long in a storm on a cliff – for, say, three weeks, supposing the ancient Greeks had weeks.

He put his hand gently on *The Marriage Of Heaven And Hell*, particularly at the wound area. It did feel secure, despite the undeniable sign of restoration. Naturally, a fondness for the Blake had established itself in Ralph. It had helped take care of his safety for quite a while now and had more or less come through that deplorable Enzyme savagery intact. But Ralph refused to sentimentalize for more than a couple of moments. Progress might require brave, hard action. To have the Blake scraped off and discarded would be rather like taking a loved old dog or cat to the vet to be put down. He hated to think of the noise caused by the removal. It would be metal on metal, a chisel or something like and the steel of the barrier. The sound would be so impersonal – a screeching, insistent, heartless din, a sort of suitably atrocious background music to betrayal of the Blakeian figure.

Occasionally, though, decisions about change must be resolutely taken. He'd do some Googling to see if he could find an illustrated volume about the history of Sparta and its conquest of Messina. He wondered whether those Spartan children who survived had a warrior look to them, even as toddlers. This kind of classical example would show club members that, yes, life was difficult and challenging – to take a modish term – but, also, that ways of dealing with those difficulties, these challenges, could be, and should be, prepared in advance.

True, some Monty members wilfully brought difficulties on themselves via lawless and/or violent lives, and probably no amount of lessons from legendary, BC Greece would impress them. But these were the kind of members he wanted to be rid of as The Monty developed. Ralph would rigorously apply his own survival tests then in deciding which requests for membership should be accepted. Clearly, no cliffs or mountainsides would be involved, but he meant to use a strict selection procedure just the same. He had something precious to look after here – namely, The Monty – just as those children who beat pneumonia and croup grew up to look after their precious homeland, Sparta.

'Why, Mr Ember, you look as if you're giving the kiss of life to a stranded whale.'

He recognized the mix of British and US accents and intonations at once in this boom-boom, heckling voice. 'Mrs Lamb!' he said, looking up from the doctored rip. 'This is a surprise.' So true: she plainly wasn't a member personally, but nor had her son Jack ever come to the club.

'Well, no, not a stranded whale,' she replied. 'Nothing like so defeated and helpless. This is the celebrated flying buttress there's been so much gossip and laughter about, isn't it, as featured mischievously in "I Spy"?'

'I wouldn't call it gossip and laughter,' Ralph said. 'There has certainly been a report in the Press of certain rumours, but rumours of a really quite unpardonable, serious incident.' He realized he must sound heavy and plonking but, fuck it, he wasn't going to have this noisy old baggage mess him about. 'I don't feel "mischievous" is the term for that Press tone,' he said. 'Flippant and irresponsible, rather. Yes, made something of in "I Spy", but how does the rhyme "I Spy" go on? It's "I spy with my little eye", isn't it? This little eye is incapable of seeing large, grave issues. It's a kind of pathetic blindness.'

'And now you've brought it down to give a health check to the star of the depiction, yes? You must feel almost as naked as he is to be without your usual sentry in the upper reaches, Ralph.'

She had on a sort of Sherlock Holmesian long, tan greatcoat with anti-storm panels fronting each shoulder. She wore a big-peaked navy cap and navy and white training boots. She must be around six feet, thin faced, too juttingly aquiline. 'Is there some way I can help you, Mrs Lamb?' Ember replied.

'Alice.'

'Alice.' He hadn't wanted first names. She'd started just now with 'Mr Ember', which was fine and proper. But she must feel they had already progressed in comradeliness during their talk: stupid of her. She shouldn't be here at all, and especially not to make fun of the grounded, special – in fact, probably unique – literary fitment. Ralph had an idea, though, that this was how a certain kind of American woman would behave by nature – just breezing in to a private facility because she wanted to, no other justification, never mind how unappealingly dressed, and because to her an open door said she would be welcome to go through it. Presumptuous. Boundaryless. She might answer that she wasn't American, only an American import; but enough of her was that full US thing to explain the casualness and cheek of her approach now. None of her clothes would have been big enough for Jack, so they were not borrowed, she had actually bought them somewhere, and sales staff must have kept a straight face until she was out of the store. Although foul, the items did not look cheap. 'I need a private confab, Ralph, if you don't mind,' she said.

If you don't mind. But her thinking plainly was that he *wouldn't* mind. This was more of that cool, egomaniac audacity. 'The club will start to get into its stride soon, and I—'

'*Before* it gets into its stride. Why I came early. This shouldn't take us more than fifteen minutes.'

Ralph gave orders that the fortification should be hoisted back for the rest of the evening and night. It was occupying too much space and the three bar chairs. He showed Alice Lamb to his office.

'Our attitude in the States to some events is not at all like yours, Ralph,' she said, almost as soon as she'd sat down. 'When I say "yours", I'm not getting at you as an individual. I'm talking of Brits in general. OK, once again I have to say, yes, I'm a Brit, too, but other factors have affected me during my years over there.'

'That's natural.' Regrettable, but natural.

'I want to mention something to see how you evaluate it – that is, you as a Brit, but also you as you.'

Him as him. Who else could he be? 'Interesting,' he said. Ralph kept a bottle of Kressmann Armagnac and some brandy glasses in the office, and he poured drinks for her and himself now.

'I do quite a bit of horse riding while I'm with Jack on holiday,' she said, after taking a sip and nodding to show that she recognized the quality: very smooth, slightly and satisfyingly dry, sugarless. 'He keeps several very fine mounts at Darien. Sometimes I'm alone, sometimes with Jack's live-in, Helen, a sweet, bright kid. Very occasionally Jack will join us. Well, Helen and I were out the other day, Chase Woods area, and what did we come upon, d'you think?'

She did a deep, theatrical, *mea culpa* groan. 'That's a stupid thing to ask you, because you can't have any idea of what we came upon. It's me doing my nursery tale performance, from when I used to make up stories for Jack as a kid, some years ago now, keeping him alert with the question. Often I slip back into that mother mood when I'm visiting GB.' She paused, smiled for a moment, perhaps enjoying memories of Jack as a small boy, well before he reached six foot five and over 250lbs. Ralph found it almost touching and almost genuine.

She left that mood. 'Anyway, what we come across is – you know Chase Woods, naturally. Not far from your house, Low Pastures. On a slope. Part of it overlooks Jack's place. Darien.

We're nearing the end of our ride when we sort of surprise a woman doing what that explorer does in the poem that Jack took the name of his home from. You'll remember, Ralph. "Stout Cortez" in the Keats sonnet gazes at the Pacific from his spot up that mountain in Darien, Panama. This woman is gazing – is gazing with field glasses – not at the Pacific, no, but gazing at the property. This is a thorough, methodical examination of the building and grounds. Alongside her, there's a green Peugeot. She's solo.'

'There are great views of three counties from the edge of the woods,' Ember said.

'Yeah, maybe. But she's not concerned with great views of the counties. She's casing Darien.'

'Famous for the views. In guidebooks. She's a tourist, maybe.'

'This tourist isn't aware of us until too late. The horses are walking only, not much noise. We can see her before she knows we're there. Suddenly, she does hear. What does she do? She turns and – very fast, but not fast enough – opens a rear door of the car and shoves the field glasses under a coat on the rear seat. Also, while the door is open, she leans in and adjusts something on the front passenger seat. Then she closes the door very softly, so as not to pull our eyes in that direction. But this is a case of shutting the door after the horses have turned up behind her. If a visitor is simply out looking for vintage views, why should she worry about being caught taking the views through field glasses? That's one of the things field glasses are for – helping with views, wouldn't you say, Ralph?'

'It's a fine, old manor house. She might be interested in the history of important country dwellings, as are many. And this particular country property apparently had quite a role in the Civil War, on the king's side. Perhaps the woman is a student, doing a thesis and looking to see how Darien would be placed strategically if there was a seventeenth-century skirmish in, say, Chase Woods.'

'We talked total shit,' Alice Lamb replied, 'the three of us. No surnames. No mention of Darien. Van Gogh, yes. Wind farms, yes. San Francisco, where I have a condo, yes. Nature, yes, my ex-husband, yes. Your place, Low Pastures and its chimneys, *yes*; power stations, yes.' Her voice rose like an oration. She took some more Kressmann's. 'Jack's place, under our noses, impressive and significant, no. Helen gets down and has a stroll around the Peugeot but sees nothing out of the ordinary. A closed ring binder on the passenger seat. This woman's mapping Darien and its surrounds? Was she shutting the ring binder in that move after hiding the field glasses? She doesn't intend us to see maybe notes and sketches that might give away her focus on Darien? She's made sure nothing can be read there from outside. There's a bulge under the coat on the back seat, according to Helen. Of course, Ralph, you'll remember that Conan Doyle, Sherlock Holmes tale?'

Was that why she had the coat on? Did she dress to suit a forthcoming topic? Perhaps Jack's occasional taste for army surplus was inherited, with a slight amendment, from his mother. 'Which?' he said.

'The dog that didn't bark. Normally, in mysteries a dog that *does* bark helps the detective deduce something vital. Here, the opposite. It's silent. That seeming negative turns out to be a priceless, positive clue for Sherlock. Same kind of thing in the Barbara Stanwyck *Double Indemnity* film. Why didn't the murdered husband make a claim on an accident insurance policy although he'd broken his leg? Answer: he didn't know the policy existed. His wife wanted to cash in on his death. Likewise, Ralph, why didn't this woman refer even for a moment to Darien*?* I'll tell you: because it was Darien alone that concerned her, and she excluded it from the conversation in case this became obvious. Well, it did become obvious, when the woman tried so blatantly to keep it *un*obvious. The omission was very flagrant, Ralph, and very meaningful.'

Ember had done the scepticism reaction to what she said, more or less by instinct. He would have discouraged anyone who floated ideas that might make a complicated situation more complicated. Alice Lamb had a badgering, unduly frank kind of approach to things, and some of those things could involve him. Well, already involved him. She'd done all that 'I Spy' rubbish and the stranded fucking whale. Ralph considered her brashness and lack of tact could be dangerous. He decided she'd better not have any more Kressmann's although her balloon was empty. 'What was she like, this woman?' he asked.

'When we read in the Press of private art collections getting pillaged, the report will almost always carry the cliché "well-organized",' she replied. 'But of course well-organized. It's not like stealing an apple from a greengrocer's pavement stall, is it? The account will often say that there must have been a long spell of observation pre-strike. What the Peugeot woman seemed to be doing, Ralph, was one part of that "spell of observation" – getting and noting down all aspects of the building – doors, windows, especially, of course. Any ladders about? Dogs? And perhaps she tried to estimate how many people were around the house and grounds and where exactly they seemed to operate. This type of work is her speciality. A pathfinder. She's young for it – twenties. Slim, squarish face, happy-looking, but that could be put on, couldn't it, to back up her pretence at being simply a simple-minded excited visitor, simply delighted by the views? The job is a high skill, I should imagine. She'll report back to associates. They'll act, or not, on her say-so. It's a responsibility.'

'Act?'

'Act to lift some of Jack's art. Maybe all.'

'Have you told him about Peugeot woman?'

'Of course. Immediately we got back, still smelling of horse.'

'And what response?'

She glanced at her empty glass. That fitted the kind of character sketch of her Ralph had formed in his head. If she wanted a drink, another drink, she was the sort who'd more or less say she wanted another drink. Sod politeness and restraint. He poured for both of them. She took a tiny sip. Perhaps she just wanted the Armagnac at hand, reliably available. A weakness? 'Helen had warned me,' she said.

'In what sense?' Ralph said.

'Warned me that Jack wouldn't say or show what he thought of the news. That's how he often is, apparently. There exist bits of his life she doesn't get to know about – all kinds of hidden concerns for him to take care of. Something weird with the cop, Harpur, perhaps? He's up at Darien not long ago and apparently looking at one of the pictures, but obviously not seeing what was actually there. If you ask me, he was getting a terrible vision of something awful that had happened to Jack.

Helen's friendly with Harpur's girlfriend, Denise, but that's no help, I gather.

'Anyway, Helen was right about Jack's attitude to this new info. We mentioned Peugeot woman, gave him the car reg in case he had ways of tracing it. "Thanks," he said, "you've done remarkably well, Ma, Helen." Like, "share top prize for good conduct at school". So I said, "Remarkably well, how, Jack?"

'"Really, remarkably well," he replied, as if that explained everything.

'So, I'm his mother, I don't put up with such evasiveness from him, big as he might be now, and I say, "But what does it tell you, Jack?"

'"What does what tell me?" he replies, if you can call it a reply.

'And Helen says, "I think we'd better leave it there, Alice. Jack's not going to elucidate."

'"Elucidate what?" Jack asks.'

'There are a lot of conversations like that around here,' Ralph replied.

'It wasn't totally negative: Jack goes out into the grounds and looks up at the spot where we'd seen the woman, as though trying to work out what she might have spied. Then he comes back and starts talking about something else altogether, like us up the hill with the wind farms and Van Gogh. And Helen goes along with his useless chit-chat, as though she's seen Jack choke off a topic many times before and realized this was as far as we were going to get.'

'Yes, lots of conversations are ended or switched around here,' Ralph said.

'And you're content with that?' she said.

'It's how it is. You'd get used to it.'

'No, I damn well wouldn't,' she replied.

As she spoke about Jack's mysteriousness and refusal to behave like an obedient son and cough the lot to his mummy, who'd crossed the Atlantic just to be with him, Ember felt a kind of pity for her. She wanted to help her lad, had tried to help him, but he'd brushed her and Helen off with a formal, blank, 'Thanks, you've done remarkably well.' And, as anyone might have followed up if given that treatment, she'd come back with something like, 'OK, we've done remarkably well. Tell me exactly how, would you, please?' His answer, though, had amounted to, 'Fuck off, Mummy, dear.'

Some words of hers came back to Ralph from a telephone conversation a while ago. The Kressmann could sometime sharpen his recall, as now, and sometimes blot it out totally. She'd spoken then like an American moll rather than a mixed-nationality ma. The Monty had been mentioned, and she'd suggested it was the kind of club where '*sotto voce*', illicit, illegal gun deals could take place. Ralph hadn't bothered to contradict her because the remark seemed too ludicrous, so melodramatic. He'd wondered if, possibly, she came from a San Francisco district where clubs had that kind of reputation. He'd decided she probably didn't know, or had forgotten, about the great tradition of English clubs such as Boodle's or The Athenaeum, a tradition Ralph intended to make The Monty a worthy part of in due course, possibly with the help of art.

He still felt like that, but today, in the club with her, he had the sudden conviction that she continued to think The Monty a source of firearms, and she was here to get one. Alice Lamb had come to accept that Helen, the sweet, bright girl who saw Jack virtually every day, was more likely to know his present ways than Alice did. The mother era was over. And Helen had pronounced from her special insights that Jack would not 'elucidate'. But, no, the mother era was not over. Only half over. She retained those feelings towards Jack, but in adulthood Jack's feelings towards her had naturally changed. Something like that happened in all families. Never mind: Alice was determined to do everything possible to look after him. She couldn't tell whether Jack would prepare to counter the possible threat from Peugeot woman and her mates, whoever and wherever they were. Accordingly, Alice had come searching for a piece to protect her boy, Jack, Helen, herself and the art, but above all her boy. How mothers were.

She took quite a pull this time at the Kressmann. 'I expect you can guess why I've come here, Ralph,' she said.

'I feel flattered,' he replied. 'You wanted to talk over a problem – as you perceive it – yes, talk over a perceived problem with someone who knows the general scene, but can bring impartiality and balance.'

'To hell with "talk over". To hell with "impartiality and balance". I want a gun.'

'A gun?' Ralph exclaimed, his voice quite believably taut with shock. 'You want a *gun*?'

TWENTY-FOUR

After that high-security session with Jack in the launderette, Harpur sent for the personnel records of all staff at the Silver Bells And Cockleshells nursery. The owner and everyone who worked there had been deep-vetted before being allowed contact with children; very deep-vetted, following a crop of scandals nationwide. Maybe it was media publicity for these cases that activated the two Oxfam vigilante slobs: Albert with his baseball bat, and Vernon. They'd prevented him from talking to the woman who yelled, from the tree house, to the Peugeot driver to come back. Harpur considered that anyone who yelled from a tree house might be worth talking to, but especially this woman.

He could remember fairly accurately the start of the bellowed message. Two children were standing near her. 'Come back, oh, do come back,' the woman had cried. 'Leave not in such circs, please.' He'd thought of that summons as heartfelt, urgent, poignant. Which 'circs' did she have in mind? Would they justify the quaint syntax of 'leave not'? But he'd had no time then to investigate because he'd needed to get into the Peugeot's slipstream – hopelessly, uselessly, as it turned out: a conversation instead with the Georgian terrace woman who yearned to shed her sarong, preferably with a young electrician, but Harpur would have been OK.

Among the vetting papers he found the dossier he wanted. A photograph was captioned 'Fern Jocelyn Beatty, aged fifty-three' and gave an address in Daynton Gardens. Harpur had been too far away from the tree house for him to make out detail of her appearance, but the photograph confirmed his impression of her: Rounded, chubby features, grey hair inexpertly cut, a burly neck and wide shoulders. She was in her fourth year at Silver Bells. Before that she'd been employed as a local-authority carer and had a five-year spell in another children's nursery. The vetting had produced nothing dubious. The earlier nursery described her conduct as 'exemplary, if sometimes slightly combative'. She was married, with a grown-up daughter who had moved out.

The Beatty address was not far from Silver Bells And Cockleshells, and Harpur drove over and decided he would drop in at the Oxfam shop en route. He might be able to get a brief giggle at Albert and Vernon, who possibly still sported damage brought by Iles responding briskly to their call. Harpur hoped they'd be on duty.

He parked at what he'd come to think of as his personal timed spot and went into the shop. They were both there behind the counter, Albert not at all facially marked but with what looked like a wrist in plaster. He must have tried to break his fall with one hand when Iles crash-tackled him. Vernon had bruising on one cheek near his ear, a reminder of the ACC's punch. 'Well, lads,' Harpur said, 'you're a worthy couple. No malingering, despite injuries.' He studied the used-book shelves. 'Damn it,' he said, 'would you believe this, not one copy of *The Practical Guide To Pederasty*?' He left the shop muttering disappointed curses and drove to Daynton Gardens. It was a Saturday and the nursery would be closed. Fern might be at home.

She answered the door when Harpur rang the bell. 'Harpur,' he said. 'Detective Chief Superintendent. Routine. Nothing to get anxious about. We do a vetting update after a four-year period in any post. New legislation owing to some of the bad instances we've all heard about and deplored, I'm sure.'

'Oh, certainly.'

'Absolutely. And there's an incident I'd like to discuss, which may or may not be of relevance. Best deal with it, though. Clear it out of the way if it is something isolated and harmless.'

'Incident?'

'An incident not actually within the nursery; more a kind of street incident.'

'Will you come in?' she said.

'Thank you.'

She took Harpur to a pleasant sitting room. It was very simply furnished, the floorboards sanded and varnished, no carpet, two big settees in leather and two matching armchairs. Three abstract paintings in broad white frames hung on the walls, not an artistic style Harpur normally went for, but he found the bright coloured blobs, wisps, and rectangles very nicely ordered here. Fern might have her strange mouthy moments and spells of combativeness, as the dossier alleged, but somebody in the house had taste.

A man of about Fern's age, heavily built, lantern jawed, was in one of the armchairs reading the *New Statesman,* a Leftish political magazine. He stood to shake hands with Harpur and spoke his name, 'Leonard Beatty.'

Harpur said: 'Colin Harpur.' He took the other armchair.

Fern sat opposite on a settee. 'My husband, Leonard,' she said. 'This is Mr Harpur, a police officer, Len. About the nursery.'

'Private?' Leonard said.

'A formality, that's all,' Harpur said.

'Mr Harpur says an incident,' Fern said.

'Could mean nothing or anything,' Harpur replied.

'Right,' Leonard said.

Harpur saw that Beatty meant to stay. He sat down again and put the magazine on the floor. Harpur guessed Beatty wanted to hear and remember what was said: no police interview trickery. When he'd asked, 'Private?' he'd seemed about to leave her and Harpur alone. That was before Fern announced 'an incident', though. He'd obviously grown wary, suspicious. Perhaps he knew of Fern's tendency to sound off, maybe sound off recklessly. Leonard would watch and witness, maybe make her apply the brakes now and then. Leonard was a *New Statesman* reader.

Harpur had made some basic notes from Fern's file and went over these with her now, as if they needed checking and possible revising. He had also written down his recollection of the full Fern statement from the tree house to the Peugeot woman.

'What incident, exactly?' Beatty asked. He might have recognized that the run-through of elementary dossier information was a cover only, an excuse for calling. Leonard was a *New Statesman* reader.

'Yes,' Harpur replied. 'One of our people, a girl called Margot, happened to be in Brendan Street at the time – had been dropping some unwanted clothes off at the charity shop. There's an Oxfam outlet near the nursery, you know.'

'One of whose people?' Leonard asked.

'As she emerged on to the pavement she heard a woman calling out in a rather unusual way,' Harpur replied. 'She looked about and saw that the shouted requests were coming from a woman standing with two children in the nursery's tree house. She appeared to be addressing – at a distance – a younger woman, who was about to get into a green Peugeot saloon car and who stood for a while listening and then waved and left. Margot said the message from the tree house had what she called "a plaintive undertow".' Harpur read from his notes. 'She memorized the words as something like this: "Come back, oh, do. Leave not in such circs, please."' Harpur looked up from his papers. 'Margot was certain about having that last sentence verbatim because of the strange "leave not" and the shortening – "circs".'

'You think this woman in the tree house, broadcasting, was Fern?' Beatty asked Harpur. 'You called out that, Fern?' Leonard asked. 'But who to?'

'Sometimes I get very frustrated at the nursery,' she said.

'That "leave not" – it could be adapted from a Shakespeare construction with the imperative, couldn't it?' Leonard said.

'Could it?' Harpur replied.

'But sort of reversed,' Leonard said. 'Lady Macbeth wanting to clear a room where Banquo's ghost has, in fact, been messing up the circs, says, "Stand not upon the order of your going, but go!"'

Harpur went back to his notes. 'The tree house shouting continued: "Oh, please. I've a lot to say. We didn't speak, did we? Do, do return. So much to comment on about him and various matters. Yes, re him and various matters."'

'Would you say "re", Fern?' Leonard asked.

Harpur had thought 're' the kind of term someone called Margot might use. He said: 'It could have been "about", I suppose. Margot didn't claim perfect recall.' He read again:

'"Yes, re him and various matters. Who are you? Who *really* are you? Is there truly a prospective Christine?"'

'You said all this, Fern? Has Harpur got it right? Who's "him"? Who's Christine?'

'Margot's pretty sure that's what she said,' Harpur replied.

'A *prospective* Christine?' Beatty said. 'What the hell does it mean, Fern?'

She paused for a while, staring at one of the abstracts, as if that were the topic. Then she shrugged. She'd decided to talk. 'Well, yes, there'd been some trouble at the nursery,' she said. 'Why I spoke of frustration. But very minor trouble. Something not worth boring you with at the time, Len.'

'I'd have preferred to hear,' Beatty said.

Harpur had the notion that Fern might fall into strange outbursts and then come to regret them, feel ashamed of them, keep quiet about them. The spells of 'combativeness' might produce one of these outbursts. So might 'frustration'.

'Well, of course, everyone's very sensitive to things about children's nurseries these days, so Margot mentions this incident to me as baffling,' Harpur said. 'I sent for the vetting documents, and Margot was able to identify Fern from the photograph there.' Harpur refolded his papers. Nice work, Margot. 'And so I opted to look into the situation myself. Why I'm here. Just to make sure everything is OK.'

'*Is* everything OK, Fern?' Len sounded angry, as if fiercely offended that Harpur should know more about his wife's behaviour at work than he did. Harpur *and* Margot that would be. Leonard probably resented that he'd been put at a disadvantage with police. Len read the *New Statesman*.

'The "him"?' Fern said. 'That's a man called Loam who comes to the nursery now and then and something goes on between him and Judy Timmins.'

'What goes on?' Beatty asked.

'Something very private,' Fern said.

'Goes on where?' Beatty replied.

'In her office,' Fern said.

'Judy Timmins is the proprietor, yes?' Harpur said.

'Loam's family are supposed to be something special,' Fern said. 'Tea.'

'Yes,' Leonard said. 'Well-known. Very big-time capitalist merchants in the past.'

'This is taking place within metres of the children,' Fern said.

'What is?' Beatty asked.

'But today there was some sort of quarrel, and he stamped off in a rage. I was afraid this might upset a very charming young woman who was in the nursery at the time about bringing a child there. She left, probably puzzled by it all, perhaps unfavourably impressed by Silver Bells.'

'Christine?' Beatty said.

'Yes, her daughter, Christine. So I tried to call her back. It struck me as a duty to try and convince her that, despite what had happened, her daughter would be fine in the nursery. She waved, but drove away.'

Yes, she did, didn't she? 'That explains things,' Harpur said. 'But I did need to check. I can tell Margot now what it was all about and put her mind at ease.' Harpur, also, was glad to get the tree house episode interpreted by Fern, and to learn that Basil Loam had been involved in some sort of disturbance there. Sexual? Or, if Jack Lamb's launderette confidences were correct, it could be to do with something different. Harpur stood. 'Thanks,' he said. 'Interview over.'

Beatty said: 'I feel we've been so remiss, offering no refreshment.'

Leonard had been determined to stay in the room throughout the meeting with Fern. He'd undoubtedly have regarded it as slack and irresponsible if he'd gone to boil a kettle. Leonard read the *New Statesman*.

TWENTY-FIVE

Enzyme thought of going out to Ralph Ember's home, Low Pastures, to ask for the return of the .38 Smith and Wesson automatic following that brazen, odiously antisocial refusal of Timmins to provide a replacement. He felt it was the kind of transaction that might need a special, delicate approach, and The Monty couldn't always be relied on to provide these conditions. Also, of course, The Monty was where Enz had blasted the Blake. Theoretically, Enz knew he was still banned from the club, although he had tried to smooth things at that previous visit when they'd discussed art for The Monty and Enz had generously undertaken to help find the right kind of paintings.

It might not be wise or effective to make a plea to Ember beneath what he'd probably regard as the grievously insulted *Marriage Of Heaven And Hell*. Enzyme thought Ralph kept his anger at that escapade very strong in his memory, despite later developments. Enzyme's couple of jokey shots at the Blake were coming to seem more significant than the ones that assassinated the Archduke Ferdinand and his wife in Sarajevo, starting the Great War in 1914.

If Enz went to see Ember at the club he would be more or less saying, 'OK, Ralph, I handed over the pistol to you as genuine proof of utter regret, so it's all totally dealt with. Now, I'd like it back, please, on account of that creature Timmins turning grossly obstructive, regardless of my fine customer record there and the general respect due to my name and family.' The reconstituted Blake would be present, reminding Ralph of the beard injury to some ancient naked guy on all fours and signalling to him that there should be no forgiveness, *could* be no forgiveness.

Enz recognized that Ralph might not have taken the gun home from The Monty and wouldn't be able immediately to give it back. This wasn't important. Enz could drop in to the club and pick it up discreetly once everything had been agreed. It was the negotiations, the agreement, that he considered would be best carried out at Low Pastures, the actual transfer being a formality only. He considered that at Ralph's historic manor house there would be an atmosphere of good fellowship and gentlemanly mutual respect. This would lead to swift and trustworthy concord between two men of widely acknowledged, imperishable status. The fact that Enz's children were at the same private school as Ralph's would obviously strengthen that feeling of social similarity between Ember and him. Enzyme had heard that in some parts of Low Pastures the walls had been left as bare, original stone, no tarting up with plaster, paper and/or paint. He liked this idea. It went to the rugged, durable essence of things. The talk between him and Ralph would be of that wholly honest and reliable quality.

He told Irene of his plan. At once he could see it troubled her. In fact, he'd considered *not* telling her. That would have been untypical, but he'd sensed somehow that she would have doubts. He thought of simply going ahead and then producing the gun at home when the children were not about, and recounting to an astonished Irene how he had done it – explaining to her the kind of four-square, honest understanding that could come into play between two men of very parallel civic standing. Enz would have ensured, though, that he did not make this sound like a male boast. Some women were probably almost capable of a similar, good experience, and he would have certainly stressed this, so as not to irritate her. He knew Irene could get touchy about all that sort of tripe.

However, habit had been too powerful for Enzyme. It would have entailed quite a break from usual practice for him to take on something as large-scale and chancy as this without consulting Irene. So he mentioned the Low Pastures strategy he fancied and made himself ready to listen to her reaction, but also, perhaps, to argue for his idea if she were sceptical. And he suspected she'd be sceptical.

It was evening again, the children in bed, the TV off. She sat curled up on a chair holding a rum and black as a change, he in another chair with a large vodka and tonic again. 'Obviously, I don't know Ralph Ember as well as you do, Bas, but I wonder if going to his house is the right way to approach him about something like this.'

Meaning, of course, that she didn't wonder at all. She clearly believed it the *wrong* way to approach him about something like this. 'Oh, Ralphy has his difficult sides. Who doesn't? But he can be managed,' Enz said.

'You always make him sound so implacable in his attitude to the William Blake shemozzle.'

Enz saw that the choice of the slangy word 'shemozzle' was clever. It made her sound as if she backed Enz's notion that the rampart incident was trivial, but also let her smuggle in another word, 'implacable', which said something like the direct opposite – and which came before shemozzle in her comment, and so had more impact. 'Ralph has to show a bit of temper,' Enz replied. 'A macho thing. Pride. Image. Face. But what we have to remember, Irene, is that Ralphy is a proprietor who longs to introduce some class into the club. Under that obligatory, tedious show of landlordism, he'll appreciate that people of some breeding will occasionally do things when in a relaxed mood that they would usually quite disapprove of. But high-jinks, nothing more. For me to talk to him at his home would be a sort of boys-will-be-boys situation, not a small-minded, niggly blame interlude about rumpled decor and a couple of sauce bottle ricochets.'

'Always when you spoke of Ember in the past, I had an impression of someone very compartmentalized,' she replied.

'In what way?'

'His home and his family and the kids' schooling are one area of his life, and the club and his trafficking business are a different area: a very definite and unbridgeable division. The gun is surely very much a club matter. There was the shooting and then the surrender of the pistol, as you've described it to me. Both happened in The Monty. If you go out to his home hunting for a point thirty-eight automatic pistol that lately did some illicit pop-pops, won't you be trying to bring those two very calculatedly separate aspects of his existence together, a sort of shotgun marriage of heaven and hell?

'Don't you think he'll resist that? I fear he might, Bas. He'll see it as your sly, wholly unacceptable way of getting around the Monty ban and tell you to sod off from Low Pastures and its acres. I'm not saying that would be justifiable. But I *am* saying it would probably happen, given the kind of man you're dealing with. Of course, the gun wasn't always identified with The Monty. I became aware you had a pistol, but it was never used, as far as I knew. I could tolerate that. In your line of work some self-protection might be necessary, even though possession is illegal. Like in the Cold War, this was a dormant deterrent. But it moved into a different category, didn't it, once you opened up on Ember's pet parapet?'

'But, look, Irene, I've put things right with Ralph by promising to give him max help with art acquisitions for The Monty. He really appreciated that offer.'

'Did he?'

'The art game is totally strange for him. We're talking very big money here – perhaps. He could make catastrophic mistakes if he acts alone. He thinks of buying from Jack Lamb. That might or might not be sensible. Jack generally has some rather unprovenanced stuff to market, though. I've said I'll check any possible purchase. I know Ralph is grateful. He recognizes there are far bigger issues involved in picture buying than in an admittedly foolish moment banging off at an illustrated print.'

'You sure?'

TWENTY-SIX

They met where they sometimes met – as an alternative to George Dinnick's Kensington flat – in the restaurant-coffee bar of the Oss Gallery in Piccadilly, not far from Hyde Park. George had a half share with a cousin in the Oss and apparently liked to run some of their confabs here because the setting would remind him that they were in a worthwhile, even noble, trade. There were good, authentic works for sale on the gallery walls under suitable lighting and a constant parade of potential buyers.

Liz enjoyed something of the same feelings, but there would be occasions when this cheerful, slightly smug mood didn't last. It was the thing about moods – they came and went. And this one didn't last today. Liz hadn't been stupid enough to suppose that it would. She knew that what she would say was not what George wanted to hear. She'd say it anyway, though. She believed she had to, for Justin's sake. But if George came to suspect it was for Justin's sake and not the firm's, she thought he could become very unforgiving.

The three of them had their customary coffees and their customary table. Liz gave them her final fieldwork report. 'Much as previously,' she said, 'but some serious new factors, in my view. They stem from what would seem at first of no account, even absurd. Someone, probably drunk, fired a gun in a rough-house club one night. No injuries, but damage to a William Blake illustration that seems to have been emblematic of something for the club owner. It gave a sort of cultural tinge to a place that could badly do with it. So, there were repercussions – why I said, "serious new factors". They led to what I have to describe as a lot of unfortunate activity.'

'Oh?' George said, and Liz could sense at once that she'd been sharp to expect trouble.

Justin seemed to sense something wrong, too, and tried to give her some help. He said: 'Liz has come across some real potential difficulties, George. We're probably very lucky she went on this second scouring. But that's just like Liz, isn't it?'

'You two have talked about these supposed "serious new factors", have you?' George replied.

'Liz did give me an outline,' Justin said.

Naturally, she had spoken to Justin about her new information. Didn't her anxieties ultimately centre on him?

'Sometimes I feel like an outsider with you two,' George said.

'No, George, no. Liz and I think constantly about the firm, its health, its future,' Justin said.

'Yes?' George replied. 'So, what "serious new factors", Liz?'

His tone hammered her. 'I was doing a standard re-look at the possible target property, Jack Lamb's Darien, when two women on horseback suddenly appeared out of woodland, sort of stealthy, sneaky.'

'They're on horseback, but you didn't hear them approach?' George said.

'Well, yes, I did, but not in time,' Liz said.

'How not in time?' George asked.

'I was using field glasses on Darien to get a full result and extend our familiarity with it. I hid the field glasses fast when I heard their approach, but it might not have been quickly enough.'

'Who were they?' George asked.

'This is the point, George,' Justin said. 'They didn't tell Liz that. She thinks they actually avoided telling her that.'

She saw that Justin was doing what he could to divert some of George's hostility from her, and she was grateful. She didn't think it would work, though. Always there had been this hazard. George wouldn't worry about Justin and her being lovers, as long as this didn't hurt Cog. She could tell he suspected now that their affair, and Justin's safety, were getting priority.

'I recognized them from before, of course,' Liz said. 'We've got them on film. Almost certainly these two were Lamb's live-in partner, Surtees, and his mother over from the States. She actually spoke of her home in San Francisco.'

Justin said: 'They would tell Jack what they'd seen, wouldn't they, George – a woman surveying the property? Sure to.' He spoke without any great emphasis or drama, as though he considered the changed situation so obvious that argument was superfluous. She'd call it Justin's seminar voice. 'Jack will get himself ready for trouble,' Justin said. 'This is bad, George. I usually feel pretty positive at the start of one of our expeditions, even foolishly positive. Not this one.'

'She's got at you. Liz has got at you, Justin,' George replied 'You're fucking windy.'

Liz thought it good tactics to get away from the horse women. 'There's something else, George,' she said. 'I had what seemed to be the police on my tail at one point, possibly that burly guy we also have on film. I got rid of him, yes, but he'd trace the car and get my name as hirer.'

'Got on your tail how?' George said.

'I don't know. He'd picked me up, though.'

'It's a mess, George.'

'The two women on the horses,' Dinnick said. 'Did they give their names?'

'As I've said, nothing like that,' Justin said. 'And they didn't ask for Liz's name either. As I say, that's the point, isn't it? No introductions.'

'Why is it the point?' Dinnick replied.

'They conceal they're from Darien – or try to – because, suppose she's casing the property, they'd prefer she didn't know they've rumbled her. If she's been sent to prepare for some operation against the house and Lamb's gallery they will be ready for it – but without forewarning her they'll be ready for it. They want surprise.'

George had done no eating and drinking, though Liz and Justin had. Liz saw George was keeping himself focused. 'Justin, why can't she tell me these things herself?' he said. 'You her priest, her intercessor, as well as her bedmate?'

Yes, George could get very evil. She'd witnessed that once or twice before. It might be necessary if you headed a firm.

'She *could* tell you, *would* tell you, of course she could, would, George,' Justin said, 'but I've listened to Liz, gone over her account of things, asked all the questions I imagine you'd like to ask. So, I can bring you information I've got straight in my own head, and maybe I can put things a little clearer than she might.'

'Yes, I'm glad of Justin's help,' Liz said. She thought he'd lost some of his calm, though. He sounded flustered, alarmed.

'You're in cooperation, you two. Sure you are,' Dinnick replied. 'In cooperation against me. She puts these trivial "factors" to you – the supposed cop trailing her, the horsey women – because she's somehow taken big fright over this project – fright not so much on her own part, but yours. The lover "factor" has become more important than the Cog, Darien factor, despite the very reliable murmurs I get that Lamb has some great prizes there for us, including *Amelia With Flask* itself. Those "factors" are nothings, are pretexts to get the raid killed off. She's turned you yellow, Justin.'

Dinnick's voice stayed very low. There were customers about. Very low, but very clear.

Liz could tell Justin was hit off balance. That wasn't a normal state of mind for him, not how he saw himself and how he expected others to see him – nerveless, capable, magnificently decisive. 'I'll get down there at the end of the week and check on Lamb's stuff, George,' he said. He'd gone conversational again, matter-of-fact, as though promising to pop into the shop for a packet of biscuits. George had riled him, shamed him, manoeuvred him: clever, professional, ruthless George.

Justin and Liz made love that night. Or it would be more meaningful to say she made love to him. There was joy to it, as ever, and there was also a touch of despair to it this time.

She'd hare back to the realm of Darien tomorrow, well ahead of him, and make such an obvious and crazy assault on the place that even he and George would see the operation had become unarguably hopeless, unquestionably impossible. Some risk would be entailed. Justin deserved it.

TWENTY-SEVEN

Harpur drove out to Darien, this time in an official car and with Iles as passenger. 'Do you know what I think all this dates back to, Col, the killing included?'

'All which, sir?'

'Yes, all this, the killing included.'

'What do you think it dates back to, sir?'

'That Blake incident at Ralphy's club. Or, rather, the "I Spy" version of it.'

'How?' Harpur replied.

'How what, Col?'

'How is it connected to all this, the killing included?'

'Yes, that's how I see it, Col.'

Lamb let them into the house himself. Harpur thought he looked very shattered. No pictures hung on the drawing room wall. To Harpur, this seemed a house that had suddenly lost its purpose, its focus. Chaos had moved in. Lamb's mother was seated, un-handcuffed, between a female police sergeant and Helen Surtees, on one of the big settees. 'Hi guys,' Alice Lamb said. She gave a pained, token grin and raised her right hand in greeting, as if she wanted to demonstrate very clearly that her arms were free. 'I acted in defence of the property and everyone in it, including staff.'

'Well, maybe a court will understand and go gently,' Iles said, in a mild, considerate voice that he kept on standby somewhere, as with Albert and Vernon. 'But this is not the States,' he said.

'It was dark, I hear breaking glass,' Alice Lamb replied. 'OK, OK, it turns out to be an unarmed solo woman, but I'm not to know that, am I? She'd planned this. It wasn't just some silly adventure.'

Helen said: 'We'd seen her taking a really thorough look at Darien and the estate. Field glasses.'

'And a rush to hide them,' Alice Lamb said. 'What I had to keep in mind was she might have been a vanguard, a trailblazer for a gang. I couldn't tell how many people had broken in.'

'Where did you get the gun?' Iles asked. 'You couldn't have brought it through airport screening.'

'In the States, many households keep a gun. To kill a burglar is often regarded as justified,' Alice said. 'One thing my second husband taught me – be on guard. For him, that meant buy off the threat. For me, it meant legitimate gunfire.'

'I don't think she was a burglar,' Harpur said.

'She breaks a window. There are valuables here,' Alice said.

'I believe Col thinks a display of some sort,' Iles said.

'Which sort?' Lamb asked.

'Maybe Col's not clear on that,' Iles said. 'But I wonder if she was protecting someone.'

'"Protecting someone"?' Jack Lamb said. 'How, for God's sake? Whom?'

'Think of the clumsiness, the obviousness,' Iles said.

'I don't understand,' Jack replied.

'Yes, the clumsiness, the obviousness,' Iles replied. 'They negate the possibility of any future raid. Make a din, cause some breakages, then disappear. Word gets around there's been a foray into the grounds and property, meaning extra vigilance by the Lambs, Helen and staff in case of a future attempt. In these circumstances any outfit considering an attempt would drop the idea. Perhaps that's what she wanted. Of course, she wouldn't have expected there to be a gun here and someone ready to use it. She wouldn't be allowed to carry out her little incursion and then buzz off, unidentified.'

'Protect a lover, do you mean?' Alice Lamb said. 'Oh, God, and I've killed her.'

TWENTY-EIGHT

The ten o'clock evening news was on one of The Monty's television screens. Sitting at his accounting desk behind the bar, Ralph Ember watched now and then but mainly gave his mind to some personal deep thinking. He believed ardently in regular periods of personal deep thinking. They helped him get a steady hold on life and annulled the rotten slurs contained in those vicious nicknames 'Panicking Ralph' and 'Panicking Ralphy'.

He'd decided to keep *The Marriage Of Heaven And Hell* after all and not go for Sparta and baby exposure. Ralph felt a kind of bond, a fellowship, with that Blake figure. Together, they'd gone through plenty, some of it damn dire. There was comradeship across the centuries, the millennia, even. Someone on the radio not long ago had said life on earth started four billion years ago, so Blake would have plenty of space to niche his *Marriage Of Heaven And Hell.* Abandonment of the shot male because of someone like Enz would be pathetic, a cultural collapse. Ember hadn't read the full Blake work yet, but he was pretty certain the figure would be on the *Heaven* side of the *Marriage*. Ralph had come to accept that the slight evidence of patching up of the illustration could surely be regarded as a noble sign of hardships encountered jointly by the white bearded man and Ralph – yes, hardships encountered, endured and eventually dispelled. Ralph no longer considered that the restored picture reflected poorly on Monty standards.

For the present, Ralph couldn't face any more upheavals. The death of that woman, Rossol, at Lamb's place had badly shaken him. He realized now it had been a crazy error to let Jack's mother have the .38, though an error based in some ways on kindness. He'd tried something of a gamble, and it hadn't worked; it had come near to working, but, crucially, not on the right person.

A few days ago Enzyme had turned up looking for the return

of that Smith and Wesson, and Ralph had apologized unstintingly and told him he'd got rid of it in the river: said he didn't like having an unlicensed gun on Monty premises. This had seemed to Ralph a totally reasonable explanation for the gun's absence, no matter how symbolic and semi-holy the .38 had become for Enz. A court wouldn't have listened to any of that crap if Ralph was hauled up for illegal possession of a firearm. Most probably Enz had been somewhere trying to get a replacement weapon and, because of his aura of madness, had been refused. So, he'd thought, *Must get back to Ralph and say the surrendering of the .38 has adequately symbolized my regrets, and now I'd like the gun back, please.* Get stuffed, Enz.

But, in fact, the gun had not been absent when Loam arrived so damn pleaful and slimy. It was still nestling there, a sacrificial emblem in the chiffonier drawer. Ralph had an idea that Enz would consider the word 'chiffonier' highfalutin' and showy when used by Ralph. Well, fair enough, Enz, let's not upset you further. Ember hadn't spoken of the chiffonier when Loam returned, no, because if the gun was in the river it couldn't be in the chiffonier, could it? Although, in fact, it was, of course. Loam had actually said he'd considered calling at Low Pastures to get 'a more conducive atmosphere' for gun discussions! He seemed to imagine this was some sort of compliment! God, the crudity of such an attitude – the foul presumption and insensitivity. Low Pastures was Ralph's home, a family home, his wife and children and their ponies were there. Would secret firearms be a suitable topic in this innocent, prestige setting? 'Conducive'!

Enz said he'd revised that plan, though, after a talk with his wife, and he'd arrived once more at the club, despite the continuing absolute ban. And so it had been, 'Awfully sorry, Enz.'

Ralph did get rid of the pistol, however, when Alice Lamb came a little later looking for armament. She was pleaful, then, too, but not slimy pleaful: practical pleaful, sturdily pleaful, worried about security, or non-security at Darien. It had been Ember's very hearty, and very genuine, wish that Enz, still profoundly eager to redeem himself with Ralph, would try and lift those paintings he'd promised for the club from Lamb's place one night, Lamb being deliciously unable to report a theft, because so much of his stock had come lawlessly. And Alice

Lamb, wisely belligerent and alert to possible break-ins – taught by her ex-husband to expect menace and stand ready to dispose of it – would hear Enz and, in her view justifiably, put a defensive bullet or two into his head from what had once been his own weapon. *From what had once been his own weapon!* The cosy neatness of that had delighted Ralph, the inspiring circular nature of it. You couldn't get a better instance of someone hoist with his own petard – blown apart by his own weapon – a phrase he'd run into during his university Foundation Year. Things hadn't taken that direction, however. A pity about Rossol, the shot Londoner. Also in his Foundation Year, students had read a novel called *Nostromo* where there was a terrible shooting of the wrong person by mistake. Ditto. What the hell had Rossol been up to, blundering about like that at Darien? How did she manage to collect the bullets very specifically intended for someone else? But this wasn't a question he needed to trouble himself with now.

No, he could enjoy a spell of relaxation, even if acute gloom clearly affected several club members tonight. Alec (Leitmotif) Wagstaff, a regular of The Monty in its present, very transitional social state, bought a triple Jameson's whisky, perhaps to soothe himself. For a while his grief was such that he seemed unable to speak and explain it. But then he said there'd been a police raid on Silver Bells And Cockleshells nursery and an armoury of true, positive repute arbitrarily and permanently shut down, with very, very worrying implications for what he called 'the dear little kiddie section of the business'. Leitmotif shook his head in dejection and gave himself a second gulp of Jameson's. 'I always think of guns as sort of in their own, particular way, clean, Ralph. Whereas, look and listen.' He pointed a skinny, accusing finger at the TV News.

The camera showed the frontage of the famous Oss Gallery in Piccadilly, London. A reporter's voice-over said Mr George Dinnick, part owner of the gallery, with rumoured connections to the 'seedy side of international art trafficking', had been murdered by at least three blows to the head with an axe in what police assumed was an attack connected with the trade. They were urgently seeking information from Mr Justin Benoit, aged twenty-six a long-time colleague of the dead man in the 'facilitator' firm, Cog, who had not been at his normal address for some while. Mr Benoit's partner, Elizabeth May Rossol, another Cog staff member, was herself recently murdered in what might also have been an art-related dispute. Police could not say at this stage whether they'd found a link between the two deaths, though a revenge killing was one possibility they would investigate. 'Three bonce chops or more with an axe!' Leitmotif said. 'So comparatively fucking unkempt, Ralph.'